BILLION DOLLAR MISTAKE

SHARON WOODS

Chrissy because of you I'm now more present with the people in my life. Thank you for giving me the biggest wake-up call of my life x

.

Content Information

My book contains spicy scenes and language. It also involves cancer and an on-page car accident.

CHAPTER 1

NOVA

"Don't you have anywhere else to be on a Saturday Night?"

I stiffen before returning to the soup I've prepared on the stove. "No. I like hanging out with you guys."

Mom side-eyes me.

"What?" I ask.

"I didn't say anything," she says, walking away from me to open the fridge.

"No, but you want to," I reply, before tasting the soup. The minestrone is cooked to perfection if I do say so myself. I won't be able to come over to their house much this week since I need to prepare for my upcoming job interviews. Which means I need to make sure they have leftovers.

"I worry about you. You're turning twenty-five this year and all you do is hang around with us on the weekends."

I look away from her accusing gaze and focus on the stacked white bowls she's bringing over to me.

"Thanks," I mumble, grabbing the bowls one at a time and filling each with soup. Because I can't afford to waste any of it, I concentrate so I don't spill a drop.

"I don't want to go out. I'm too tired," I lie.

Lying is not something I like to do. And I refuse to tell her I can't afford to go out. The moment she learns I'm giving her and Dad all my money, they'll stop taking it. And I don't want that. Since Dad's colon cancer diagnosis, he hasn't been able to work, and Mom's department store wage isn't enough for them to survive on. I want to be able to contribute and since I've finally finished college, I've been applying for full-time accounting jobs, and with some luck, I'll get a job this week.

"But don't you want to spend more time with friends or find a special friend." Her voice hitches with hope.

We carry the bowls to the table and set them in front of our seats, the ones we've sat in since I was little.

"I spend plenty of time with my friends. I live with them," I say, as I move to the cupboard to grab crusty bread and then to the fridge for the butter.

"It's not enough. And you're avoiding the topic. What about a man?"

I groan as I walk back over to join them at the table. Most people are not this close to their parents. But I am. "Mom, I only connect with guys on a surface level. You know there's only one thing they want. And I don't feel like being used when all I want is to focus on my career."

I know she worries about me being alone, but I know it won't be forever. I can't tell her that I'm trying to enjoy every moment I can get with Dad, because I don't know how to take time for myself without feeling guilty. I worry if I miss a moment with him and he passes then I'll live with regret. So, that's why I give my every waking moment to them. I can worry about myself later.

"That's a shame. You're beautiful."

"You have to say that, I'm your daughter," I tease.

She reaches across the table to touch my face in a soft stroke. "My very beautiful and very single daughter."

"Alright I get it," I say, pulling my head away from her hand with a giggle.

Before I pour myself soup, I remember something. "I brought a new book for you to read. I just finished it and I need you to read it so we can discuss it," I say, feeling relief now that we put the relationship talk behind us.

Loving fictional men is all I can handle right now.

Mom and I have always shared a love of reading. When I was fourteen, I read my first fantasy novel, and I haven't been able to stop since then. Now we share books and discuss our thoughts when we finish them. It's a good distraction. It slows down the chaos of life, giving us a reprieve, even if for just a moment in time, and helps us not dwell too much on Dad's health.

"Oh good. I finished book one already and I need to know what happens after that cliffhanger," she replies as she sits down.

"Hey kiddo," Dad says, wandering out of his room after his nap. He usually naps in the afternoon and wakes at dinnertime. Coming close to me, he lays a kiss on my cheek before moving to pull out his chair at the table.

"Hey, Dad. How are you feeling?" I ask.

We've always been close. Growing up, he taught me how to ride my bike, watched every swimming lesson, and signed me up for my first boxing class. He quizzed me for my first spelling exam all the way through my accounting exams in college. Even when he told me he had colon cancer, he did so with a grin, making sure to emphasize how it wouldn't bring this old man down, because he had too much to do. He's always been a happy and positive man; I can't recall ever hearing him complain. I'd like to think I got my patience and understanding from him.

"Strong as a horse," he says, taking a large slurp of his soup.

I eye him critically. He's an adult. There's nothing I can do to get a different answer out of him. If he's doing ok, I usually believe him. Even though I shouldn't.

I bring a spoonful of soup to my mouth, enjoying the salty taste.

"Are you ready for your job interviews this week?" Dad asks.

The way he looks at me, as if he wants to help, has me saying, "I think so. But would you help me prepare?"

He lowers his spoon and sits up straighter in his chair. These days the roles have reversed. Dad used to be the man of the house, always caring for the two of us, and now he feels like a burden. I know he does.

He's worked in a few different warehouses over his working years. One being at the department store where he met my mom. He was meant to be working on the floor, but on his lunch break, he saw Mom struggling to move shoe boxes, so he offered to give her a hand. They got to chatting, and because he is good at convincing people of just about anything, he asked her on a date and she agreed. And like they say, the rest is history.

"Alright. Hit me," I say eagerly.

I eat another spoonful of dinner before he asks, "Why do you want the job?"

"Jeez. Hitting me with the hard questions fast." I laugh.

But, in my mind the words *I need this job* scream out loud.

I don't know how I'm going to afford the gas bill. But I keep my lips firmly together. Those words won't leave my lips. They're my problem to solve, and right now, getting a job will fix it.

"I have to. You need to be able to answer these easily," he replies.

"I have gathered invaluable skills during my studies and my good marks are proof of how valuable I could be as a new hire. I am a fast learner, and I am ready to face new challenges," I answer, hoping he likes my prepared reply.

He nods as he takes another mouthful of dinner and so do I.

"Are you a hunter or a gatherer?"

My brows pull together.

"Just answer it," Dad counters, obviously reading my confused face.

"Gatherer. I think," I say, watching him to see if I'm correct.

"Yeah, you are. You're good at collecting data."

I exhale. "Give me an easy one now."

"They've all been easy. But okay. What motivates you?"

Money. Financial freedom. Happiness. But I don't say those. Instead, I think for a minute, watching my dad finish the soup. He's always loved my cooking, so seeing him finish it makes me happy.

"I enjoy working with numbers and my attention to detail is my greatest strength. I am excited about the opportunity of being here and learning more about your company."

Mom claps from her seat. "Good answer."

"Calm down, Lydia," Dad responds. But his soft smile and longing look make my gut twist.

I worry about Mom. If I am scared out of my mind right now, I wonder what she's feeling. Does she fear she'll have no money for herself if she becomes a widow? Maybe there's a fear of having the relationship with her only daughter change because of grief. Or is it the fear of losing the person you love?

Unfortunately, as much as I wish I could be there for her and tell her I know exactly how she is feeling, I can't. I've never been in love.

CHAPTER 2

JEREMY

"This is one way to conduct a meeting," I mutter to myself as I step onto the obnoxiously large white yacht. Don't get me wrong, I own one too, but the difference with me is, I'm not showing off what I have to potential business associates. Even thinking about it makes me want to spin right around and walk off this yacht. But I can't. Business is business, no matter how much I dislike the person. And right now, I'm dreading meeting Bentley Spencer.

Walking across timber floors, I follow the sound of the latest pop music. I can hear a lot of people, and I swallow hard as I get closer to the loud wails and laughter. I do my best to simmer the annoyance bubbling beneath the surface of my skin.

I stride toward the crowd, and I can't help but notice the alcohol.

Fuck, I need a drink.

How did Bentley become this successful?

He probably gets everyone drunk and then makes them sign important papers.

My hands are firmly planted in my pockets as I weave through the scantily clad crowd. Seems Bentley failed to tell me it's a pool party. Women are in bikinis and men in shorts and tees; whereas I'm in my suit, which is usually what I wear to a meeting. Now I'm feeling out of place and I fucking hate it. Hate that I'm the only one dressed differently. I wouldn't have worn a bathing suit, but I could've been in a nice pair of shorts and a shirt. I still need people to take me seriously, but I would've blended in better.

I narrow my gaze as I look for Bentley. It takes me two seconds to figure out who he is. The guy has a big fat disgusting cigar sitting on the edge of his lip and one arm draped around two women. One on either side of him. I want to make this quick. I need to get the fuck out of here and get back home. I avoid parties at all costs. I've never been into them or big group gatherings, unless it's for events or fundraisers. This time I was forced to show up because it's urgent and Bentley has been out of the country.

I don't care for the ass kissing that happens in these parties. I've managed to conquer just about everything I've set out to do, and I did it by myself, so the validation doesn't matter to me. I enjoy having my own company and setting my own goals. That's a major difference between Bentley and me. I don't need people to make me feel good about myself. I like myself. Scratch that. I love myself and my life. I work hard for it.

As I get closer to the two women in bikinis, more of Bentley's outfit comes into view. Caramel chino shorts with a white shirt unbuttoned halfway. We definitely don't present ourselves the same way. I remove a hand from my pocket and swipe it down the sides of my lips before taking a drink from a nearby waitress. She seems to be the only woman on this yacht who is completely dressed and sober.

"Thanks," I mumble and take a big sip of the rum. I enjoy the warm sensation it fills me with. At least the liquor is expensive; I'll give him that.

A touch on my suited arm has my gaze flicking sideways. It's a brunette woman with brown eyes wearing the skimpiest yellow bikini and holding a half-drunk mojito. She has had so much plastic surgery that she looks unnatural. She's pretty, I'm just not interested. When I'm in work mode, nothing can distract me. My eyes are on the prize and discussing the medical speculums proposal for my hospitals is the priority today.

"Hi," she purrs. "I see you've got a drink and you're ready for a good time."

"Sorry, I'm here for business. I was headed somewhere else," I reply firmly.

"Are you sure I can't change your mind into having a drink with me?" She flutters her lashes in a desperate beg.

"I'm sure. I hope you have a good night." I pull my arm out of her grasp, and she pops out her bottom lip. It does nothing for me. I shake my head and walk off.

I grip the glass tighter as I continue to my destination, only a few steps away. Suddenly, I come to an abrupt stop. "Bentley Spencer?"

His eyes slowly move to me, and his face scrunches up before it softens when he meets my stare.

"Mr. Lincoln?"

I give him a curt nod. "Mr. Spencer. Would you mind if we find a private place to chat? Wasn't exactly expecting an audience," I demand. I don't care if he thinks it's rude. This is rude. I didn't ask for a party. I hate going out. I'm pissed off and feel like I was tricked into coming here today. When Bentley called it was quick because he was about to board a flight home. He requested I join him on his yacht at seven with no other information.

"Are you—" His words cease immediately.

The flat stare I'm giving him must be exactly the right expression. He peels his arms off the girls and kisses each of their temples before telling them he'll be right back.

I swallow the bile coming up from the repulsion of knowing he will end up fucking these women tonight. I feel sorry for these girls. Honestly, I'm against fucking multiple women for the sake of it. With that, I pivot, looking for somewhere more suitable for a business discussion.

"I have an office downstairs," he slurs. I'm thankful he read my mind, but I have to bite my tongue and not comment on his drunken state as well as remind myself it's not my business.

As long as he can agree to one tiny business thing, I'm out of here—I check the time on my Rolex—in hopefully no more than ten minutes.

"Follow me," he suggests.

Once we reach the downstairs level, he opens a door that reveals a small office with dark wooden bookshelves and a matching desk.

Simple and small. But better than doing this upstairs.

"Take a—"

I sit down and cross my legs before he has a chance to finish his sentence.

He sits down across from me.

"Is this normal?" I ask.

Bentley frowns with confusion.

"Conducting business meetings on a yacht while drunk?"

"I'm not drunk..."

With his lie, I tighten my grip on the glass.

"Just had a few drinks while I was waiting for you."

More lies.

I decide to get straight to the point.

"I want to discuss having your eye speculums in all of my hospitals."

He shuffles in his seat. "Ah, yes."

"I'll need all new speculums for each operating theatre," I add.

He nods repeatedly. "Yeah. We can do that."

I lift a brow at him. "You can?" My voice totally giving my lack of confidence in him away. But the way he's been acting, can you blame me?

"Definitely. You give me a number and I'll deliver."

"Do you have a pricing contract drawn up?" I ask. Even though he doesn't have a single piece of paper out, I'm not here to mess around. And I need his words in writing. I've been around long enough to have been fucked over in business once before...I'm not letting it happen again.

"No, but—"

I run my tongue over my teeth. "How about you draw one up and send it over tomorrow?"

He sits forward and pulls open drawers to find paper. "I can write one up quickly."

"No. You need to draft a proper contract. I take this seriously, Mr. Spencer, and so should you."

"I am," he rebuts quickly.

I want to argue back, but I won't waste my breath.

"I can wait twenty-four hours. Enjoy your party and we can talk tomorrow."

He's still looking around in the desk drawers for something before he sighs and closes them again. "Yeah, that's probably best."

Knowing the chat is over, I can't bear the thought of going upstairs with him, so I ask, "Can I wait here until we pull in?"

"Are you sure you don't want to head back up and have another drink?" he replies, standing and eyeing my almost empty glass.

I shake my head. "No, thank you. I prefer to keep my mind sharp."

He looks taken aback, but I don't apologize. I quietly stand my ground.

He thrusts his hand out. "Thank you for coming today, Mr. Lincoln. I'll have the pricing contract drawn up immediately and send it over."

I want to fire back, *you should have done that a week ago so it would be ready right now,* but I don't.

I drain my glass before lowering it to his desk. Holding his gaze firmly, I ask, "When are we docking?"

"We aren't due to arrive back for an hour."

I suck in a breath. Fucking hell. I'm literally stuck here.

He stands and I ease back into the chair, remaining silent. "Help yourself if you change your mind about a drink. And say goodbye before you leave, Mr. Lincoln."

I won't change my mind, I want to say, but I don't.

He leaves the room, closing the door behind him. I'm grateful to be alone. I let out a deep audible breath and lower my leg so I can pull my phone out of my pocket. I may as well work a little while I'm stuck here.

The captain announces we're ten minutes away from docking, so I leave the room and search for Bentley. I could sneak off, but I need to close the deal first. Therefore, I suck it up and give a quick farewell.

His loud voice booms above the music so I follow it.

"I meet them online."

I know he's talking about the women he was with. My skin crawls. He should come with a warning that says, *sleazebag*.

"Look at them all," he says, flicking pictures on his phone.

I internally groan and walk away calling, "Send me the details, Mr. Spencer, and I'll visit your office to sign it. Be prepared this time."

"Alright, Lincoln," he mumbles, not bothering to lift his slimy head away from the phone.

CHAPTER 3

NOVA

I PLASTER A SMILE even though my skin is crawling. If I wasn't desperate for a good-paying job to help my parents, I wouldn't be sitting here at this job interview. But all the other interviewers ended up passing on me for a more experienced person. So this interview is very important. I *need* to get this last job.

Scratch that...I *have* to get this job.

Being able to work for a company that is within the health industry was important to me. So when this job opportunity came up, I felt a strong connection to their goals and my dad.

Bentley isn't interested in what I have to say as much as he enjoys running his gaze over me. I shuffle in my seat, trying to get comfortable even though I can't. Not in his presence. Not with his heavy gaze admiring me. Could I work like this?

I wouldn't be working directly under him. I'd just be working for his company. And right now, with the medical bills my parents are racking up, we are desperate for this kind of break.

So, no matter how slowly his eyes slide over my body, I picture my dad and mom. Imagining their happy faces helps.

"I'm still in shock, Miss Lee," he says with a slight drool.

"Why's that?"

"Beautiful and smart. I'm surprised you haven't been snatched up already."

By the tone of his voice, I know he means in a relationship, but I want to keep this talk strictly business related. There'll be no other relationship between us.

"To be honest. Your company is the best in New York. And it's offering the best package."

He leans forward in his office chair, his hand running over his chin. "I think I should be worried you're only here for the money, but I'm not. If that's how I get you here then I'll take it."

I lace my fingers together, wondering how much longer I'll have to be here. It's already been a long twenty minutes.

"Are you saying I've got the job?"

Please say yes.

"I should be interviewing more candidates…"

"But you won't." I lift a brow at him. I'm barely holding back a beaming smile.

His lips pinch together before he shakes his head. "Seems like I can't say no to you."

I don't believe anything he's saying, but if my looks win me this job, I'm alright with that.

"Which floor would I be working on?" I ask.

"Let me give you a tour."

That I like the sound of. But I don't want him to realize how excited I am so I tone down my response. "Okay."

He stands and moves beside me. His hand gestures for me to go first, even though I have no clue where I'm going.

We enter the elevator and I'm quick to stand on the opposite side. He presses level ten, and it doesn't take long til we're there. Exiting the elevator, I take in the open floor. I'm able to see all the workers behind their desks typing away and working hard.

I'm quiet as I absorb everything around me. I get a few looks as we pass by. He pauses at an empty desk.

I peer at him.

"This would be yours," he says with a smirk.

My gaze flicks back to the space. Not too small and not too large with everything I could possibly need and more. All the latest technology, pens, paper, files, folders, and a calculator. Accountant heaven.

"Our current accountant is on maternity leave, so the job is temporary, but I'm sure once she returns I can find another position for you. I wouldn't want you working anywhere else."

The way he speaks it's as if he owns me. I wonder if he is serious...I wonder if he means he wants me or if he's still talking about the job. I would never go there with my boss.

Now that I think about it, I wouldn't even have time for a normal relationship. The only time I have for myself is when I can squeeze in a workout. I've kept up with my boxing at a cheap local gym. It's an hour that's just for me and I savor it more now that my dad's sick. Instead of curling up in a ball and crying, I take that hurt and pain out on a bag. Literally punching the shit out of it until I can't feel anymore. I go home exhausted but also lighter.

"Let me introduce you to your team."

My stomach begins to flip with nerves. I follow him to a desk where a guy in his mid-30s with short, dark hair is typing furiously on his keyboard. He must hear us approach because he ceases typing and swivels in his chair to face us. His green eyes look brightly at me.

"Dalton, this is Nova. She's replacing Fern."

Dalton smiles. "Hi Nova, it's nice to meet you. When do you start?"

The question takes me off guard. I look to Mr. Spencer for the answer.

"We haven't worked out a start date but most likely in a week or two."

Dalton nods. "Well, I look forward to working with you."

Mr. Spencer touches my arm and I jolt. But I relax the moment I realize he wants me to follow him to another desk where a red-haired woman, who looks to be in her early 40s, finishes up a phone call.

"Hi, Poppy. I'm just introducing a new staff member. This is Nova, she'll start in a week or so and she's replacing Fern."

Her icy blue eyes slit at me. She's unimpressed.

I smile and she gives me a curt one back, which twists my stomach into a ball of nerves. I don't normally have issues with other women, and I really hope she's no different. I don't get long to think about it, though, because Mr. Spencer's phone rings and he hits decline before speaking to me. "Let's get to the contracts. I have a meeting soon, so I unfortunately need to end this."

Not unfortunate for me. Today has been a lot. From coming into a job interview to leaving with a job and starting in possibly a week's time. No wonder my emotions are a mess.

But this is all positive. I need this.

I can't wait to leave and tell my parents. Their proud faces and tears will be worth it.

"Nice to meet you," I say and wave to Poppy and then Dalton before following Bentley to the elevators.

Downstairs I sign papers, and before I know it, I'm leaving the office building that I'll call my workplace soon.

On my walk to my car that's parked a block away, I call home.

"Nova. How did it go?" My mom answers on the first ring.

My chest swells. I'm thrilled to be able to tell her the great news.

"I got the job!" I exclaim proudly.

"Oh, I knew it. Charles, she got the job." Mom sniffles.

"Tell me all about it," she requests.

I'm getting in the car to drive to the gym, but I know she won't let me hang up until I tell her something. "I start next week. I met my co-workers Dalton and Poppy. The boss said it's temporary while a lady named Fern is on maternity leave but after the contract is up, he'll find me a new job within the company."

I avoid saying the guy gives me an uncomfortable feeling because I don't need them to worry about me. I can handle Mr. Spencer.

"How's Dad feeling?" I ask. He had a doctor's appointment today for a check-up after his first round of chemo.

"He's okay. There's a little bit of swelling from one of his kidneys. The doctors are keeping an eye on it but other than that he's good. Don't worry about him."

"I'm fine. Don't worry about me. I'm not going anywhere." My dad's voice calls out in the background.

"You heard him," Mom adds.

"I did. Well, I'm about to drive to the gym, but I'll talk to you soon. I love you both."

"I love you too. Drive safe."

"I will. Bye, Mom. Bye, Dad." I hang up and drive away.

Entering the open-air gym, I head to my usual spot tucked away in the basement corner. I want to be alone for the next forty-five minutes, where I can feel my knuckles hit the bag and relish in the pain. The gym is packed with kids who come here after school, but I block them out by focusing on the Hip Hop music, and the feeling that punching the bag with all my strength gives me. When I'm dripping with sweat and my knuckles can't take another hit, I pack my bag and head home.

I don't live with my parents. I haven't since I went to college. There have been times when I've wanted to move back. Like the day my dad was first diagnosed with cancer. But that was my fear talking. Fear of losing him. But he insisted on me living my life and finishing college. His strength is one I look up to. Maybe that's why I refuse to give up. The thought of him not being around one day is scary, so I don't allow myself to think or feel it.

I park at the rental house and take a few exhausting steps toward the door. Entering the mudroom, I kick off my trainers and the smell of onion hits me. Someone is cooking.

"Mmm, smells good in here," I call out.

"Spaghetti," Summer calls from the kitchen. She's home from college where she's studying to become a veterinarian.

There was this one time she brought home her dissection project and put it in our fridge. She went to take a shower, forgot to tell me, and when I opened the fridge, I screamed. She came out of the shower wearing a towel and looking around frantically. I pointed at the fridge and she laughed. I didn't find it funny. I was still trying to calm my heart rate down. From then on, she promised to never bring her projects home.

"Can I help?" I ask, wandering into the kitchen.

"No. I'm just waiting for the water to boil," she replies, nudging her nose down at the pot before her brown eyes meet mine. She's wearing her usual pair of gray sweats and her wavy brown hair is tied up in a bun on her head. She seems all set for a relaxing night.

"I might jump in the shower then." I tilt my head in the direction of the bathroom.

"Go for it."

"Where's Chelsea?" I ask, surprised to find her gone.

"No idea." Summer shrugs. "Maybe still at work."

"I'll be back," I say over my shoulder and jog up the stairs.

I step into the hot shower and try to find the energy for another few hours before I can crawl into bed and sleep.

When I return to the kitchen, I notice Chelsea is home and she's setting the table for dinner. She's wearing her usual activewear, this time a bright blue, which compliments her dark hair and sun-kissed skin.

"Hey, Chels." I walk over to help her. She's taller than Summer and me at five foot nine and all legs.

"Hey!" She peers down at me with a smile. Summer lowers a bowl on the table. As I finish putting the last fork down.

We all take our seats.

"Oh. I forgot something." Summer stands. She walks to the fridge and pulls out the champagne. It's been in there for a few weeks. We have been waiting for this moment.

She stares at me. "Please tell me the interview went well."

I nod with a big smile. "I got the job."

Summer pours us a drink and they both come over and hug me. Tears prick my eyes from the support. It feels like it's been a long time coming. All my hard work at school has finally paid off. I'm an adult with a full-time job. My dream job. A job I feel I'll be good at. And it'll be nice to make my own money.

"You guys are going to make me cry." I pick up my napkin and dab my eyes.

"It's okay. I'm sure it's a lot. You've finished college and now you have a job in a fancy New York office." Summer rubs my arm. It soothes me.

"Yeah, but enough about me. What about you girls? Anything exciting happen?" I ask.

"I dissected—" Summer begins.

I wave my arms. "No vet talk at the table. I want to be able to eat my dinner."

"Yeah, save it for later," Chelsea adds.

A phone chimes. Chelsea lifts her phone from the table and winces.

"Everything okay?" I ask.

"Yeah. I was supposed to see Bobby tonight, but he's working late again."

Her eyes haven't left the screen and I want to scream and tell her to dump him. Her boyfriend of two years, Bobby, is a jerk. He never puts her first, and always finds a way to put her down. She's becoming a shell of her bubbly self. He definitely doesn't realize how special she is.

"I'm sorry, Chels," I say genuinely as I grab her forearm and gently squeeze it until she looks up at me from her phone.

My stare says what I wish I could say, but she's already heard me say *you should break up with him*. I don't want to repeat myself and push her away. I'm her safe place. She knows Summer and I are going to be here for her when that day comes. And it will come. Bobby is a liar and a cheater. An all-around douchebag.

We eat in silence and Chelsea is the first to retreat to her room. I clean up with Summer. We give each other looks but don't utter a word. We don't want Chelsea hearing us bitch about Bobby. It would hurt her more.

After the kitchen is tidy, I say goodnight and head up to my room. Lying on my double bed, I pick up my phone ready to catch up on the day, but I see a message from an unknown number.

> **Unknown:** *You never sent me the contract.*

CHAPTER 4

JEREMY

I SHOULD BE SLEEPING. But after hours of tossing and turning, I give up and reach for my phone. It's never a good idea because nights like this end up with me working through most of it. But after scrolling through emails for a while, a message pops up.

Bentley: *Who's this?*

For fuck's sake. Is he for real?

I type back furiously.

Jeremy: *You know it's me, stop fooling around.*

Bentley: *I don't know who me is.*

I pinch the bridge of my nose and close my eyes briefly before writing back. This guy does my fucking head in.

> **Jeremy:** Jeremy.

> **Bentley:** Never heard of a Jeremy.

> **Jeremy:** Bentley, stop messing around. I don't have time for this.

> **Bentley:** Bentley's my boss.

I sit up straight in the bed, tossing a pillow that's poking me in the back. It lands on the floor with a thud.

I swipe my forehead in annoyance. Why the fuck did Bentley give me an employee's number.

> **Jeremy:** Why did he give me your number?

> **Bentley:** I don't know.

I stare at the name saved, but I don't even know who I'm talking to.

Jeremy: Who's this?

Bentley: Nova.

I stare at the name again, but it doesn't ring any bells.

Jeremy: I don't know who you are.

Bentley: :(

I laugh for some reason. The whole thing makes no sense. It's actually ridiculous.

Jeremy: He was meant to send me a spec and financial contract. Do you know anything about it?

While I wait for her to respond, I change the name in my phone.

Nova: *I don't start at the company until next week.*

I don't know what to say back but I get another message.

Nova: *I'm the new accountant, maybe I'll be fixing it?*

Jeremy: *In a week's time? I hope not. I need the equipment ordered for my hospitals.*

Nova: *Your hospitals?*

Do I really want to answer her?

What else would I be doing?

It's either sleep or work.

I'm wide awake now. Would talking to Nova be classified as work? I don't know, but I never realized how much easier text conversations were until now.

Jeremy: *I'm the CEO of Lincoln Eye Hospital Group.*

Nova: *Right, I just saw it on Google. NY's largest ophthalmology chain. Fancy.*

I choke out a laugh.

Jeremy: *Did you Google me?*

Nova: *As soon as you told me your name.*

Jeremy: *I've never Googled my name. Anything interesting?*

Nova: *Why don't you have a look, Mr. Fancy Pants?*

Jeremy: *Don't call me that.*

Nova: *Why?*

Jeremy: *I don't like it.*

Nova: *Fine. What do I call you Mr. Lincoln? Jeremy? Google calls you a bachelor.*

Jeremy: *It doesn't.*

Nova: *It does. I dare you to Google yourself.*

Jeremy: *No. I don't play games.*

Nova: *It was very interesting.*

I swallow the lump that's formed in my throat. There's nothing personal there, so I don't need to worry.

Nova: *Three brothers and your parents are still together.*

Jeremy: *I'm going to Google you.*

Nova: *Go ahead, you'll find nothing. I'm boring compared to you.*

Jeremy: *Trust me, I'm the one who's boring.*

Nova: *I doubt that. Being called a bachelor…sounds fun.*

Jeremy: *I'm not a bachelor. I haven't dated in years.*

Nova: *Why?*

Jeremy: *You're nosy, aren't you?*

Nova: *No. Just curious. What does Mr. Fancy Pants Jeremy Lincoln, not a bachelor, do? Because you're currently saying everything Google says is wrong.*

I can't help but laugh out loud. She's used all the nicknames she's made up for me, and I don't like any of them.

Jeremy: *I don't like any of those names.*

Nova: *How about Jerry, Jem, Jere, Remy, Jerr, Jez, Rey. I personally like Remy.*

Jeremy: *Did you find them from Google too?*

Nova: *Totally. Choose one.*

Who are you, Nova?

Looking at all the names, I go with my gut.

Jeremy: *Call me Remy.*

Nova: *I like that.*

Jeremy: *So you've told me.*

Nova: *Now that we've got a name. Why is Google wrong?*

Jeremy: *It's not completely wrong, it got my family and business correct.*

Nova: *So you're saying the only thing that is incorrect is the bachelor title. Where did they get it from?*

Jeremy: *No idea. Maybe because I don't go out with women to events. Or have a long-term girlfriend.*

Before I think about what I'm doing, I snap a picture of myself lying in bed. Proving to her that I'm an average guy and not bachelor material. And then I send it to her. Instantly regretting doing so. I quickly type her a text.

Jeremy: *Sorry, I don't know why I did that. Other than for some dumb reason proving that Google is wrong.*

Nova: *Don't be sorry. You're kind of cute.*

> **Jeremy:** Now I'm definitely regretting sending it.

> **Nova:** Why?

> **Jeremy:** Being called cute isn't a compliment.

> **Nova:** It is. But if you prefer…I'll call you handsome.

> **Jeremy:** Send me a picture of you so I don't feel stupid.

> **Nova:** It's because you thought I was Bentley.

I bite my tongue. I can't type out what I truly think about him. He's her CEO and I want this deal. It's the most important thing to me. Well, other than my family.

Nova sends an image.

Holy fuck.

The image is of her makeup-free face. One that's unforgettable. She has the most captivating hazel eyes in the most beautiful of faces. Her wavy brown hair cascades around her shoulders as she leans back on her bed, mimicking my pose. A sexy little quirk on the side of her lip looks every bit naughty and seductive at the same time. For some reason, I find myself texting her for the rest of the night.

Jeremy: *Are you copying me?*

Nova: *What do you mean?*

Jeremy: *You copied my pose.*

Nova: *Lying in bed at night is common, you know.*

Jeremy: *You're not just pretty but cheeky.*

Nova: *I'm regretting sending my pic now.*

Jeremy: *Why?*

Nova: *Getting called pretty isn't a compliment.*

Jeremy: *Would you prefer to be called beautiful?*

Nova: *Yeah, but only if you think I am.*

I stare at the text. I can't reply. I went too far with her tonight by calling her beautiful. I'm not a relationship guy and never will be. It didn't help when she opened up to me. I'm not used to women being so earnest and honest.

I should focus on work and the deal. Not getting caught up with one of Bentley's employees. No matter how captivating her eyes are.

> **Jeremy:** Why are you still up?

> **Nova:** Now who's nosy?

My mouth curves into a smile.

> **Jeremy:** Just keeping up with you. Can't let you have all the fun with secrets, right?

> **Nova:** Then tell me something about you.

> **Jeremy:** I used to live in Chicago.

Nova: *Now you're where?*

Jeremy: *New York. Now it's your turn to answer my question.*

Nova: *I can't sleep so I'm watching a movie.*

Jeremy: *Am I allowed to ask which one?*

I flick the TV on, which is something I rarely do––because there's always work I could be doing in my office.

Nova: *It's okay we've established you're nosier than me.*

Jeremy: *I beg to differ.*

Nova: *I say caw-fee and you say Kaa-fee.*

One corner of my lip lifts, but I stifle another laugh.

Jeremy: *I say caw-fee. What movie?*

Nova: *Million Dollar Baby.*

Jeremy: *Honestly? No Notebook or Pride and Prejudice?*

Nova: *Why do you sound shocked? Should I be worried that you know the name of those movies?*

Jeremy: *They're classic romance movies. I haven't been living under a rock.*

I press the on button and search for it. It's been such a long time since I saw that movie. I play it and disbelief fills me. I can't believe she said she's watching this.

Nova: *Have you seen it?*

Jeremy: *Million Dollar Baby?*

Nova: Yeah. Bachelors don't live under rocks, this isn't The Little Mermaid.

Jeremy: You're not someone I'd pick to watch that.

Nova: You expected me to only watch Disney movies?

Jeremy: No. I'm just surprised.

Nova: Have you read the books?

Jeremy: I have. The characters were well-developed.

I have the collection of books sitting on a shelf in my office.

Nova: But Clint Eastwood and Hilary Swank made the books come to life.

Jeremy: What's your favorite part about the movie?

Nova: The relationship between Maggie and Frank. And the moment he decided to train her. You?

My eyes are getting heavy. Suddenly I'm tired.

> **Jeremy:** *Maggie's strive for success against the odds given to her.*

I glance at the TV, and the exact scene where he decides to train her is playing right now.

> **Nova:** *The whole movie is very moving and heart-warming.*

> **Jeremy:** *Did you cry at the end?*

> **Nova:** *Every. Damn. Time.*

Talking to her has relaxed me. I don't get a chance to say goodnight, or switch the TV off, because I fall asleep. But, of course, my dreams are filled with her and those alluring bedroom eyes.

CHAPTER 5

NOVA

> **Jeremy:** *It's only fair you tell me about you tonight. Google really has nothing about you.*

I STARE AT HIS text, nibbling my bottom lip, and type back. This new friendship with Jeremy feels oddly easy. For someone of his status, to be so down-to-earth and funny is unexpected. He doesn't seem snobby. And he doesn't speak like he's better than me, even though our lives couldn't be more different.

He even starred in my dreams last night. We were lying in my bed watching Million Dollar Baby together. His arm draped over me as I snuggled into his strong body. It was a very nice dream––shame it had to end.

I've not dreamt of a man, in well...*ever*. So to wake to a message from him now after thinking of him all night sends a new thrill down my spine.

Nova: *You Googled me?*

Jeremy: *I did.*

Nova: *I thought you didn't like Google.*

Jeremy: *I didn't say that. I meant I don't Google myself.*

Jeremy: *Now you know all about me. Tell me something about you.*

Nova: *Only if you Google yourself.*

Jeremy: *What if I say I do and I don't?*

Nova: *I believe in trust. Are you a liar?*

Jeremy: *No. I hate liars.*

Nova: *Then if you want to know something about me you need to Google yourself.*

I sit back, pleased at myself.

> **Jeremy:** I want something personal. Something you haven't shared with others.

> **Nova:** I'm not sending you nudes.

> **Jeremy:** I didn't ask for any but if…

> **Nova:** Not happening.

I'm typing with the stupidest grin and the giddiest feeling. The back-and-forth texting is taking my mind off my usual thoughts. Thoughts of money and my dad.

> **Jeremy:** I'm going to look now.

> **Nova:** I change my mind. Put it on video.

> **Jeremy:** You don't trust me?

> **Nova:** No, the opposite, I want to see your face as you read it.

> **Jeremy:** Fine.

My phone rings in my hand. I accept the video call and my body rushes with heat. He is wearing a simple white T-shirt and black sweats. A stark contrast to the polished image of the powerful businessman in his pictures. The T-shirt clings to his shoulders and arms, accentuating the impressive size and strength of his muscles.

He's different from the guy on Google. And even from the photo last night. Seeing him dressed down through video is a nice surprise. Don't ask me to tell you which version of him I prefer, because I hate to admit that I've envisioned ripping his button-up shirt off.

But this laid-back version is a different level of hotness. I can't stop staring. My tongue instinctively slides over my lips as I take him in, unable to tear my gaze away. A five-o'clock shadow dusting across a chiselled jaw, complementing dark blue eyes that hold a hint of mystery. His dark hair, which he runs his hands through, isn't as perfectly styled as his Google pics. But it makes my hand twitch, imagining my hands running through his hair instead. It looks soft and yet a length I could easily curl my fingers through.

"Hi," he says, pulling my mind out of the wandering thoughts it was having.

"Hi." My hands start to feel clammy.

He walks me through his house. I take in his gray walls and gray carpet. Moody and sultry. Totally suits him.

"Where are you taking me? Am I getting a guided tour of your house?"

A deep low chuckle leaves his chest. "No. I'm walking to my office so I can show you my screen and what I've found on Google."

"I know. I'm just asking to see your house," I admit.

There's a large painting of New York City on the wall, but it's the photo on the console table underneath that draws my attention.

"It's boring and unexciting, like me."

I lean forward to catch a glimpse of the image. It looks to be an old family photo. Four boys, parents, and grand-parents. His family. The boys look to be in their early 20s.

Smiling, I wonder which one is him.

"I doubt that. I like the gray...it suits you."

His eyes hit the screen and cause me to shiver. "How? I didn't design it. I paid a designer very well."

"She must've known you really well," I say, sounding a little jealous.

What is wrong with me? It's just a designer. And he isn't mine.

"I've never slept with her if that's what you're asking," he answers my silent question.

"I didn't."

"I know people think I fuck everything that moves."

I laugh. "Most men do."

"I'm not most men."

He sits down on his desk, and he hits a button on his screen and the vision of him is gone.

Damn it.

The clear-cut lines of his profile are hot. I watch him type his name.

"I did it." He talks behind the camera. I can see his computer screen. It's showing me what I already know.

"Read it," I say.

He grumbles, but I can tell he starts reading it by the way he slowly scrolls the screen up.

"I didn't break up with her, she broke up with me," he argues at the screen.

"Why did she break up with you?" I ask softly. I was curious about that information when I read it last night.

"Nova. You've got enough dirt on me."

"Ohhh, is it juicy?" I ask excitedly.

"No. Me working too much isn't juicy. It's pathetic."

Just as the words leave his mouth he curses, "Shit."

"You didn't mean to share that did you?"

A heavy sigh escapes him. "No but apparently that happens a lot when I'm around you."

I laugh, enjoying this gentle side of him.

He must have hit the button to spin the camera again because his handsome face fills the screen. His dark brows pinch together, but the determined look in his eyes has my lip falling from my teeth.

"Spill Nova." His tone is darker, and I want to give him something boring but the way he's looking at me...There's a vulnerability. It shows that me knowing more about him than he's comfortable with leaves him feeling exposed.

His vulnerability has me spilling my biggest piece of information.

"My dad's got stage three colon cancer."

I watch as his tight face drops. I see his eyes open slightly. I'm expecting pity, but I don't see it there. Only sadness.

"I'm sorry." His voice is strained.

I shrug. "Nothing anyone can do about it."

"Doesn't mean it doesn't hurt." He leans back in his black office chair.

"Oh yeah, it hurts. It's the hardest thing I've ever gone through." I shift on my bed, unable to believe I'm sharing all this with him.

All from the wrong number.

But it's freeing, being this vulnerable. Opening up to a guy for the first time, especially since he doesn't have any preconceived notions about me. His non-judgment allows me to express my true feelings without the scrutiny I would receive from my friends or family.

"Nova, food's ready." I can hear Chelsea calling out. Relief fills my body, the awkward tension of talking about my dad's diagnosis is heavy. I want to go back to the lightness between us. It takes me away from the dark.

"Down in a sec," I yell at my bedroom door.

Then turn to face the phone again. I can see him frowning.

His thin lips move. "You live with your family?"

"No. I live with friends. And that's all you need to know right now."

His eyes soften a tad. "I see how it is."

I smirk. "I gotta go before one of them barges in here."

"Do you live with guys?" he asks coolly.

Would he be jealous? Only one way to find out.

"Wouldn't you like to know?"

I smile as I hang up, giggling as I throw my phone on to the bed before heading downstairs to see the girls. I know he'll text, but I won't answer, just like he did to me last night.

Payback's a bitch, Remy.

CHAPTER 6

JEREMY

I'M TYPING AWAY, TRYING to organize the agenda of an upcoming meeting I have scheduled with my new hospital in Los Angeles. I don't have time for this right now, but I'm the only one who can do it right.

My phone buzzes on my desk, but I finish the email before checking it.

I ease back in my chair as the name Nova sits on my screen. I swivel around in my office chair away from my computer, knowing I won't be sending just one text.

Texting with her makes me feel young again. I don't have friends who share the same interests, but with Nova, the racing heart and warm feeling I get when we text makes me feel like a giddy teenager.

Nova: *Heard your family is hosting a charity gala. What should I wear? lol.*

My lips curve up.

> **Jeremy:** *How did you find out?*

> **Nova:** *Google notifications.*

Now my mouth parts into a full stupid grin. Putting notifications on just to hear about me. I wish I was more exciting, but currently, my life mainly involves working and playing poker with my brothers and friends.

However, I was not always like this. Growing up, I maintained a better work-life balance.

I studied hard––when necessary––but I also actively participated in social activities like attending college parties, dating girls, and going on many family holidays. I miss that fun and carefree part of my life.

I tilt forward, my arms leaning on the newspaper I've been reading between meetings and work.

> **Jeremy:** *Are you serious?*

> **Nova:** *Didn't know you were James Bond ;)*

I swipe the sides of my lips and shake my head. She kills me.

> **Jeremy:** *I'm not going, but I think it's important to give back.*

> **Nova:** *Not just a pretty face, are you, Remy?*

My heart thumps whenever she calls me Remy. It feels personal, considering my parents call me Jeremy. They've never used a nickname. They think a nickname isn't prestigious enough. In fact, they've never used one for any of my brothers either. But her calling me Remy is special because there's only one other person who does, and she has an important place in my heart. My grams.

> **Jeremy:** *Are you calling me pretty? Didn't we talk about names?*

> **Nova:** *Okay. How about Doctor Linc oln...is that better?*

My dick hardens at the thought of how that would sound leaving her mouth. *Doctor Lincoln.*

> **Jeremy:** *Much.*

> **Nova:** Why aren't you going?

I attend several charity gala's every year, which may surprise some, but I genuinely enjoy them. It's not the type of event I loathe, like a party; rather, it's an opportunity to support a cause, celebrate achievements, raise awareness and leave feeling incredibly inspired.

> **Jeremy:** *I have work in Boston.*

> **Nova:** *I was hoping to read about the non-playboy…playboy.*

> **Jeremy:** *Sorry to disappoint.*

> **Nova**: *Yeah, I am a little disappointed. Plus, I was hoping to get an invite.*

I sit up straighter as my desk phone rings. I pick it up and

Kirstie is letting me know my brother Evan is here. I tell her to let him in. Kirstie has been with me for the last five years. She's in her forties and keeps me organized. I'd be lost without her.

I hang up and type back quickly.

> **Jeremy:** Maybe next year?

> **Nova:** Will we still be talking next year?

I turn my head away and rub the back of my neck in thought before I type back.

> **Jeremy:** Sure. We're friends.

My office door opens as I put my phone away. My older brother appears wearing his usual serious face. I'd scowl, but he scares me.

"You work too much."

My body tenses. I'm used to hearing that. Especially from women. They sneer or roll their eyes at me every time I grab my phone.

Maybe it's my fault. I never actually had my heart in the same place they did.

"You work more than me, dickhead," I reply defensively. He closes the door behind him.

"Touché."

They all try to rile me up. But being one of four brothers, it's bound to happen.

"Are you coming to dinner on Sunday?" he asks, making himself a drink.

"I don't know. I'm in the middle of a big deal." I exhale.

He strides over from the drink trolley to the large windows overlooking New York City. "That's a good thing, isn't it?"

He cradles a crystal glass with amber liquid and ice. My mouth suddenly dries. I stand and stroll to the cart, pouring my own. "It is, if the guy wasn't a clown."

Evan turns around and leans his hip against the window frame. "What do you mean?"

I suck in a breath, recalling the meeting––or lack thereof, I should say.

"This guy is just––" I fill my glass and cradle it back to my office chair, tapping the glass with my fingernail. "An unprofessional amateur. He doesn't take other people's time seriously."

A smirk forms on the corner of his lips. "Can only imagine how much that would piss you off."

My eyes narrow at my brother. "You have no idea," I mumble.

Looking around my office, I take in how I went from becoming a doctor to a CEO. I was unable to practice medicine and own a chain of hospitals at the same time, so I decided to step away from my chosen career to follow a new passion.

I've worked hard to get here. My brother is no different as the owner of the family's newspaper, Lincoln Media. He is sharp and successful in the business world, which is why we have these business conversations. And missing occasional family events is understood. Our mother, on the other hand, takes more sweetening.

"Is it worth it? Can't you find someone else?"

I shake my head. "I fucking wish." I swirl my glass of liquid, the ice hitting the sides.

"He's the only one who designed and manufactures these speculums. If I had another option, I would've taken it by now," I admit.

"I'm sure I can put in a good word for you. You know it's our mother, not Dad or Iris."

Hearing Grams' name makes me think of Nova. The little spark of fun in her even though she's losing her dad hits me differently. We share something in common and she doesn't even know it.

It's not something I've told people about because saying it out loud means it's real. And I'm not ready to accept

it. I like to control things and Grams' breast cancer is out
of my control. How is she so brave about something so
crippling?

"How's Grams today?" I ask, swirling the ice cube in my
glass.

"Same feisty woman. You wouldn't know anything's
wrong with her."

I snort, picturing her smile and the wrinkle in between
her brows as she gets a read on you. "I can imagine her
giving you shit for asking."

"Yep," he mutters before taking a drink.

"I'll call her before poker. Are you coming tonight?" I
ask. Usually, I play poker with my brothers and friends on
Thursday nights.

"Not this time, I've got a meeting with one of my employees," he gruffs.

Anytime he uses that tone it's when he's angry. He's not
a big talker. Growing up, he was picked on at school for
being quiet. He prefers small groups, and even then, he
communicates sparingly. However, I'm used to him that
way, and, in fact, I appreciate the serenity he brings.

His obvious hatred of this guy has my interest piqued.

"What's wrong with him?"

"He's odd. I can't put my finger on it, but when I figure
it out, I'll let you know."

"Sounds fair," I reply smartly.

A wrinkle forms between his brows. "I'm telling you there's something off about him."

I put my hands up in the air like I'm surrendering. "I didn't say there wasn't."

"But you've got that skeptical look on your face."

Confused, I let my expression fall. "What look?"

"It's a face you pull when you don't believe someone."

I tilt my glass back and finish it. Placing it on the table with a thud, I say, "I don't know what you're talking about."

My phone chimes with a new email, distracting me from our conversation. It's the Director of Education from my hospital in Chicago. I can't ignore this.

"I've got to read this email, it's urgent."

"Of course," he responds, standing. "I'll talk to you tomorrow."

I don't wait for him to even leave my office before I spin around to my computer and read the details of the email. I decide to make a call to my friend from Chicago, Doctor Damien Gray, to get his thoughts on it. I'm going to have to get my assistant to schedule a visit.

I spend longer on the phone catching up with Damien and his family than I usually do with normal clients.

After I hang up, I get Kirstie to organize the trip.

I check my watch and I have half an hour before I need to leave my office to get to my friend Richard's house.

But, of course, work holds me up and I end up running forty-five minutes late for poker.

When I arrive, it's only a small group of five of us tonight. My younger brothers, Harvey and Oliver. Our friend Lukas, Richard, and me. We sit in the den of Richard's house. It's dimly lit, with a soft glow of overhead lights casting a warm hue on the green felt of the poker table. The air is thick with a mixture of tension and excitement. The only sounds are from servers or the occasional chips shuffling.

We drink, smoke and eat. I don't smoke, but I will drink alcohol. I experimented as a teenager, but studying medicine showed me the harmful effects smoking can have on a person, so I quit immediately.

The cards are drawn, and I scoop them up and lean back in my chair. My game face is on.

Over my cards, I eye each of the guys. Poker night always starts out serious but after we settle into a few games we spend most of the time talking shit and drinking.

On occasion, all my brothers join, but tonight, two out of the three came. I enjoy spending time with my brothers. I'm close with Evan and Harvey. Oliver is a hard one to spend time with, but when we do, it's always light-hearted. He's the joker out of all of us. He'll have you laughing even on your shittiest day.

We haven't all been together playing poker in a couple of months. Someone's schedule is always not lining up with the rest, but at Grams', we all make it. None of us would ever miss a dinner with her.

I choose not to miss poker nights because it's the only activity I engage in outside of work. That's why I always look forward to Thursdays; it's a welcomed break from the monotony.

It's my turn, so I'm looking at my cards and deciding my options when my phone vibrates in my pocket. Tossing a card down, I pull out my phone and see her name across the screen. My lip twitches, but I tuck my phone away, planning to respond after the game, and return my focus to the game. It's Harvey's turn, and he's currently staring at his cards, contemplating his move. Knowing she's messaged eats away at me. I'm desperate to know what's in her text, so I give myself another minute before I can't wait any longer.

After my turn, I pull my phone out and read it.

> **Nova:** What does Remy do on a Thursday night?

> **Jeremy:** Plays poker with his friends and brothers.

> **Nova:** I thought you didn't play games.

I let out a short chuckle. I'm about to type back when Lukas interrupts me.

"Who's making you laugh?" His brow is up to his hairline.

I drop my phone into my lap and refocus on the game.

"No one," I reply.

Because who is Nova? A friend? Colleague?

Other than beautiful, funny and charismatic, I don't have an answer. Honesty would only cause more questions. And she's none of anyone's business but mine.

After another turn, the boys start discussing the Chicago Eels' latest football game, so I take the opportunity to reply to her text.

> **Jeremy:** I only play certain games.

> **Nova:** Like?

> **Jeremy:** The fun ones.

> **Nova:** And truth or dare isn't?

> **Jeremy:** No.

Nova: Why?

Jeremy: You ask a lot of questions, Nova.

Nova: And you avoid a lot of them, Remy.

Jeremy: Not on purpose.

There's been a burning question I can't shake. I'm a straightforward guy, so before she responds, I type another message and hit send.

Jeremy: How are you so brave about your dad?

It takes her a while to respond this time, so I just set my phone face down on the table and shift my focus toward the game once again.

It vibrates. She responded. I pick it up and swipe it open.

Nova: *Truthfully, I'm not. I hide it well.*

Jeremy: *But you don't let it affect you.*

Nova: *I box as a workout and find it relieves my frustration and sadness. I'm then too tired to feel.*

I know what she means... Anger surged through me when I discovered Grams had it. That day remains etched in my memory, vividly, as if it was yesterday. The doctor in me vanished, and my feelings as a grandson took over. In a fit of rage, I threw the glass of rum I was holding, called her doctor, demanding a cure. Despite attempts from my parents and brothers to calm me down, it was only when Grams visited my office that I finally gave in. She understood my fear––the gut-wrenching terror fear––that cancer equated to a death sentence. When it comes to cancer, feelings can get overwhelming and hard to understand. It's like every emotion thrown at you and you're hit with every single one at different times. One minute you're happy and the next you're gutted and scared. It's a fucking roller coaster.

Jeremy: *I am also close to losing someone I love very much and I don't know what to do with myself.*

Nova: *If you ever feel like you don't want to do this alone, you have me.*

Jeremy: *I do?*

Nova: *We're friends, aren't we?*

Jeremy: *We are. Do you have anyone who's been there for you?*

I type *anyone* as a way to find out if she lives with a guy. I know I shouldn't care, but she still hasn't answered me about who lives with her, and it's knotting me up inside.

Nova: *I am good at being alone.*

Jeremy: *No siblings?*

Nova: *No, just me.*

I exhale and ease back into the chair. No mention of

a boyfriend or fiancé or husband. Nothing. I know I shouldn't be happy she's single, but I am. I'm fucking ecstatic.

CHAPTER 7

NOVA

"WHERE ARE WE GOING?" I ask, tearing my place apart looking for my phone.

"Away," Summer says, standing at the door watching me.

"That's not helpful," I reply, standing up with my hands on my hips and peering around the room.

"Where else have you been today?" she asks. "We don't have much time; Chelsea will be back soon, and we need to hit the road."

I want to ask again where we're going, but it's pointless because she's tight-lipped.

I start work on Monday, so I have three days off and my friends have decided to organize a spontaneous trip away. I've already packed, but I lost my phone. And for the life of me, I can't remember where I left it. The last thing I remember was messaging Remy last night and saying goodnight.

We've tried to call it, but it's on silent.

This morning I went to the gym then the florist to pick up some red roses and bring my mom her favorite bouquet. I don't have a lot of money, but I find enough to buy my mom flowers. Small things can bring you happiness during dark times.

"I went to the gym, and no one handed it in. Went to where I box, nothing was there. Then I went to the florist, same thing. It wasn't there, and the sales assistant hadn't seen it. It wasn't at my parents either."

"So, you're tearing the sofa apart, hoping it's here because?"

The hint of humor in her voice makes me giggle. "I don't know. I'm losing my mind. I need my phone." I sigh.

"Do you?" She says with a smirk forming on her face.

I roll my eyes. "I'm going to keep looking in my room until Chelsea's home."

Ever since I started texting Jeremy, I look forward to our interactions. I can't admit that to Summer, but I really need my phone to keep talking to him. I'm not going to fall in love with him. No, I can't do that. His rich lifestyle is the opposite of mine. I don't have anything to offer a billionaire. It's just he's the first guy to genuinely care about my deep-rooted pain when it comes to my dad. I usually keep it buried. But I feel at ease sharing it with him. He's going through something similar so it's a connection I didn't expect and didn't know I desperately needed.

At this rate, I'm going to have to accept I won't have my phone on this trip. I just hope I find it because I can't afford to buy a new one; it has everything on there. Photos, messages, and most importantly memories.

"Looks like you won't have a chance to keep looking for your phone," Summer says, and I peer up to see Chelsea enter the house. I sigh.

"What's happened?" Chelsea asks, obviously the stress written across my face.

I follow her into the kitchen and see it next to the coffee machine.

My tired brain clearly forgot I made a coffee today.

"There it is." I scoop it up and wave it in the air.

"Alright then. We're all set, let's go," Summer announces with so much enthusiasm, I wonder if I should make another coffee for the road.

If I thought that was the end of my phone drama, I was wrong. Upon reaching the cabin, the girls organized a hiking expedition. The mountain trail led to the most stunning waterfall. But disaster struck when my sweaty palms dropped my phone, and it landed on a rock and cracked. Now I have an unresponsive screen and because it's an old phone, it's not worth repairing.

I spent the rest of the trip without a phone. Despite calling my parents, who wished me a good time, the inability to contact Jeremy weighs heavily on me.

I wish I had memorized his number, but I didn't. And I can't help the way that crushes me inside.

During my girls' weekend, I kept wondering if he texted me at all or wondered where I was. Thankfully, I start my new job today, so I can stop thinking about all the different scenarios for a bit.

I arrive at the office ten minutes earlier than needed because I wanted to get settled before Dalton and Poppy came in. The nerves are choking me, but I try to focus on this great opportunity. I'm working in the career I tried so hard to get. This is a huge company and I have to make a good impression to keep my job longer than the contract.

I've still not been able to replace my phone and I can't ask Dalton to give me Jeremy's phone number. I don't have a phone to call him from anyway and I don't want Summer and Chelsea to share theirs with me. But with my first paycheck, I'll buy myself a new phone.

"Well, hello hello," Dalton says. I swivel in my chair to the sound of his voice.

"Already kissing ass," Poppy mumbles.

"Hey Dalton. Hey Poppy," I say, my eyes flicking between them.

"You ready to work?" Dalton asks.

My face splits wider at his question. "Born ready."

"God. So cheesy," Poppy mutters and walks off toward her desk.

"Oh yeah. I lay it on thick," I call back with a smile.

Dalton places his hands on the desk, wearing a goofy grin. "She'll warm up. She's a hard bitch on the outside, but I promise she is really sweet, and you'll get along so well."

I doubt that...

"I'm new, I get it. She had a relationship with the previous girl, right?"

He nods. "Nailed it," he says, pushing off the desk.

"Let me check emails and then let's make coffee in the break room and catch up on our weekend before we start talking work. I need some time to wake up on a Monday morning."

"But what about Bentley? Won't he want us to start on time?"

"He's easy going. As long as you get your work done on time, you're alright."

That knowledge baffles me.

"How long have you worked here?"

"Five years," Dalton says.

"Too long." A grumble sounds from behind Poppy, and it makes me giggle.

Dalton tilts his head to look over in her direction, calling out, "Oh, don't be like that. You secretly love it and wouldn't work anywhere else."

She mumbles, "Whatever."

He turns with a smirk. "Told you," he whispers.

"I heard that," she barks back, and I pinch my lips together holding in a laugh.

"Let me get settled and I'll come grab you afterwards."

"Okay," I say, returning to my computer.

It's new, but fairly easy to use. I play around and open my email to find a new one from Mr. Spencer.

To Nova,

I hope you're settling into your desk. HR and your colleagues will answer any questions. I'll check in with you later.

I have a project you need to get started on, and if you need help Dalton and Poppy will be able to assist you.

I've attached everything you could possibly need, but I require a well-contracted pricing agreement. I already have the spec sheet, so you don't need to worry about that.

This is to impress a hard client.

Bentley Spencer

Spencer Health CEO

I blink rapidly at the words. An empty feeling in the pit of my stomach settles as I'm delivered my first official task. There's so much new information to consume that I'm afraid to fail. I need to write the perfect pricing contract because I don't know if Bentley allows employees to make mistakes. I trust my gut and my abilities as an accountant, but the fear of getting fired still consumes me.

Hitting the reply button, I quickly type out.

Good morning, Mr. Spencer,

It's been a lovely morning, thank you. What
information about the client do you think
would be useful for me to know about before
I get started on this project?

Sincerely,

Miss Lee

I hit send and try to shake my nerves out of my hands and open the attachment on the email. Scanning the contents, I see it's fairly basic, but I print it out and begin making notes. My head is buried in the papers for ages before a throat clears and I look up into the eyes of Dalton. "You're going to make us look bad if you finish your work before morning coffee."

I bite my bottom lip. "It's an important deal for Mr. Spencer."

"Call him Bentley. He's not that serious. He's a chill guy."

I don't remember feeling 'chill' with Bentley, but if Dalton says to call him that I guess I can. He's been here longer than I have.

"Are you ready for a coffee?"

I check the time and I'm surprised I've been working for three hours without even realizing I haven't had my coffee yet.

"I'd love to."

I stand and we walk off.

"Wait up you two," Poppy calls out. And knowing she wants to join, warms my heart a little. Maybe I can get her to like me. I don't think she hates me. She just doesn't know me. I'm just the person replacing her friend. But I'm going to prove myself. I need this job. It's important to me and my family. More than they know.

CHAPTER 8

JEREMY

I'VE BEEN TEXTING NOVA for the last three days, but I've had no response.

Has she ghosted me?

She could've told me to back off. But I didn't get that feeling from her. She seemed interested in our conversation. To have her disappear and be unresponsive leaves me a little rattled. If she wasn't anyone of importance, I would've forgotten about her and focused on my work. Work is usually the one consuming me, not a woman.

Nova's interesting, and there's a lightness in my chest when we talk. We have so many common interests.

But since she hasn't responded, I haven't been able to concentrate on a single project. Even hearing Blue Morgan on the damn radio this morning on my drive into work reminds me of her and the time we texted while we discussed our love of Million Dollar Baby.

"When will the final pricing contract be ready?" I ask, pinching the bridge of my nose.

"We're almost done," he replies easily. I can imagine him reclining back in his chair all casual.

"What's almost done?" I rebut, annoyed.

"How about you come in tomorrow for a meeting to go over it. I'm sure it will be done." He tries to sound convincing, but I'm not.

"What time tomorrow?" I ask as I open the calendar on my laptop. Casting my eyes over the day.

I could do it at 7a.m., but it sounds like they'll need the day to organize the paperwork.

"How about 5?"

"P.M.?"

I could move the meeting with the local hospital. It just means I'll need to eat when I get home.

"Yeah. I'll have dr—water or coffee."

I'm grateful he remembered I prefer not to drink alcohol during work meetings.

"Water."

"Of course."

"I'll be in your office at 5p.m. sharp, don't be late, Mr. Spencer." Turning in my chair, I'm ready to hang up after moving meetings for him.

"I won't," he says.

I want to sign the contract to buy his micro instruments. I need the details of the instrument and the prices on paper. It will take some time for them to be manufactured and then delivered to each hospital. So I want to secure this contract and get the production started asap.

I hang up not knowing and hit the button to call my PA Kirstie.

"Mr. Lincoln?" she answers politely.

"Can you come here for a second?" I ask down the line.

"Of course."

I hang up, and a second later, she knocks and enters. Her shoes are soft along the carpet. She wears her usual black suit and black hair pinned back. I gesture for her to take a seat in front of me as we discuss tomorrow's full day.

"Hi. How can I help?" she says, her brown eyes meet mine as she takes a seat and pushes her glasses up her nose.

"We need to move the final meeting. I have a new one scheduled for Spencer Health."

"Do you need me to get anything prepared?"

I know the papers she had organized for me already sit inside my briefcase, waiting for him to be ready.

"No. What you prepared last time will work. Just check if there's a date on it and if there is, can you amend that and print it out?"

"Sure. I'll get that one rescheduled. What time are you meeting Mr. Spencer, so I can add that to your calendar and let the driver know."

"I'm meeting him at 5. And thanks, Kirstie, that will be great."

"Do you want me to organize dinner?"

A small smile turns up at the corner of my lip. "I don't intend to stay that long. And I'm sure my housekeeper will have a spare meal in my fridge at home."

"Is there anything else?"

I shake my head and sit back in my chair, ready to get back to my emails. I shouldn't have many as I keep updated on them all throughout the day.

"No. Thanks. That's all."

She dips her chin and stands. Silently, she leaves the room and shuts the door behind her. I check the time because I need to leave in time to visit Grams before she goes to bed. She saw the doctor today and I want to hear all about it.

I finish the last of my work before I switch off my computer and drive to the house.

Three hours later, I arrive at the three-story limestone house with a small porch. But it's her back garden that's spectacular. The flowers, grass, and trees are what I love most about her place.

I knock on the door, expecting it to be my mom opening the door, but I'm surprised to see it's Grams.

"Where's Mom?" I ask, my tone louder and clearly unhappy.

She widens her eyes and then rolls them before grabbing my arm and dragging me in.

"I'm not dying yet. Get in here and give me a kiss. Your mother went to the grocery store to grab me some things I need."

I let out a deep exhale. Relieved she wasn't here alone. What if she was by herself and something happened?

Heaviness sits in my gut.

Moving toward her, I lean in and kiss her cheek, noticing her skin is thin like tissue paper and paler than usual. I note how fragile she is.

She closes the door and links her arm through mine. We walk through the house, and I guide her to her armchair.

"It's so cold in here. Did you want a blanket or the heater on?" I ask after she settles herself into the brown chair.

"No. Come sit down, Remy. Tell me about your day," she says, patting the sofa beside her.

"Mine is the same. I want to know how it went at the doctor's appointment." I ease down onto the sofa. Sitting back but tilting so I face her.

"That's why you're here early," she accuses with a humorous expression.

"I wasn't able to concentrate on work..." I trail off.

Her face pinches. "Why?"

"A girl?"

"You're avoiding my question," I say, dodging her soon-to-be interrogation.

"So are you." She quirks a brow.

I smile softly at Grams. The witty comebacks are always on point. And just when I think I can forget all about Miss Lee, I know with Grams I can't not be honest.

"There's no girl." My voice lacks conviction. I bring my leg up onto the opposite thigh and tap my fingers on my shin.

She hums. "You're still holding something back. Tell me."

I stare at her, hoping she drops it, but the challenge on her face lets me know she's not dropping the topic.

"How did you know?" I ask.

"Remy, I've known you for your whole life. You have tell-tale signs when you are bothered by something."

I sigh. She's right. I may think I'm unreadable but not to people who've known me my entire life. Which gets me thinking.

"Not a word to Mother about this."

She pretends to zip her mouth with her hands, causing a deep chuckle to leave my chest. "My lips are sealed."

"There's not much to say other than I had messaged a number who I thought was the CEO of a medical instrument company. He somehow gave me the wrong number."

"Hmm," she says, leaning to one side of the armchair, her hand sitting under her chin. Already invested in my story.

"It ended up being one of his new accountants. Who happens to be funny, and we were talking but—"

Her face screws up. "I hate the word but."

So do I...

I sigh as I seize the opportunity to get her advice. She's never steered me wrong. "I haven't heard from her since Thursday night."

"And she seemed normal?"

I shrug, remembering all our conversations. "Yeah."

"Have you tried to call or text?"

"Both. But it goes straight to her voicemail. For some reason, I can't stop myself wondering what happened."

I scrub my face, still trying to wrap my head around it all.

Her hand slips from under her chin as she sits up. "I think you've caught some feelings."

"But we've only chatted a couple of times," I argue, disbelieving I have any feelings for a woman. I'm married to my job.

"Great relationships always start from a friendship. You need to have solid groundwork before you date; otherwise, it's just chemistry. And this sounds like you have more than just attraction."

"I thought our brief conversations were good. Easy and fun. I'm just confused."

"Well, how about you ask her boss if everything's okay?"

I frown. "I can't do that."

"Why?"

"He'll think more of it, and I don't like him. And frankly, I don't want him anywhere near my personal business."

"Mm. Would you see her at work?"

Would I?

"I don't think so. I deal with her boss," I reply. Wishing I was dealing with her and not him. "But I say things to her that I've never been able to say to anyone else."

"Such a shame. This one seems special," she whispers, and pinches my cheek like she always does.

Nova is something...I just don't know what.

CHAPTER 9

JEREMY

"WE'RE HERE, SIR," MY driver says, pulling me from an email.

I lean forward to peer out my window and take in the glass building. Not as big as I thought. Not compared to mine.

"I'll be back soon," I mutter as he opens the door for me.

"Yes, sir. I'll wait here until you return."

I slip out of the car and onto the sidewalk. I hit send on the reply email, before sliding my phone into my pocket, and enter the building. I need to mentally prepare myself for Bentley, the guy is a total dick. And no matter how many times I have to deal with him, it never gets easier. But this deal will help all my hospitals and their patients. The micro-instruments will enhance the efficiency of micro-surgery, which means it can help maneuver into obstructed view areas and be able to successfully treat more challenging patients. When it comes to business, I'll put up with his shit just to close a deal. Which is why I'm putting aside any thoughts of Nova. She works in this building and maybe the ghosting is what I needed to remind me of my goal today.

Yeah, she did me a favor.

I don't have to wait long for the elevator.

Entering, I stand in the very back corner as a few people join, but they all hit different levels, so we make multiple stops before I get to the top. Finally, the doors open, and I exit. The loud voice that makes me grit my teeth echoes through the whole floor. Ten minutes and I'm out of here.

Not a fucking minute later.

I stroll in and the young blonde receptionist greets me. "Hello. Can I help you?"

I stop in front of her desk. "I'm here to see Mr. Spencer."

"Do you have an appointment?" she asks.

"Mr. Lincoln doesn't need one," he calls out in the most unprofessional way. As if we're friends.

I follow the sound of Bentley's voice. He's walking toward me like a smug peacock.

"Oh. Sorry, Mr. Spencer," she quickly replies.

"Follow me." He waves me over.

Ignoring her.

Rude prick.

He better be prepared this time. Because I'm already wired up.

"I had the pricing contract drafted," he says, gesturing to the seat in front of his large glass desk. I sit as he continues speaking, "Take a look and let me know what you think."

He slides the papers across the desk toward me. I reach over and swipe them. Leaning back, I carefully read them.

He's trying to talk, but I'm focused on reading the details.

When I'm finished, I ask for the spec sheet. I want more details of the speculums in writing.

"Do you have an updated spec sheet? This has last year's date." I ask, readjusting my suit jacket.

"Let me look." He frowns, taking the paper from me and reading it for himself. "Seems you're right."

"You doubted me?" I say darkly.

"No. No. Our wrong. My accountant went on leave, and she did this just before she left. So, it must have slipped through. No biggie, right?"

I nod. Not happy, but I can't be angry with someone I haven't met or allowed to explain themselves.

"I'll get it updated," he says, picking up the receiver. My phone vibrates and I glance at my wrist. I moved my meeting with the local hospital to earlier today to allow plenty of time for tonight, so I'm not leaving until it's done.

"Excuse me, Mr. Spencer. While you organize the update, I've got a quick call to make outside," I say.

He glances at me as he still holds the phone to his ear but reclines in his chair. "I'll get her to do it now and bring it up."

I rise from my chair.

"See you soon," I reply coolly, turning without another look and striding out to make the call.

The call is a quick one with Kirstie. We run through tomorrow's agenda with the managers at our biggest NYC hospital with the goals and budgets for their departments. When I'm about to hang up, I turn, colliding with someone. "I am so sorry," I say as her stuff falls from her hands and spills onto the floor. I immediately crouch down and pick up...her now broken red lipstick. Noting the name of it is called Brave. Her head is down as she scrambles to pick up the other loose items. The strong waft of rose perfume fills my nostrils and sends my heart racing. I rise to my feet and blink twice, simply staring at her bewildered.

It's Nova.

Fuck.

She has makeup on today. When we talked over video, she didn't have a scrap of it on her face.

Her hazel eyes are so bright and unusual because they have beautiful flecks of gold in them. And when her red lips move they emphasize her brilliant smile, and I think I stop breathing for a second. "It's okay. It's my fault too."

My brain finally begins to work. "Your lipstick," I gruff out, handing it over. Admiring her adorable suit ensemble, a navy jacket and skirt paired elegantly with a white blouse.

She takes it back from me, and electricity hums through my veins as she holds my eye contact firmly. "Thanks," she whispers.

She's affected by this, by me too.

I clear my throat. "Your, ah, lipstick is..." I point to around my lips, and she takes the small compact mirror I hadn't realized she was holding and raises it.

"Oh, God. I shouldn't have been doing touch-ups in the damn elevator. How embarrassing," she whispers, but I catch it.

She dabs at the skin around her full lips, and I'm utterly transfixed. I can't seem to get my feet to move. I'm frozen. Watching her with fascination.

When she's finished, she gives me a shy smile. Her cheeks are flushed, and at that moment, it hits me square in the face. Nova's the new accountant working on this. He said "she," so I was expecting a woman. But I didn't expect a beautiful woman. Fuck, I should've expected her. I should warn her. She shouldn't be working with that sleazy prick. She seems too good for him.

"You're here," I blurt.

My mouth moves before my brain can think straight.

She looks around before giving me a wry smile. "Where am I supposed to be?"

The usual flirty banter that we used to share feels like a distant memory, replaced by an unspoken weight that hangs in the air.

"Where did you go, Nova?" I ask, my voice steady but laced with threaded concern.

Her eyes widen slightly, and she bites her lip shyly before meeting my gaze.

"Nova. You could've said something. This makes things—" I start, but she cuts me off as her hand lands on my chest.

"I'm so sorry. It's not that I don't want to talk to you," she rushes out, her desperate plea for understanding.

Her response has me breathing easier, but I'm still confused about her whereabouts. I know I shouldn't care. But fuck. I do.

"Then what happened?" I demand, searching for answers that seem to have slipped through the cracks of her hesitation.

A touch of pink touches her cheeks, but there's sadness in her eyes that doesn't match the playful banter we once shared.

"I dropped my phone," she confesses, and the gravity of her words pull me in.

"You smashed the screen?" I ask, inching closer.

She shakes her head slowly. "Not just the screen. But it's an old phone so it's not worth fixing."

"Did you buy a new one?"

Her hand reaches around to grab the back of her neck, rubbing it.

"I can't a—"

"There you are." Bentley's voice booms.

I close my eyes and take in a deep breath at his timing.

He's interrupting us. I needed to know that she was about to confirm what I suspected, which is that she can't afford one.

"Sorry, Mr. Spencer. I bumped into Mr. Lincoln, and we got talking," she says sheepishly.

"My fault. I held her up," I add.

I don't want her to lose her job on my account.

Bentley waves. "Come on, let's go to my office."

He ambles off. Nova dips her head and tucks a strand of hair behind her ear as she passes me. She follows behind Bentley, clutching the papers and her bag tightly.

I can't help but twist my head and watch her.

I pull out my phone and text my driver, requesting a new lipstick and phone.

My driver texts back, *a lipstick, sir? Are you sure?*

I type back, *Absolutely. Make sure it's the color BRAVE.*

I send him an image I find online.

After I hit send, I stride toward the office. Inside, I see Bentley sitting down behind his desk. Across from him, Nova sits tensely, waiting for me to take my seat beside her.

I drag the chair out to accommodate my long legs. Sneaking a glance at Nova, I see she's focused on Bentley and refusing to look my way. I like the professionalism she exudes. She clearly wants to impress Bentley. I grind down on my molars. Deep down, I wish it was for me. Leaning to the side of the chair, I position my body toward both of them.

"Have you amended the spec sheet?" I ask, trying to keep my voice level, knowing she had to fix the mess. I don't want her to think I'm blaming her.

"Yes. Nova, you did." Bentley's eyebrow rises as if he didn't know. I grind my teeth again, causing a sharp shooting pain in my temple. Fuck.

"I did. Here you go," she says. Leaning forward in her chair, she hands over the papers to Bentley. Again, I wish it was to me.

What is wrong with me?

Her navy suit jacket rises as she leans forward, allowing the curves of her ass to show.

I shake my head and focus on Bentley, who is scanning the documents. I need to get all the dirty images that are filling my brain out of my head. I need to concentrate on my job. Not on her.

My phone vibrates in my pocket. I don't bother answering. I know my driver will have what I asked for. It should be ready by the time we are done here.

Bentley's face beams as he hands over the documents. "Here you go, Jer..." He begins to say my first name before correcting himself. "Mr. Lincoln."

As I reach for the documents, I can feel her eyes watching me, and I like that they're on me.

Bentley has returned his to his computer, and as I enjoy her gaze upon me, a thought crosses my mind. I know I could teach her better than him. Well, my company could. She'd be better looked after too. I could make sure of it. Here, I don't know what they're teaching her. And fuck, do I even want to know?

I read the spec sheet carefully.

This time noting the changes. More than just the date.

She's impressive. Her attention to detail is alluring.

After scanning the document thoroughly, I read that each of my hospital's operating theatres will have a complete pack of instruments. The set includes six instruments at a total of $1,833.81. And the price includes delivery.

I lift my head and Bentley swivels in his chair. A smug expression on his face.

"Are you happy?" he asks.

I move my gaze toward Nova, her hazel eyes are wide and so fucking hopeful.

It's killing me.

I swallow hard. And turn toward Bentley, unable to look at her and think clearly. *What is she doing to me?* Those damn eyes short circuit my brain.

"More than happy. The entire contract is updated, not only the date."

Bentley's face drops and his mouth opens as if he's about to speak, but I interrupt him to finish talking. "I'm extremely impressed with the attention to detail. Nova, thank you."

A little gasp leaves her mouth. And I turn to face her. She's blinking at me. I don't think she was expecting me to notice because it's clear Bentley didn't. And again, the anger bubbles inside me as to how incompetent he really is.

After some research, I found out Bentley inherited the company from his deceased father. He didn't build the company from the ground up, which is why he's so incompetent. Maybe he never wanted it and was forced to take over.

"She's a great addition to the team."

"More than you deserve," I mutter coldly. But not loud enough for him to hear. I know she heard because a cute laugh leaves her lips.

I look back to Bentley. "Let's sign this."

He rubs his hands together and looks around. "Yes," he says and grabs a pen, then holds it out for me. "Here you go."

I lean forward, grab the pen and sign the contract. Feeling the heat of her stare on me. When I'm done signing, I lower the pen and sit back.

"Done. We're all set. Please call me when delivery is being arranged for each hospital," I say.

Bentley's brows pull down. "Sure. I can organize that."

"Good. I want to be there for each delivery. I'll need to make arrangements to ensure I can make it to each location."

"You do?" Bentley asks, shocked.

"When something is important to me like this, yes," I say. My eyes flick to Nova, and I see she is watching me with her sweet mouth parted. She looks surprised. I wonder what she's thinking.

"All right. I'll have to get someone to schedule that with you," Bentley replies.

I nod. "Sure." Looking at my watch I check the time. "Is there anything else we need to discuss?" No matter how much I want to continue sitting here with Nova, I'd prefer it if Bentley wasn't here. If I leave now, hopefully, I can grab her for a quick chat.

Bentley shakes his head and stands. He rounds his desk and holds out his hand. I shake his hand firmly. "Nice doing business with you."

"I'll see you soon," Bentley adds.

I turn, exiting his office, and stroll to the elevator, seeing myself out. Glad to be leaving. However, I do wish she was following. I pull out my phone and send a text to my driver to expect me down in a couple of minutes. He responds to tell me he left the package at reception.

"Mr. Lincoln," Nova's buttery voice calls. I pause immediately, turning slowly on my heel to face her.

CHAPTER 10

NOVA

His eyes hold mine. Dark, deep, and thoughtful. I suddenly can't find my words. But I called out for him. Why?

When he left the room, Bentley dismissed me, and I knew it was a sign to speak to Jeremy. But now that he's here in the flesh, a few steps away, wearing an impeccable designer suit and a wicked smirk, I'm wordless.

"Nova?" he pushes.

It helps. The fog in my brain lifts, and I manage to stammer, "I-I wanted to talk to you again."

He raises an eyebrow, a silent challenge in his gaze. "You did? So the broken phone wasn't on purpose?" he probes, his smirk taking on a more curious tilt.

"It wasn't on purpose. I enjoyed our conversations," I assure him.

For a moment, he remains silent, his expression shifting. Panic swirls in my chest, wondering if I said something wrong until his words silence it.

"So did I."

Relief washes over me, but the words still hang in the air. We both have admitted we like to talk to each other.

Is that all it is?

It's all that it should be...

I won't be buying a new phone for a while, so keeping our chats going is impossible. He's too busy to exchange emails with me so I won't even bother mentioning it. The reality of the situation settles in, and I reluctantly have to accept that it's over.

"Are you headed down?" I ask in a weak voice. Unable to hold back the disappointment seeping out of my words.

"Yeah, but hang on," he says as he walks past me. I don't move, just twist to watch him stride across the floor, eating up the space in the room so easily with his long legs. He stops by reception where she hands over a bag. I frown. And I can't lie, a rush of jealousy mixed with curiosity strikes me. What's in the bag?

He turns around and walks back until he's standing in front of me.

He gestures forward. "Let's go."

I should tell him not to order me around, but his tone is surprisingly gentle.

I still don't know what's in the bag and it's twisting me up, but it's not my business. I force myself to move forward and forget about it.

We're silent as we wait by the elevator, which isn't a long wait. Inside the elevator, his rich woodsy scent surrounds me. I lick my lips and try to taste it. It's intoxicating just like him. Seeing him online made my heart flutter. In real life, my entire body is fluttering.

"You're headed home now?" I ask, and I wish I didn't because it sounds so pathetic, even to my own ears. Like where else would he be going at 6 p.m.

His head tilts down to look at me. "Yeah. You?"

Staring into his eyes has me spilling the truth. "Yeah. Nothing else to do."

"No boxing?"

I shake my head. I'm surprised he remembered even the small details about me.

"Not visiting your parents?"

I swallow the guilt because now with no phone I can't do my check-ins with them. "I visit Friday to Sunday and call in between." I bite my lip before exhaling slowly. "Well, I used to..."

He dips his chin but doesn't say anything. He presses the lobby button on the elevator.

But we don't move. Another minute later, he presses the button again.

Nothing happens.

"We haven't moved," I mutter, my chest tightening, and it feels like I'm suddenly breathing through a straw.

He presses the emergency button.

"It's okay. We'll be out soon," he says, his voice trying to soothe me. There's no one else in here. I'm alone with him for the first time and this is what happens.

My pulse speeds up as the lights in the elevator flicker. My skin is dampening with perspiration as realization dawns on me: we could be stuck in here for hours.

I take slow deep breaths. I don't want to have a panic attack with him here. I'm not claustrophobic, but the panic rushing through me is from my fear of death.

"It's alright. They won't be long." His voice sounds far away, but the touch on my arm brings my thoughts to focus on him and not the situation we're in.

When he drops his hand away, I want to protest, but he hands me a bag, cutting off my line of thinking. "This is for you."

I take the bag with a shaky hand and a puzzled expression. I look at him. He nods. Encouraging me.

I open the bag and see the familiar packaging. A brand new box of my lipstick and the latest iPhone box.

I blink rapidly and blurt out, "You bought these for me?"

I reach in and grab the box and see the word *BRAVE* and it's the exact damn shade. How did he know?

"Yeah, I broke your lipstick—" he says.

"Not my phone," I reply, turning the box in my hand still in a state of shock.

"No, but I needed to put my number in somewhere. I thought if I waited for you to buy it, I wouldn't see you again."

He wants to see me again.

"I can't take this." I hold out the bag.

He shakes his head.

"You can. I'm not taking it back."

My brain hurts. It can't handle all this niceness. I'm not used to it. I've never had a guy be this thoughtful well...ever.

Yet, this man buys me two expensive gifts. I've seen the Rolex on his wrist but still. Surely, he wants something.

"What do you want?" I ask, lowering the lipstick box back in the bag.

I glance back at him. His forehead wrinkles. "What do you mean?"

His face is close to mine. His hand back on my arm. Does he know I need that right now?

I close my eyes, trying to shut out the intensity of the moment, as the weight of unspoken desire hangs thick in the air. When I open them again, I find the strength to say, "Everyone wants something."

His gaze is fixed on me. "I don't." He softly murmurs with dilated pupils. "Well, I want to talk to you."

"You could have bought me a second hand one. Not the one that's only just been released."

"I can't have it breaking on you." His words carry a tone of urgency and sincerity.

"Sure," I playfully quip, a smile tugging at the corner of my mouth. My eyes drop to his lips, and I can't help but add with a chuckle, "If I didn't know any better, I'd say you were trying to get into my pants."

"Why would I need to buy you a phone to do that?"

"I don't know," I say. I'm becoming delirious the longer I'm in here.

His finger touches my chin and tilts my head back. Our eyes hold once again. "I need to talk to you, remember?"

"Talk to me." I wink.

He shakes his head as a deep chuckle leaves his chest. I find myself wanting to lean in and kiss him. Kiss him with those lips that like to talk to me. When was the last time a guy wanted to do that?

A long time.

And as crazy as it sounds, I believe him.

Opening the lipstick as a distraction. I swipe some on my lips and rub them together. I feel like myself again.

A camera flashes the instant I turn to Jeremy.

I scrunch up my face. "What are you doing?"

"Taking a photo."

"Why?" I ask. As new butterflies swarm my stomach.

"I want your new phone number in my phone."

"You needed my face to do that?"

His eyes bore into me, and I don't expect his next word to be so calm and direct. "Yes."

A shiver runs up my spine. "I still have the SIM at home. I'll keep my old number."

"I'll save your picture to your name."

"Well then, I need a photo of you too. It's only fair."

"I don't do photos."

I roll my eyes. "Isn't that supposed to be my line?"

"No. Your face is so…" He trails off, rubbing his jaw, and looks away. I want to beg him to look at me and continue.

"So?" I press, needing his answer.

"Delicate. Exquisite," he says and turns to face me. His eyes move slowly over my face. I can't understand what he's thinking. He's so hard to read.

"And you're handsome so I need a photo too."

He smirks. "You think?"

I roll my eyes but my cheeks heat. "Stop fishing for more compliments. You're not getting them."

"Was worth a shot." His voice drops low and the way he's staring at me sends tingles down my spine.

After a moment, I reach inside the bag and grab the box. The elevator is obviously stuck, and we need to wait for help. He rang the emergency alarm, so I may as well distract myself. I try to open it, but it's too hard to do it standing up so I lower myself to the floor. I open the box and begin setting it up.

He stands next to me, but must get sick of waiting because he crouches down to sit beside me. "This is a first," he mutters, diverting my attention.

I'm waiting for the phone to be set up. I see his thin lips and deep frown between his brows and a giggle slips out of me. He's a good distraction, making me feel calmer than I did when we initially found ourselves stuck.

"Never been on the floor before?" I tease.

He looks over at me. His dark gaze becomes narrowed and glazed. "Oh, I love being on the floor, specifically on my knees."

"Then what's the problem?"

Is he insinuating what I think he is?

How often has he done that? Why do I want that right now? Sex was fine with my previous two partners––enjoyable even. But a guy going down on me has never been something I've enjoyed; it was way too awkward and clumsy. But with Jeremy, he's a man. He'd be strong yet reassuring. I bet sex with him would be amazing because I'm attracted to him. He's devastatingly handsome and kind and Jesus...Now that I think about it. When the hell did I last have sex? It's been a damn long dry spell if I'm thinking of him doing unspeakable things to me right here in this damn elevator.

"I'm in my suit."

"Can't ruin the suit." I snort.

"I don't care about the suit. I have plenty more," he argues.

I roll my eyes. "Of course you do."

"Nova, suits aren't comfortable."

I'll tell him what's not comfortable. How hot it is inside this stupid elevator. I know I should be freaking out, but part of me is hoping we get stuck here together all night long.

I blink at him. Then a smile splits my face. "Glad I don't have to wear one."

"No?" His eyes run over my navy skirt and jacket. I know he thinks I'm wearing a suit but I'm not. The scrutiny of his gaze intensifies the unease settling within me.

"They're not pants," I argue, shuffling to sit up, as the tension in the confined space of the elevator grows palpable.

"Same thing. Are you comfortable right now?" he asks, his gaze unyielding, and I resist the urge to fidget.

He knows I'm not.

"No. Are you happy?" I challenge him as I look into his eyes. Still needing to tilt slightly to hold his gaze. "No."

"No?" I repeat baffled, the air growing heavier with each passing moment.

"I want you comfortable."

I'm trembling as I peer around the elevator. "It's not going to happen in here." Panic continues to pulse through me. "Aren't you afraid of dying?"

"Seriously? You want to talk about that while we're stuck in an elevator?"

"I need to talk before I have a panic attack in here."

Without warning, his hand reaches out to grab my waist and he gently pulls me to sit between his legs. "Lean back on me," he instructs, and I cautiously follow suit.

His touch guides me until my back is pressed against his chest. His heart is pounding hard into my back while mine feels like it's on a damn treadmill. I exhale and watch him add my photo to my number on his phone then save it.

I grab the phone he bought me and swipe it open. His hand slips from my waist to my hip. Holding me there.

When I'm ready to add his photo, I lift the phone, and he holds out his other hand blocking the view. I take the photo and a couple more, but he's not letting me get a clear picture of his face.

"Just let me have one," I moan. My eyes drop to his pink lips and automatically my tongue sweeps over my bottom lip as my eyes move back to his heavy ones. He's reading my face, and as if there is a magnet between us, I'm drawn to him. The room feels hot and heavy. My body moves closer to his, at the same time he moves his head down and his eyes lock with mine. This close, his scent overwhelms me. My heart is thumping inside my rib cage like I've been boxing for an hour. I'm about to touch my lips to his, when a loud deep voice booms outside the elevator. "Are you two okay in there?"

I close my eyes briefly before calling out, "Yep."

"Stay calm. We'll get you out," the stranger says.

I slip out of Jeremy's embrace, dusting off my skirt as I straighten up. I feel movement behind me as Jeremy rises. Goosebumps erupt across my skin as Jeremy's heavy breath tickles the shell of my ear as he whispers, "I wish he didn't. Because I've been thinking about fucking you in this elevator since the moment we walked in."

CHAPTER 11

NOVA

THE ELEVATOR DOORS OPEN, revealing one technician and one building maintenance worker. It's easy to tell who is who when the maintenance guy has a work shirt, pants, and a safety vest with the company logo stitched on it; whereas, the technician is in his safety gear holding tools. They both stand there assessing us.

"Is everything all right?" the technician asks. And I notice his hair is styled neatly with product. The maintenance worker is wearing a hard hat instead.

I clear my throat and then swallow hard. "Yeah," I say, disregarding the tumultuous emotions within me. Jeremy's words are still ringing loudly in my ear. I'm not sure I would have turned him down. He's obviously hot, but he's also incredibly generous, thoughtful, kind and compelling.

"Okay. Good. I've got someone here to check you both over," he replies.

"Thank you," I say shakily.

"You're out and safe now." The stranger smiles kindly at me. I must be wearing my feelings on my face because he told me what I needed to hear.

A large gentle touch on my back surprises me. Jeremy offers it as a way of giving me comfort again. I don't know if he knows how much his touch soothes me.

I move my heavy feet across the floor. I do wish we could spend more time together...well, more than just we did. Once we're outside and in the hall, Jeremy and I are separated and asked numerous questions. I answer the worker on autopilot, my brain still back in the elevator.

"Are you feeling any pain?"

"No," I reply.

"Are you feeling, okay? You're quite pale."

"Yes," I answer. I can't hear Jeremy's voice and I wonder if he left. My eyes flick across to where he was, and I'm relieved he's getting the same treatment. A smile spreads across my face at his unimpressed expression and stance.

After a couple of minutes, the worker leaves and I awkwardly turn around, wondering if I should say goodbye. I move closer to Jeremy, deciding that I want to have one last conversation with him.

"Thanks for calming me down in the elevator," I say.

His dark gaze is hard on mine. "Let's go eat."

My heart beats faster in my chest at his offer. Eat, as in dinner? As in a date?

"Is that a good idea?" I say, trying to mumble through words getting my brain to work out. "I don't know...it's like nine o'clock––"

"Exactly," he interrupts. "You need to eat."

His directness makes my stomach flip. I am hungry now that I think about it. And I definitely need to eat. "Yeah."

"Come on. I'm taking you to dinner."

My lips part and I stare at him bewildered.

Why does he keep helping me? I work hard to help my family; do I give off a vibe that I want free things?

He senses my hesitation. "Come eat with me, Nova. Please."

The beg of his please makes my breath momentarily falter.

I am hungry...

"Okay. Let's go."

"Good," he says, with a confident smile playing on his lips as he grabs my hand. His grip is firm and purposeful. We leave the building together.

New York City's streets are less crowded now, but the pace is slow. The glow of the streetlights cast a warm hue on the sidewalk where locals and tourists leisurely explore.

"Where are we going?" I ask.

"I've got the perfect place," he replies easily, his response carrying confidence that leaves me rolling my eyes and chuckling.

"Of course you do. Is there anything you can't do?"

He rubs along his jaw, looking out onto the street, before back into my eyes. "There is, but I haven't figured that out yet." He pauses before continuing in a low and husky voice. "I always get what I want."

He sure does.

I don't mind because giving up control and power to somebody else is actually refreshing. I feel like I can finally breathe. Not doing or thinking about everything. The silence is bliss. We walk along the sidewalk, the warm lampposts, the luminescent moon and glittering stars sparkling in the sky. "It's so pretty out here," I mumble to myself.

"It certainly is. There is nowhere else like New York City," he says.

I agree. Some days I still can't believe that I live here. I've never lived anywhere else before, and I wouldn't now because of my parents. But I couldn't see myself ever moving permanently. Spending the holidays in another state or country is one thing, but full time living? I couldn't picture my life anywhere else. New York has the best cuisine, career opportunities and world-class entertainment. I love it here.

We walk another block. I'm tired and getting hungry. I want to sit down and drink some water. The medic gave me a bottle of water, but I feel like I need more.

"Just here." Jeremy speaks, and his voice makes me alert. However, looking around, I frown. It looks like an average building. No lights on. I'm confused.

"Is this place still open?" I ask.

"Yes. I messaged the chef and had it arranged while you were talking to the worker. Our table should be ready."

I'm just not used to this kind of treatment from a man. It's normally me. I'm the helper. No one helps me. Yet. He's helping me. My mind is spinning.

I'm a proud woman who can hold her own and I have for a long time now. But Jeremy insists on breaking down that wall. Throwing his money, lifestyle and accessibility at me. He's buying me things, taking care of me, can I really welcome his help into my life?

We step into the building and head back near a pair of elevators.

I freeze. He stops and looks at me. "You don't want to go in." It's not a question. He's stating it.

I look up at him and dip my chin, ashamed of the wash of terror creeping in. His dark eyes narrow with a worried expression.

"We can take the stairs. There's just a lot of them," he offers.

I shake my head slowly. "No, it's fine."

I don't feel fine, but I can be brave just like my dad is.

His face hovers just a few inches away from mine. His gaze flicks from my eyes to my lips. I feel the heat of his breath on my skin, the anticipation of a kiss lingering be-tween us. He inches forward, his move deliberate, stopping just short of sealing our lips together. But he doesn't kiss me.

"I've got you. I promise nothing will happen to you while I'm with you," he reassures me with words I can feel. That cut deeply into my veins.

I know I can do this.

"I've got you," he repeats, his fingers intertwined with mine as he grabs my hand. Reminding me how surprisingly soft but strong his hand is.

Only a couple of calluses, from weights maybe? But otherwise, it's large and warm, and it encapsulates mine. He's making me feel wanted and safe, just by simply holding my hand and keeping me close to him.

We step into the elevator as I concentrate on my slow steady breaths.

"Keep breathing. I've got you. It'll only be a short trip up," he adds softly. His thumb running over my knuckles.

"You'll be free soon."

The fear is bubbling back in my throat. "Keep talking to me," I beg. Panic is definitely hitting hard again.

"What's your favorite color?"

I frown and turn my head to look at him. "What a silly question."

"Just do it," he says with a deep and bossy tone.

I keep looking up at him as I exhale and answer, "Black."

He stares down at me, an unreadable expression settling on his face. "Do you seriously like black?"

"Yeah, what's wrong with black?"

"Nothing," he mumbles.

"What's your favorite color?"

His eyes hold mine as something passes between us. "Black."

My heart hammers hard in my chest as I whisper, "No."

"It is."

"Are you just saying that? Because it feels a lot like you're copying me," I tease, desperate to lighten the mood. The air is getting heavy in here with the electricity bouncing between us in this elevator.

"Do I look like I need to copy a woman to impress her?" he retorts, his response carrying a hint of challenge.

"No. But I just feel like you're messing with me or telling me what I want to hear."

To keep me from spiralling out of control again.

"I'm telling you the truth," he asserts with sincerity in his eyes.

"I trust you," I admit.

"We are connected in such a strange, unique way that I can't even understand myself. It's never happened to me before..." It's like he's talking to himself. Yet, it's out loud.

I don't really know how to respond, other than, "Me too."

The elevator doors open, and the relief floods my body. I'm okay now. I try to slip my hand out of his, but he grips me tighter. I look up at him and he shakes his head no, as if to he's going to continue holding my hand. End of discussion.

Today has been full of emotions and I don't have much food in my stomach.

The hunger. The highs and lows make me suddenly feel faint.

"Nova, you're awfully pale. Do you need to sit down?"

"Jeez, thanks for the compliment. But I'm fine."

"No, you're not."

No, I'm not.

He really is good at reading me...

"Yeah, I feel a bit light-headed. I need a glass of water."

"Let's go," he orders darkly, and I'm moving faster on my legs. Clearly, not fast enough for him because in the next minute, my feet are lifted off the floor.

"What are you doing?" I gasp.

"I don't want you to faint."

I don't want to make a scene but... "You're carrying me through a fancy restaurant." I look around. The mood is ambient, sexy, and dark with warm lights. There are couples everywhere talking over candlelight dinners. I grimace. Are they watching me being carried bridal style by this handsome man like an idiot? I hope not.

Not that Jeremy cares. He holds me without a care in the world.

I want to enjoy this moment, but I can't because I'm just so in my head.

Seriously. What the hell is he doing?

I'm about to tell him to put me down when I'm lowered to the ground slowly anyway. I'm next to a table and chair that overlooks the city. It's beautiful.

"Wow, that's a gorgeous view," I mutter to myself.

"Can I have a glass of water and some starters?" Jeremy speaks.

"What would you like, sir?"

I didn't even hear the waiter come over.

"A selection. Nova. Are you allergic to anything?"

I shake my head. "No, but you don't need to order the whole menu." I widen my eyes at Jeremy, trying to tell him through my eyes not to be ridiculous.

"The portions are small."

I gape at him as I take my seat.

His burning gaze is waiting on an answer. "Order for me."

His lips lift with amusement.

I shake my head as he orders and take my seat. Sitting across from him, I simply enjoy the view. I still feel dizzy, and I'm not sold that it's just because of the lack of food.

I think it's him.

I shuffle forward and grab a glass of water and gulp it down. Enjoying the cold refreshing feeling.

"Better," he says, watching me with approval.

"Yes, much."

The waiter comes back quickly with some starters, and my mouth waters at the sight.

I grab a piece of bread and dip it in the spinach-artichoke dip. Eating happily now.

He grabs a piece and eats alongside me. "You should feel better soon."

I nod, unable to respond because my mouth is full. But also, I'm a little lost for words. Jeremy is too much. Other than my dad, I haven't had a guy in years worry about taking care of me. I know the bubble will burst soon. Both of us are terrified of losing someone we love. It's not worth falling for someone who will leave you one day.

We should enjoy tonight as friends. I passed my first task at work successfully, and he signed the contract.

Thinking about work, a question for him comes to my mind.

"Do you ever regret the path you chose?" I ask, his dark brows pinch so I add, "Your life path. Like what if you stayed working as a doctor."

He shrugs off his jacket, and it's captivating. My own personal show under the dim lights. I can't drag my eyes away. His strong body fitted with only a snug white shirt. Every vein on his arm outlined and drawing attention.

"Not at all."

He drapes the jacket on the back of his chair, giving me a second to think.

"How did you know to take that risk?"

I meet his eyes, and he rubs his jaw, looking thoughtful.

"One choice can change everything. It's both terrifying and exhilarating. But without risks, there's no change."

"And do you think it's changed you?" Curiosity laces my tone.

He leans forward, arms on the table, a subtle pause emphasizing his openness.

"Definitely. I'm more mature than I was, say, three years ago. Why'd you ask?"

"Being here with you is not what I had planned."

"Do you regret it?" His eyes hold a mixture of curiosity and concern.

"No. It's scary to go off the path and off expectations, you know?" I admit, the weight of my choices and the unpredictability of the moment hanging in the air.

He nods understandingly. "I do. But vulnerability is where our true strength lies. It's the courage we share to be imperfect." He reaches forward, laying his hand on top of mine. The touch is intimate, a silent reassurance clasping my hand, and his gaze softens as he looks into my eyes. "You're good for me."

My body tingles with warmth from not just his touch but his words. My eyes drop to his fingers that are mindlessly skimming my hand in a soft pattern.

"You're good for me too," I murmur under my breath.

I'm surprised by how much he makes my dad's cancer journey less lonely.

I look up to find him watching me with his lips parted.

He grabs his drink and his gold and diamond cufflink catches my attention. It makes me giggle.

His brows draw in again. "What?"

"Your cufflinks. Cards. Really?"

He twists his wrists giving both of us a better view. A flair of playing cards, gold with black details.

"Custom made."

I roll my eyes playfully. "I bet the pens on your desk have Jeremy engraved on them."

He sucks in a breath, shaking his head. "Close."

I raise a brow.

"Just Lincoln."

We laugh and continue eating the starters.

After a couple of minutes, I look back at him and he seems satisfied. I hear this rumble in his chest.

"You got some dip on your lip."

My hand wipes at my mouth. He's watching with a dark, intense stare. It makes me flush.

"Did I get it?"

He shakes his head. "No. Come here." He leans forward and I mimic his position. My eyes watch his drop to my lips. His own are parted and he's enthralled with my mouth.

His fingers tilt my chin up, giving him better access. I welcome his touch on my skin. My breath hitches the moment his thumb swipes over my top lip. The brush is rough enough that it drags my lip.

His thumb pauses at the corner of my mouth and I think he's about to pull back so I lean into his touch begging for more.

He's still so fascinated with my mouth that my silent plea causes him to follow my request. He drags his thumb over my bottom lip slowly, as if he's memorizing the feel of it. My eyes don't leave his face. And if we weren't in a restaurant, I'd let him kiss me. He drops his hand from my face when his phone pings. Quickly, he retrieves it and types frantically on it.

I'm left panting and craving more of his touch. "Is everything okay?" I breathe.

"Yep." He grabs his glass and drinks.

His eyes return to mine. A blaze staring back at me.

The way he's drinking, I can't help the shiver that runs down my spine.

"I had something to ask you."

"Hmm. What's that?" I ask, my voice returning to normal.

"Would you be interested in the boxing weigh-in at Madison Square?"

My mouth opens and closes. I know what he's insinuating, and it would be a dream. He's given me so much today that it's making my head spin. "Those tickets sold out in minutes."

He grins proudly. "You free at 3?"

I'm taken aback. "You're serious."

He nods. "Yes."

While I truly am grateful for the thoughtful gift, it's making me uneasy. "Don't be ridiculous. I can't accept that."

His brows furrow. "Why not?"

I try to get him to understand how I'm not the usual girl who expects a guy to buy me lavish gifts. "You don't need to pay for my ticket. I can afford it."

"No, I take you, I pay," he insists, making it sound simple.

I scratch at my temple, searching for the right words. "Your generosity is touching, but I'm not comfortable receiving multiple expensive gifts without contributing."

His stern expression softens. "I don't mean to make you feel that way. Maybe you can buy the merch?"

I smile in response. "Deal."

It's not about spending the same. I just don't want to feel like a transaction or that I can't afford anything. My new job will bring in more income. It's nothing extravagant, but it's certainly an improvement.

He dips his chin as he grabs more food and eats.

"Have you been before?" I ask.

"Surprisingly no."

That makes my lips part into a wider smile. I love knowing that I'll be showing him something I love that he hasn't experienced before.

"You have?"

"Yes," I reply.

"When?"

"My dad took me. He introduced me to boxing."

Before he got diagnosed and our lives changed.

"I look forward to it."

I'm excited for Friday. Not only seeing the weigh-in, but to be able to spend more time with Jeremy. It reminds me of how my mom keeps telling me I need to get out more.

Maybe she was right after all...

The waiter brings more plates of food. Things that I've never seen before. Oysters, antipasto, and soups. There's so much food. The portions are small but presented beautifully. This is money. Money that I don't have. Will never have. I want more money to be able to buy a house on my own. I'd also like to upgrade my car. I'm grateful that my parents handed it down to me when I was eighteen, but I'm envious of his life, and the freedom money brings.

The waiter comes over and we order our main entrees.

"It's going to be hard to get home at 11 and go to work tomorrow with very little sleep in me."

He shrugs, picking up food to eat. "I'm used to it. I live off little sleep."

"What time do you wake up then?"

"I go to bed around midnight and wake up at 4 a.m. to work out."

"You're only getting four hours of sleep."

He shuffles in his chair, picking up his glass and swirling the liquid around. "I work a lot. It's why my last relationship didn't work."

His drive and passion for work is something I admire.

"Did you do this with her?"

His brows knit together. "Dinner?"

"Yeah."

"Sure. Not as regularly as she'd like."

"Monthly?"

"If it was monthly, I'd have worked with that. She wanted it twice a week."

I couldn't imagine having this type of dinner twice a week. I'd prefer a low-key dinner at home. A cuddle on the sofa. I drop my gaze from the powerful man across from me. His hand runs through his perfectly styled hair. He messes it up slightly. Would I want a dinner like this with him? Sure. I feel special with his eyes and attention all on me. Who wouldn't. But not all the time.

I lick my lips as I look at him.

"She never cared about my lack of sleep," he murmurs. "Probably because she got to benefit from the money I earned." His fingers rubbing against the bottom of the glass.

"I care. That's so unhealthy."

He stares blankly at me. He leans back in his chair with a slight twist in his lips and a raised brow. 'Really?"

"Yes, really," I reply. "You should be getting eight hours minimum."

He chuckles. "I've never had eight hours of sleep. Ever."

"Oh, you're missing out. Sleep is my favorite thing to do on the weekend."

He picks up his glass and takes a drink then lowers it as he speaks. "I'll have to take your word for it."

"Hey," I say. "That's our first difference."

He chuckles again. "You make me laugh, Nova."

My cheeks tickle. And I think I'm blushing.

We eat in silence for a little bit before we order another glass of wine each. I let him choose because the menu was too long, and there was an abundance of wine brands I've never heard of. When it arrives, I take a healthy sip. It's delicious.

The entrees arrive and we eat. Afterwards, I feel relaxed. With a full stomach, from the abundance of food, water, and alcohol. And if it was the weekend, I could see myself sleeping for 10 hours, but tomorrow I have to work.

When we leave the restaurant, he follows me back to the parking lot. As we get closer, I worry he'll see my beat-up car.

"Where did you park?" I ask, trying to think of a way to get him away from it.

"I didn't. I have a driver," he admits.

This is why he doesn't need to see my car. Not only can I not afford a phone, but my car is also in need of replacing. It's a gold 2005 Honda Civic with rust and a missing fuel cap.

"I'm just over there." I wave in the general direction of my car and a few others. "I'll be fine, call your driver."

"He's here, but I'll walk you to your car."

The tone in his voice already lets me know I don't have a choice, so with a sigh, I force my legs to move toward it.

Pausing beside it, he wears an unimpressed expression, but before he speaks, I remember the phone.

I hold out the bag toward him. "Thanks again for the kind offer but I want to earn the things I have. I've never had things handed to me."

"No," he says. "Take it or leave it here on the floor. Either way I'm not taking it back."

I'm trying to find another reason not to accept it, but I've got nothing. I sigh, grabbing the phone. "Well, let me get that photo of you."

"I don't do photos."

Yet, I still try to snap one, but he's quick to put his hand up again.

I pretend to scrunch up my face and be angry, but I can't. My mouth is moving into a smile and he gives me a wry one back.

"I'm gonna get one," I say, as I keep clicking the button, snapping lots of pictures.

"Is that a challenge?"

I shrug. "Whatever you want to call it."

"Fine. But you didn't say just of me," he says, encircling an arm around my waist, while his hand rests on my stomach.

"Can you take it?" I breathe. My hands are too shaky from his close proximity to snap a picture right now.

He slides the phone out of my hand and lifts it up. He leans into my neck and my breath catches in my lungs at his sudden nearness.

His nose tickles behind my ear and his breath warms my neck. He snaps a picture and pulls his face away then lowers the phone.

Slipping his body away from me.

"Here you go," he murmurs, handing back my phone. His voice carries a subtle tremor that hints at how our closeness unsettles him, adding to the already palpable tension. I take it and check the photo. It's a hot picture, but his face is out of it again. Only his side profile. It's a damn good one. Especially when even in the photo he looks like he wants to devour me.

I don't have it in me to argue. I need to breathe the night air. And hear the city sounds to calm me down. I open the car door, taking one last look at him. "Goodnight."

"Goodnight, Nova. Message me when you get home," he replies with his hands now firmly inside his suit pockets. His stance wide and his eyes still watching me.

He's not going to move until I leave. He's worried about my safety. No one other than my family and friends have worried about my safety. Hell, even my friends wouldn't send a text until the next day. So for him to care this much, it rattles me.

I drive slowly out of the parking lot and watch him in my rear view mirror until he's out of sight. I may not physically see him now, but he's still firmly implanted in my mind.

CHAPTER 12

NOVA

WE ENTER THE SLEEK, high tech Madison Square facility, which is buzzing with eager fans. The smell of buttery, slightly nutty popcorn and the sharp, tangy note of cheese waft through the air. Around the sides of the hall are the merchandise stalls, so I purchase the memorabilia T-shirts. Jeremy is on his second work call, so I take in the facility. Memories flood me. I loved it when my dad and I came here together to watch a fight. It's the only time I've ever seen one in person. Those memories fill me with happiness. We had the best night and our fighter won.

Jeremy is talking to a suited gentleman with sandy blond hair. He nods and turns. Jeremy grabs my hand, and we follow.

The man points at our seats.

I gasp when I take in the seats illuminated by bright theatre lights. "These are ours?"

I stare at the two empty ones in Row A. The front. My heart is beating so hard. This is unbelievable.

"Yes. Come," he says.

We take our seats. Jeremy checks his watch.

"When does it start?" I ask.

"Soon."

I frown and as I sit there and minutes pass, no one else enters.

A hard lump forms in my stomach. Something feels off.

"What's going on?" I breathe.

His gaze leaves mine at the sound of footsteps. "You'll see in one minute."

A man in all black athletic wear comes closer, and when his face hits the light, I feel lightheaded.

It's Eddie Cus.

"What's he doing here?" I ask.

"He's training you."

He organized a professional boxing coach to train me?

He trains champions. This is sure to be embarrassing. But I push it aside and know it's only me and Jeremy in here with Eddie. There's no point in being self-conscious; it's a once in a lifetime opportunity.

I can't wait to tell my dad.

Eddie approaches us. We stand. Jeremy shakes his hand and I follow. We exchange hellos.

Jeremy turns toward me, his gaze unwavering. "Why don't you get changed?"

"But I don't–" I begin, but the words catch in my throat when he holds out a brand-new gym bag.

"Inside is a change of clothes and gloves."

The bag dangles between us, a silent invitation and a challenge, leaving me breathless and caught off guard.

I take the bag, our fingers brushing against the cool fabric. My mouth is parted, trying to suck in deep breaths, because the surprise has overwhelmed me.

Inside the changing room, I open the bag to find a pair of custom-made gloves initialled with gold NL letters.

I pull out the stylish athletic wear. I hesitate but not for long because I don't want Jeremy coming in here, or worse, Eddie.

I put on the black tights and green top that feel like butter against my skin. I tie my hair up but leave my bangs out because I don't have pins.

I head out a little shaky, but as soon as Jeremy spots me, he licks his lips and gives me a wolfish grin.

He likes this outfit.

My liners and gloves are already on.

"I'm ready."

"You are." He winks.

He guides me up into the center of the ring, where Eddie stands holding pads and a harsh frown.

Jeremy leaves the ring and I follow his steps until I see him take a seat in one of our seats.

"You ready?" Eddie asks, pulling my eyes back up.

"Yeah, Coach."

He holds the pads up and begins instructing me on the art of boxing.

At first, it's a friendly sparring session. But as I hit the pad and the echoes surround the ring, a new enthusiasm at the challenge hits my veins. As he shouts his next order, I follow. Hitting the leather hard. The atmosphere is electric. My usual poised and sophisticated hit transforms into a determined fighter, showing Eddie my strength and agility.

Even with Jeremy's eyes on me, shouting or clapping, his passion doesn't deter me.

The smell of leather and sweat fills my nostrils. It's a display of resilience and determination.

When Eddie tells me we're done, I straighten and catch my breath before thanking him. My body is perspiring and the skin on my knuckles is broken, but I smile at the weight that's been lifted from my shoulders from the session.

I exit the ring and trot down the stairs, my legs shaking.

I reach Jeremy who grins at me. "You really shined out there."

Eddie flipped a switch in me. He knew what to say and do to bring the fighter in me out.

"You think?"

"Like a star." His fingers graze my temple and I lean into it.

"You captivated me with your intensity and focus."

I'm high from adrenaline and his touch. I'm speechless so he speaks again.

"I wanted you to have a private session before the official weigh-in starts."

"So we're still seeing it?" I ask in a daze. Unable to believe I am getting more tonight.

"Yes. But head to the changing rooms and freshen up. I'll wait here. Take your time."

I walk into the bathroom, ready to take a nice shower. After I soak my muscles in the hot water, I step out to get changed, but to my surprise, there's a massage therapist waiting for me, a setup arranged by Jeremy.

After the massage, I enjoy the snacks and refreshments that are laid out. Then slip back into my blue jeans, brown boots, cream knit sweater, and walk back out to find Jeremy.

I take the chair beside him, and he immediately kisses my temple. "You good?" he asks, his voice low and soothing.

"More than good."

He nods in acknowledgment, and we settle in waiting for the weigh-in to start. The arena gradually fills with people, their movement and loud conversations create a buzz of excitement.

I steal a glance at Jeremy, noticing how his usually hard face is softer tonight. He tilts his chin down, catching me checking him out. A smirk plays on his lips, and with deliberate movement, he shifts his hand to my shoulder, pulling me closer to him.

I wonder what else tonight will bring, but disappointment floods me when he has to leave to deal with a major power outage at work.

"Is it just me, or has today just dragged on?" Dalton sighs loudly from his desk.

"Just today or do you mean this entire week?" Poppy adds.

"Tell me about it. I've aged about ten years since Monday," Dalton says.

"You and me both," Poppy says.

"So, any exciting plans this weekend?" I ask, peering over at their desks.

Poppy is slumped over hers, looking between Dalton and me. She's warmed to me now. Less rigid. She still scares me though. "Nope. The usual. Sleeping in. Binge-watching Netflix and tackling my laundry. You?"

I wait for Dalton to answer. He's squirming in his chair with a smirk. "I've got a date lined up."

"A hot date, huh? Who's the lucky person?" I smile.

"Well, you know how I went to Chicago, Poppy?"

Poppy raises her brows. "Mmhmm."

"I met a cute guy named Blake in line for coffee. We got talking and hit it off but he had to go before we could finish our conversation."

"Did he move here?" I ask.

He shakes his head. "Nope."

"You met him on a dating app."

"Wrong again." He smirks.

"Tell us," I say.

He grins. "He dm'd me on Insta. Said he saw me in a pic that came up on one of his friends' stories."

"Smooth," Poppy says.

"We've been chatting back and forth for a while now," he continues. His chair swivels side to side, and his gaze flicks between Poppy and mine.

"So he's in town and you're going out. Where?" I ask.

"We both love sushi. There's a nice but casual place just off 7th Avenue near the library."

"I know the place. Best smoked salmon I've ever had," Poppy adds.

"What about you?" Poppy asks me, sitting back up in her chair.

"Just the usual. Netflix and chill with my roommates."

Dalton smiles. "Hey, that sounds pretty good too."

"Definitely. But I expect a full debrief about your date on Monday."

Poppy mumbles her agreement too. But her eyes are on her computer screen. "Hey, did you just get the email about a team building workshop happening upstairs right now?"

Dalton grumbles and turns around. I swivel in my chair and open my email to find I've got it too.

"Another afternoon with awkward icebreaker questions," Dalton says.

I giggle, knowing exactly what he means, but for me, it'll be good to meet everyone since I'm still new.

"But we might be able to find out everyone's spirit animal or most embarrassing childhood memory."

I laugh.

"But seriously, these things are a bit of a drag, aren't they?" Poppy murmurs.

"You know what will get us through it?" Dalton perks up, rising from his chair.

"The coffee machine on the top floor." Poppy stands and walks toward the door, pausing at my desk. "And donuts."

"That sounds good." I smile as I pack up my desk.

"What on earth happened to your hands?" Poppy gasps at me as she leans over my desk.

I look at my healing knuckles, remembering the date Jeremy organized. I hold my hands out and stare at them. They look better than they did that night. I busted them open.

"Shit," Dalton says, coming to stand beside Poppy.

I giggle. "I'm fine."

It's what I had to tell Jeremy too who insisted I have a doctor look at them post session.

"Looks like you were in a fight," Poppy hisses. Her face is tight and disapproving.

"I was, but in a professional way. For a date." I lower my hands to my lap.

"You're telling me you went on a date and he organized this?" Poppy asks aghast. Unable to believe what she's hearing.

"Yep," I say proudly.

I know it's strange to others, but to me, it was perfect.

"He organized a celebrity trainer and had boxing gloves made with my initials engraved on them."

"That doesn't make this any better," she mumbles.

"You need to come to the gym with me and try it," I say.

Poppy snorts. "You'll never catch me boxing."

"Come on," I beg.

She shakes her head and pushes her bag higher up on her shoulder.

"You're weird. It should've been romantic," Dalton says.

"We are, but it helped us bond," I reply, with a smile.

Dalton sits on the edge of my desk. "How?"

"Not only did he organize the date but hearing him cheer and encourage me from the side of the ring was something else. It definitely made our connection deeper."

Dalton grimaces. "I would have taken a spa day."

I laugh. "He did organize a massage therapist afterward. The hot stones and oils felt amazing."

"Now we're talking," Poppy says, nodding.

"Boxing relieves so much stress. It's better than a massage," I say.

Dalton chuckles. "We're going to have to agree to disagree."

"I'll change your minds one day," I say as I walk around my desk and we leave the office for our team workshop.

"Good luck with that!" Dalton replies.

CHAPTER 13

JEREMY

I STAND BY MY office window, staring out at Central Park. The sun's shining down on kids skateboarding and people hustling about.

I've been clutching my coffee cup Kirstie brought me. I finally take a sip when there's a knock on the door. Lowering my cup, I stand up and walk toward the door.

It must be someone familiar because Kirstie didn't call or knock.

Leaning back against the window frame, I take another sip of my coffee, welcoming the warm liquid along with the caffeine hit.

My brother Harvey enters.

I push away from the window, wander across my office, and head toward one of the sofas. On the table my laptop is open and papers for my next meeting are laid out. Grabbing the top paper, I ease back into the soft fabric and prop my leg up on my opposite thigh, getting comfortable.

"Harvey," I say, resting my coffee cup on my thigh. The warm cup heats my leg as I wait for him to sit down on the other sofa.

I'm surprised to see him so early on a Monday morning. He's usually as deep into work as I am.

"Brother," he says with a hard expression. "I know it's early."

I twist my wrist and read the time. "Yeah. It's not even nine a.m."

"I know. It's an early visit, but I need your help," he answers, taking a seat on the cream sofa, but instead of relaxing, he's sitting on the edge of it.

"Do you need a drink?" I ask, casting my eyes across the room to the drink trolley before facing him again.

He shakes his head. "No. I'm good."

"What could you need my help for?" I ask curiously.

Harvey, who is four years younger than me, and a brilliant guy, is someone I'm proud of. He pushes me business-wise to focus hard. To not give up and never back down. And to not take no for an answer.

I sip my coffee, wondering what could possibly have my brother on edge like this. He's never had to ask for help, especially from me.

"What about coffee? Can I get Kirstie to get you one?" I ask. His knee is bouncing up and down and it's causing me to tap my coffee cup.

He shakes his head again. "No. I just had one. But I changed my mind about alcohol..."

My eyes narrow as I watch him stand and then stride toward the drink trolley. With his shoulders up tight to his ears, he seems tense.

He grabs a glass, fills it with ice then pours a decent helping of whiskey.

I watch him take a drink and then walk back to the seat. This time settling a little farther into the sofa.

I'm still wondering what the fuck is going on with him, but I'm grateful to him for pulling me away from my earlier thoughts of Nova.

I've only been able to sleep about two hours tops. Just thinking of her beat-up, shitty old car has me grinding hard on my molars. Is it too much to think about buying her a new car? I knew the moment I spotted the car why she insisted I call my driver and not follow her. She was embarrassed. I don't want her to feel like that with me. Does she think it would make me think of her differently?

Because it doesn't. If anything, it makes me want to protect her more. I don't want to scare her off, but that dump of a so-called car looks like it could blow up at any moment.

I hate the thought of her driving the thing to God knows where, but thankfully, I did get a text last night.

> **Nova:** *Remy, I'm home. Get some sleep. More than four hours, please.*

Reading her message made me happy. But also, I had to hold myself back. Fighting my emotions for her and her damn safety. I barely know her. I can't buy her a fucking car.

A phone, easy. But a car? I'm scared she'd run for the hills.

I'm only just starting to get to know her. And what I've seen so far, I really like. So having Harvey here today is a great distraction.

Harvey shuffles on the sofa, cradling his glass. "I have a problem with a company that I'm planning to work with."

I drop the paper in my lap and run my hand over my freshly shaven jaw. "What problem do you have?" I ask, baffled. How does he have a problem buying a company? He buys and sells companies every single day.

"I went in to help this company that's on the edge of bankruptcy and..." he says but pauses to take a sip of his drink. "I didn't expect to meet the feisty daughter who is trying to save it."

The gleam in his eye now makes sense.

"Hmm. There's something about this one then?" I state, biting back a grin. Glad I'm not the only one messed up over a woman.

He mumbles words I can't catch. Other than a simple, "Yeah."

"Is there any way that she can save the company on her own?" I ask.

"Maybe, but I doubt it," he answers unconvincingly. "It's a multimillion-dollar debt. I don't see how she could save it." He sighs. "But the look of determination in her eyes. The fire, the sassy attitude. And yet, this sense of fear I get from her that she's hiding something makes me soften for her," he admits.

I can read his face. He doesn't like that she makes him feel vulnerable.

Harvey usually walks in determined to buy the company. He's the youngest Lincoln yet the most ruthless. He'll take what he wants with no fucks given.

So for a woman to stop him...I wish I could have seen it.

It makes a small smirk rise on my face. "So she's hot. I get it. But why is she being stubborn?"

"It's her parents' company. Her dad died. And she's trying to save it."

I wince with sympathy. I'd hate to lose anyone from our family. We're close. Yes, we fight like all families do but overall, we love each other. We're a tight knit family who actually enjoy each other's company.

"Does she have time?" I ask, feeling oddly sad for this woman. It's strange. I'm wondering why I'm so fucking soft these days.

His knee is still bouncing erratically up and down. "I could probably buy her some time. But not much."

It's obviously tearing him up.

"What do you want to do? Do you just want to take it from her?" I ask. I know the answer, but he needs to admit it out loud. He wants reassurance, that's why he's here. He wants to be told it's okay not to be a dick.

"That's the problem," he grumbles.

He drains his glass and tips it toward me. "Need a drink?"

I hold up my coffee cup. "I'm okay with just coffee this morning, thanks." I chuckle. "Help yourself. Drink as much as you want."

He doesn't bother waiting. He's up and on the move, already adding more ice and a splash of whiskey.

He takes a swig before he rejoins me.

"This is the fucked-up part." He exhales audibly. "I want to give her more time and I don't even know why."

I grin wider. I get what he's saying, I really do. It's how I feel about Nova.

"There's just something about the way she wants to fight for her parents that I find attractive."

"Our family is close. And you see yourself in her. We would do anything for our family."

"Exactly," he counters. "And she's doing the same thing in the only way she knows how."

"So her standing up for her parents' legacy is a trigger," I reply. "Were they in this situation before the dad died?"

"They were," he replies, taking a sip before looking solemnly at the floor.

"That's fucked. Even I feel sorry for her," I admit.

"Yeah, see my problem," he says, lifting his chin back up to face me.

"If she's making you feel something in that cold heart, I say give her the time."

His knee finally stops bouncing. "But what if nothing changes?"

I suck in a breath. "Be kind. But take the business if her time's up."

"Or I could pay the debt for her..." He trails off looking at the empty glass.

"Fuck, Harvey. No," I say. Here I was thinking I was the only one with woman issues. I was thinking of buying Nova a car and Harvey here wants to buy this woman a company.

"You can't be that stupid. You don't know this woman," I add.

He sighs. "I know. I'm being ridiculous. I'll just have to be firm and not think about her and do my job."

Hearing him talk about a woman is strange. He's always been the outgoing, playful brother, especially when it comes to relationships. But I've always wondered whether he was just protecting himself. To hear that a woman is affecting him in this way, it makes me naturally curious.

"What does she look like?" I ask.

He rises to take the glass to the trolley, setting it down.

"I don't know," he says, taking his seat again.

I give him a look that says I'm not buying this shit.

"Fine," he says, annoyed.

She's hot.

I can guarantee that.

"She's beautiful and has this unique heart-shaped face," he explains it as if she's here in this room and he's picturing her. "Even though she's determined, there's this softness about her."

"Oh, you've got it bad," I tease.

I'm soft about Nova but I'm keeping my mouth closed. For now anyways.

"Shit. She's getting in my head now."

I laugh and he gives me a shut-the-fuck-up look. Which makes me laugh harder.

"Shut up, dickhead. I better go and get to work now," he says standing up.

I glance at my watch and check the time. "Yeah. I need to get across town for a meeting."

"Will I see you tomorrow night?" Harvey asks.

I stack the papers on top of my laptop and rise from the sofa, taking my cup with me and walking to my desk. Lowering the coffee, I check my calendar. "No," I say.

"Why?" he asks, approaching the desk. "Do you need to work?"

"Yeah. I'm going out for celebratory drinks. I signed the contract with Mr. Spencer. The one for the ophthalmology instruments."

I know we've discussed this before.

"Nice, brother," he says.

"Yeah, massive deal. This is going to change my hospitals. And more importantly, it will allow us to treat more complex patients."

"So proud of you," he adds with sincerity.

"You too, Harvey. You too. And keep me updated."

"I will. I will," he says, raising a brow at me. "And any news with you?"

"About what?" I ask, confused.

"Women."

I swallow hard. He doesn't know about Nova, so I don't know why there's a lump in my throat.

I want to tell someone about Nova, but it seems a bit too early. He's shared about his dilemma, but I don't have time right now. I'm lucky if I've got five minutes to explain Nova. And Nova is not a five-minute conversation. No, she's so much more. We have so much in common. Yet I don't want to share all these little things. I want to keep them private for a little longer.

Because if I explain everything, he'll jump to the conclusion that I'm falling in love with her. But that's impossible. I'm dedicated to my job; I don't have time for love.

Friends talk on the phone, go to events together, and buy each other things. There's nothing more to it. But if I try to tell Harvey or any of my brothers that I want to spend time with a woman, they'll ask more questions. And fuck, I have questions I need to answer first.

What makes me want to protect her and keep her safe?

Protect her from the sadness of the world.

Yep. Fuck. I'm getting soft. Definitely not telling my brother.

And anyway, after the celebratory drinks, we'd be done. There'd be no reason to see her again. So there's no reason I need to tell my brother because there's no relationship to explain. Other than my pathetic crush on the beautiful brunette.

"Unfortunately, no. Nothing to report yet," I lie through my teeth but know it's for the best.

"So it's only me. Well, thanks for your opinion. And don't say a word to anyone, you hear me?"

I keep my mouth closed even though it wants to smile widely. I do the zip sign my Grams does over my lips.

"My lips are sealed," I say.

"Good. I'll keep you updated," he says, turning around and making his way out of my office.

Before leaving, I check my email and read a new one about the need to hire new accounting staff. Immediately, thoughts of Nova come to mind, prompting me to impulsively text her.

Jeremy: *Do you want a new job?*

I regret it the moment I send it. Why did I fucking do that?

Nova: *No. I just got one. Why?*

The regret worsens when she replies with a no.

Jeremy: *I'm offering you one here.*

Nova: *Thanks, but I'm happy here.*

Jeremy: *If you change your mind.*

Nova: *Thanks, Remy.*

With disappointment sitting heavy in my gut, I refocus on work. Standing up, I get ready for my meeting and hit the button on the telephone to tell Kirstie I'm ready to leave.

But as I grab my things, my mind drifts. And I can't help but wonder why she'd rather work for Bentley than for me.

CHAPTER 14

NOVA

HE OFFERED ME AN accounting position at his work, but I could never take it. I couldn't work for someone I had feelings for or that I'm attracted to. It'd be a conflict of interest. Whether he feels that or not, I couldn't accept his offer.

Would it be better to work for his company than Bentley's? Of course, but working for him is not an option. I need to focus on being here. Not worry about another job opportunity.

Since I started, Bentley has been better. He's much more professional. His eyes stay on my face and there's no flirty behavior.

As I stand there, I look at my wardrobe, wondering what the heck I'm going to wear to this work celebratory yacht party.

Like seriously, who the hell throws these types of things?

Bentley Spencer does.

His description of attire was casual. I can't dress casually at a work event. Even though the way Mr. Spencer describes it is less work and more play.

I get confused by Mr. Spencer. My dad always taught me, bosses are not lenient and carefree ever, and they often have very strict rules. Plus, I like structure. It makes sense to me. His way comes with added stress.

Even though Dalton and Poppy both insist I go casual, and that Mr Spencer is serious when he says it's a celebration.

Dalton is wearing black skinny jeans and a white shirt and sneakers, of course. Poppy said she's wearing a flowy dress and some wedges. She still barely looks in my direction or says more than a few sentences, but it's more than what I got when we first met.

My eyes run across every single item hanging in my closet and then I prowl through drawers of clothes. Nothing. I'm not happy with anything in my wardrobe. I typically don't wear dresses. You're more likely to find me in jeans and a top. Or shorts and a top.

But now I'm second-guessing myself.

As I take the stairs, I'm hit with a rich buttery smell. Eggs and bacon. I inhale deeply as I hit the final step and enter the kitchen.

"Good morning," Summer says.

"Morning," I say, twisting my hands together. "Can I ask a favor?" I add.

She turns her head from the stove. She's still stirring briefly to look at me. "Yeah, what's up?" she says.

I walk closer and she turns to stir the eggs once more before switching off the burner.

"You know how I have the yacht party for the celebratory drinks for Mr. Spencer selling 200 million dollars worth of product?" I explain.

"Yeah. What about it?"

"I don't have anything to wear and since you're the most fashionable and fun friend I have...Will you help?"

Summer rolls her eyes. "Stop trying to kiss my ass."

My brows rise and a grin stretches across my mouth. "Is that a yes?"

"Yes, I'll help your lost cause."

She brings the pan to the plate and looks at me, lifting it higher as if to offer me some. I shrug. "Please."

She grabs another plate and then serves me some as she answers, "Don't stress. I'll help you find something to wear, but let's eat first."

"You're the best. I knew you were the right one to ask."

I turn to get some forks out for us but pause to ask, "Where's Chelsea?"

"She stayed at the douchebag's house," Summer spits.

We sit down across from each other with our plates of food.

I get her hesitation, so I can't blame her for the attitude. "Ah, right. Well, I hope for her sake, he's treating her better."

Summer looks at me like I've got rocks in my head. "People don't change. And definitely not him. He needs a new personality," she mutters.

I can't help but agree with her.

"So anyway, what are you going to do with your hair and makeup?" She shifts the subject back to the party.

"My usual," I say, already having that part figured out.

"Nice. But wear your red lipstick."

I smile. I love the red lips too. And the fact people think it's a me thing makes me happy.

My mind suddenly goes to Jeremy. He bought me a brand new one, in the exact shade I like. Now, I can't help but think of the way his fingers grazed my hands every single morning when I put it on.

Summer narrows her gaze at me. "Something's up with you."

"Nothing's up with me."

"Chelsea can lie about being happy in that relationship all she wants, but you... You can't lie straight to my face."

I sigh. It would be amazing to finally share something about Jeremy with my best friend.

"Last week, I ended up stuck in an elevator for two hours with one of our richest clients. That's usually not a big deal, but in this case, it was. Because we had been flirting through text for days before that," I blurt.

Her fork hits the plate with a bang, and I wince at the sound.

"Sorry. What? Who?"

"Jeremy." I'm unable to help the smile that forms on my face, remembering the electricity we had.

She makes a tut sound. "I can't believe you kept this from me. Now, you're not leaving until you tell me every single detail."

I laugh and explain, "I freaked out in the elevator, so he held me and calmed me down."

Her eyes widen slightly. "What happened after you were out?"

"We had dinner together."

I return to eating before it goes cold.

"Did you kiss him?" She wiggles her brows.

"No."

"Did you want to?"

I'm chewing eggs, so I nod. "Mmhmm."

Her shoulders shake as she laughs.

I swallow. "Stop laughing at me."

There's this weird attraction I have to him, but even with our few commonalities, our lives are too different.

"Sorry. Tell me more."

"He found out I lost my phone and broke my lipstick, so he bought me new ones."

Her mouth opens and closes before she murmurs, "He's generous."

I look down at my food.

"You're not happy?" she says.

I can't deny it, my silence and disapproving look gave it away.

"I'm trying to be, but I can't help feeling slightly offended."

"What did he say when he gave it to you?"

I frown, wondering why that matters.

"That he wanted to talk to me."

She quirks a brow at me. "He seems caring. It's better than dating someone like Bobby."

The mention of Chelsea's boyfriend makes my skin crawl. He doesn't buy her anything. Ever. Not even a card or gift for her birthday, their anniversary, or Christmas.

"True..."

"Do you think he's buying you all this stuff just to sleep with you?" She winks.

My teeth scrape my bottom lip as I ponder. "I don't know."

"Does it matter? You could just have some fun." She wiggles her brows.

I laugh at her insinuation. "I could use some fun."

"That's my girl."

I shake my head. "I need to be cautious, but it's a nice distraction."

"So he'll be there tonight?"

"Yeah." I bite the corner of my lip.

She smirks. "Then you better wear something hot."

We finish eating, clean up, and head into her room.

I'm suddenly feeling lighter having told someone about Jeremy.

After a shower, I walk out and find her opening her wardrobe and pulling out a couple of dresses. As she is about to grab more, I wave my hands out in front. "Stop. stop. stop. This is plenty," I say.

"We can never have too many options."

"Can we just start with what we have here? I just don't want to get overwhelmed and I'm on a time crunch. I've got to be on the yacht by six."

"Of course. Let's just start with this one. I feel like your red lip, dark hair, hazel eyes and the green and white summery dress will look beautiful together."

My mind immediately drifts to Jeremy. He's going to be there, and I'm hit with a sudden adrenaline rush. I smooth down my top, ready to find the perfect outfit. A mix of sophistication yet sexy. I picture the way his eyes will linger on my lips and then drop over my body. I already know if he kissed me tonight, I would kiss him back. I'm so attracted to him and I'm ready to live a little.

It dawns on me that he's not going to be wearing a suit. And then I wonder what he is going to be wearing.

Getting to see him in casual clothes excites me.

He excites me.

"Yep, let me try this on," I say, heading to my room to quickly change.

Once the dress is on, I look at myself in the mirror and smile. I run my hands over my hips, loving how soft the fabric is.

Summer comes beside me. "It looks amazing on you," she says with a pause. "Even better than it looks on me. Which is so not fair," she adds with humor.

I giggle, which then turns into a sigh. "Nothing looks better on me."

She rolls her eyes. "Oh, shut up. You really don't know how gorgeous you are. Jeremy won't know what to do with himself when he sees you," she says with excitement.

"I feel like I want to vomit." I start, before she spins me around to fix my hair on our way to the bathroom.

"I get it, I do Nova, but it doesn't mean you can't live. After everything you've been through this year, you deserve to have a good time, give yourself permission, just this once."

I douse myself in my rose-scented perfume and carefully add my red lip.

"You are going to a party on a big yacht, with a guy you happen to be attracted to. Please, don't fuck this up. I'm so excited."

"Glad you are. I'm shitting myself," I say, taking a seat on my bed. "He's rich and can have anyone he wants. I don't get why a man like him would want me. I have nothing to offer," I say.

She sits down beside me, running her hands up my arms. "Nova, I will not let you talk about yourself this way. Just because a guy has money doesn't mean he's better than you."

"I know but—"

She shakes her head. "No buts. You're one of the kindest, most generous people I've ever met. I can see exactly why he would fall for someone like you."

"No one said anything about falling."

"Yes, but a crush can turn," she adds.

"I know but let's not get ahead of ourselves."

We hug and she whispers in my ear, "Well, you're all ready to go. So there's only one way to find out. Nova, please go have some fun. Go celebrate and maybe get to know your colleagues a bit better."

"One of them hates me. I'm sure of it."

"Well, then tonight let them get to know you the way we know you. Show them how fun Nova can be."

I smile. "Thanks, Summer. I really needed this chat. But please, don't say anything to Chelsea. I don't want to discuss him with anyone unless it is something, you know...I don't want to get my hopes up. I think that's what I'm trying to say."

"I totally get it. You can tell her whenever you're ready. It's your business. But please keep me updated. This is the most exciting thing that has happened to me all week."

"I better get going," I say, checking the time. I want to call my parents on the way to check in and maybe I'll go see them tomorrow night.

"I'll be home late tonight so don't wait up for me."

"Maybe you're going to have such a good time that you won't come home at all," she says, wiggling her brows at me.

CHAPTER 15

NOVA

I STEP ONTO THE stairs that lead onto the large yacht. I made it just before it departed.

When I look around, my mouth drops open...it's huge. There are people everywhere. On the deck, in the cabins and main salons. I scan around to see if I can recognize anyone. I wonder if Dalton and Poppy are already here.

I need to make a decision quickly. Do I head left or do I go right?

I decide right, which is the back of the yacht, where there seems to be more people. Following the latest pop song. I can't believe I am here. I've never been on a yacht before. And I'll probably never be again. Glancing around at people as I pass them toasting drinks, I wonder if this is the norm for them. It's definitely more of a party than quiet celebratory drinks.

Who are all these people? Do they work for Spencer's company? Or do they work for Lincoln's?

Speaking of. I wonder where he is...

I focus on walking and not slipping in summer sandals. Even though they're low heeled, I'm still getting used to them. I'm glad I chose this dress as everyone has a similar outfit on, so at least I can pretend I fit in.

I wonder if everyone here has Bentley's kind of money. I feel a little out of place since I don't and will never make crazy amounts of money like them. But if there's one thing my parents taught me growing up it's that those things don't matter. More money would be nice, but it's not necessary for happiness. With my dad being sick, I'm content with what I have right now.

I take one step at a time looking around. The people in the group beside me tip their heads back laughing. I walk around them and head toward the bar; some are sipping drinks while others are swinging their hips and dancing to the music.

I walk slowly through the crowd of people, searching for a familiar face. The longer I look around, the more uneasy I become because I don't see anyone I know.

However, once I arrive at the very back, I take in the view. I've never seen New York like this before. The city lights, the bridge, the landmarks like the Statue of Liberty that are softly illuminated in the distance. The gentle sound of the water lapping against the hull as we glide through it.

"Nova?" Bentley's voice booms loudly.

I search the faces until I find his before answering, "Yeah?"

He gestures me over. "Come here. Let me introduce you to some people," he says, obnoxiously louder than normal. He's wearing a white dress shirt and tan chinos with his long, messy blond and gray hair tucked behind his ears.

I wander over the wooden floor, and when I'm close, he slips his hand over my shoulders. In a friendly way. I welcome his arm because I don't know anyone else here. And the relief I feel flooding my body just from knowing him hits me.

He begins pointing at people and introducing them. Then I ask him questions about his yacht. He's obviously seen my awe of it.

"My parents gifted it to me when they upgraded," he answers easily. As if that's a normal thing. To him it would be; to me, it's unheard of.

"Lucky you," I say. "You have some nice parents then."

"I wouldn't say that, but you know, things like this have its perks." He shrugs, but the tone of his voice makes me wonder if he's not close with his parents.

That saddens me. I can't imagine not calling my parents every day or swapping fantasy books and stories with my mom. I've always had this soft spot for people who aren't as close to their parents as me. I know it's a dumb fantasy and I understand not everyone has the relationship I do with mine. And sometimes it's for the best. I guess I just can't relate.

"Well, it's a beautiful yacht," I say.

After some research, I discovered that he also inherited the business from his father. He had been working for his father since he left college, but the articles I found referred to him as a notorious party boy. Bentley gives me the impression that he only cares about making money to support his lifestyle.

"Grab a drink. And have some fun. The sale is done. We need to celebrate."

He is the boss and he's being insistent, but I don't feel comfortable letting loose.

As a server passes by, I ask what drinks they have. I decide on some champagne. One of the only two drinks I'll have tonight.

I look around at the men and women. Everyone is holding a drink or eating as they engage in conversation. Servers walk around with trays of small yet delicious looking food.

The chatter isn't too loud, and I can hear a new pop song playing in the background.

"Who are all these people?" I ask, feeling calm now that I'm here on the yacht.

Bentley drops his arm and takes another glass from the tray before the server walks away. Then, turning to scan the crowd, he shrugs. "A mix of people. My staff and Mr. Lincoln's. Even a couple of existing and future clients."

"Well, this is some celebration," I say, not really knowing how to put into words how overwhelming this feels.

"Come over here. Let me introduce you to more people. I don't think anyone else you know is here."

Great...

"Okay," I say, following behind him.

But as we walk, I see Dalton and Poppy sitting there. They spot me and I wave. My eyes widen as if to say, *please come and save me*. A silent conversation. Of course, Poppy rolls her eyes as if I'm a burden and she really doesn't want to. But Dalton excitedly waves and then jumps up, grabbing her hand and dragging her along. He gives me a wry smile as they come over.

"Hi. Um. Mr. Spencer's showing me around," I explain. My voice carries a pleading tone that I hope they pick up on. I want them to come with me.

"Yes, exactly what Nova said," Bentley says. "Come with me and I'll introduce you to some important people."

I'm thrilled he has asked them to join.

Bentley inspects their drink and says, "I see you all got drinks. Perfect. Let's go."

We walk, but it doesn't take very long to find the people he's looking for. We are down one side of the yacht now, where a guy sits there leaning back, drink in hand. He has wavy blond hair that's swept to the side, almost a little too long for my taste. He can tuck it behind his ears. He may be wearing sunglasses but I can tell his eyes are zeroed in on me.

Oh, no. I think to myself.

I take a sip of my bubbles, wondering where Jeremy is?

I had a feeling he was as excited to see me in a social setting as I was to see him.

I'm sure he's late.

He would be a nice friendly face to have around, but also, yeah, I can't lie to myself, the only reason I am here––and all dolled up––is because he is also going to be here.

If I don't find him soon, I'll text him.

"Grant, I'd like to introduce you to my colleagues," Bentley says as he waves a hand over each of us and introduces us. "This is Nova, Dalton, and Poppy. They work in my financial and accounting department."

"Nice," Grant says. "You're trying to get me to talk numbers before we've spoken about design or any other finer details, Mr. Spencer. Smooth, very smooth." He laughs.

"I never stop working," Bentley replies, tossing his head back and letting out his own chuckle. "But never, Grant. I'd never do that to you. I'm just getting you familiar with my team. I know you'll be working with me. There's no one better than us."

I can't help but laugh inside. Bentley is good at talking business, I'll give him that.

"Take a seat, everyone," Grant says.

"I'm going to grab us some food. I'll be back in a moment," Bentley says.

Dalton and Poppy have already taken their seats, so there's only one spot left, and that's between Poppy and this Grant guy that I've never heard of. Grant leans back with his arms straight out over the back of both chairs.

I take a breath and sit down. Careful not to lean my back too far into the chair because his arm would be just behind my neck. I don't know this guy and wouldn't feel comfortable being that close.

"Your boss is smooth, isn't he?" Grant asks me.

I turn to face him. "Yeah, he's very subtle," I say sarcastically.

The other two are talking amongst themselves. I want to interrupt and ask them if they can talk to this guy instead. I'm so new to the company. Jesus. It's like they're just feeding me to the wolves right now. I don't want to say the wrong thing or reveal too much. He could be a potential client. I want to prove I am worthy of my spot in the company.

"His company has been a really good place to work for. So I think you'd be making a mistake not working with Bentley."

A deep rumble leaves his chest. "He seems to really know how to hire people. I sense you're being completely honest."

"I am," I respond. I believe I try to always be kind and honest.

I take a sip of my drink, but it goes down the wrong hole. I choke on a bubble. I'm coughing when Grant's hand touches my back, and he leans forward. Close to my face. "Are you okay? Do you want some water?"

My eyes prickle with tears from the bubbles of the champagne. Oh, God. What a great impression.

I nod. "Please."

His hand is still on my back as he tries to wave down a server. I look too until my gaze lands on dark, pissed-off eyes from across the yacht.

Jeremy.

I struggle to catch my breath. The air thickens with an unspoken tension. His arms, tense and unmoving, are crossed over his chest. His gaze, icy and piercing, bores into me as if he can read every thought running through my mind. My heart races, but it's not from his obvious dislike of the man beside me. No, it's something deeper, something electric that sparks between us. My eyes sweep over his impeccable body. He's stupidly gorgeous.

The way his muscles strain against the fabric of his shirt makes my fingers twitch with an undeniable desire to touch him, to trace over the contours of his tight jaw, up his neck, and into that perfectly-styled dark hair.

He's frowning, an expression of displeasure is etched across his stunning features. The sunglasses that had been on his face now rest on top of his head. They must have covered his eyes until he spotted me.

Oh, crap! Panicking, I attempt to remove the guy's unwanted hand that still rests on my back. Leaning forward, I'm relieved when Grant's touch slips from me.

I stand in a rush. "I don't want to bother you. I'll go find myself some water," I say to Grant and then tell Dalton and Poppy I'll be back.

I hurry off toward Jeremy. I don't want him to think... If roles were reversed, I'd be devastated, so I do what I'd like to be done to me. I move toward him and really take in his outfit. Tan-colored loafers that match perfectly his tan shorts. My favorite is his white linen shirt rolled up his forearms. It looks delectable against his sun-kissed skin, with the dusting of chest hair peeking out of the top of his shirt.

He's manly, warm, and apparently extremely sexy when pissed off.

He meets me with his chest rising and falling. I'm still holding my glass, but he doesn't have one, so I lower it to a nearby table. When we stand toe to toe, he stares down at me. "Who was that guy?"

"I don't know," I answer honestly.

Luckily there's not too many people around us on the deck of the boat. And the ones that are around, are too engrossed in their own conversations to focus on us.

My throat dries in panic. I've hurt him. I swallow and explain. "Bentley introduced me to him. I think he's going to be a potential client."

His features don't change. "Why did he... Fuck, why was he touching you?" His tone is annoyed. Not in anger but hurt.

"I was choking on stupid champagne bubbles," I mumble. "I'm such a mess."

"You're not a mess, Nova." We stay silent. "I just didn't like seeing his hands on you."

You don't say...

"I don't want anyone else touching you." I feel every word under my skin.

"Why?" I ask, unable to hold back.

He inclines his face, so his mouth meets my ear. "You know why," he whispers, his breath tickling my ear. I shake my head softly, but I don't breathe. I hold it as I wait for him to explain.

My skin prickles at his words. I want him to touch me.

"Who wants a drink?" Bentley calls out, moving through people near us.

I suck in a deep breath and take a step back. *That was close.*

I can't believe I was going to let him kiss me in front of my co-workers and boss. I'm supposed to be making a good first impression as an employee. Tonight means everything to me. And as much as I want to kiss, I can't. I need to think about my parents, and if I lose this job what it means for them.

"Can I get you a drink?" Jeremy asks.

Jeremy plus alcohol seems like a lethal mix.

"I don't think I should drink anymore," I say.

"Are you sure? You didn't get to enjoy your champagne."

"Mm true. One more won't hurt anyone."

I wouldn't mind having something to take the edge off.

Jeremy nods to Bentley who beams back at him.

"Here's the man I was looking for," Bentley says coming to stand next to Jeremy. We take our drinks. I grab a new champagne and Jeremy grabs a drink with amber liquid.

"There's someone I wanted to introduce you to," Bentley continues.

I sip my champagne, watching the interaction over my glass.

Bentley waves over a serious looking short, dark-haired man. He's wearing a similar outfit to Jeremy.

I wonder if I should stay or go.

Bentley goes to open his mouth, but Jeremy's voice cuts in. "Asher. Nice to see you again."

"It's been a long time between meetings," Asher says, in a low gravelly tone. Not a hint of a smile on this man's face.

"I'll leave you boys to it," Bentley says and strolls to the next group of people, offering them more drinks. I must admit, he is a good host when it comes to parties.

"How are your new Primary Care Clinics going?" Jeremy asks.

Asher's eyes widen a fraction, under the night lights, I see a hint of glimmer in his eye as he's asked about his business.

I watch them talk, sipping my drink, my gaze ping pongs between them in fascination.

"I've opened another ten with expansion plans."

Jeremy offers some advice, and they organize to catch up. I can't close my mouth.

I'm in awe of how fluid he is with business. I'm so transfixed that I swipe a new glass of champagne from the tray passing by.

I finish my drink in a few sips as the guys continue talking. When my glass is empty, I decide it's a good time to find my friends and colleagues, Poppy and Dalton, who I haven't spoken to much tonight.

Moving around the yacht, I'm about to head up the stairs to the upper deck when I hear his sexy, husky voice just behind me. One of the speakers is above, so I didn't hear him approach. I turn around to face him.

"I was looking for you earlier." His hand circles my wrist. "And now I am doing it again."

The corners of my mouth turn up. "I didn't want to interrupt you before, so I thought I'd take a walk."

The touch on my wrist makes it hard to think when he draws lazy circles over my beating pulse. The alcohol has definitely kicked in. I feel like I'm floating. He stares at me, and with his heavy cologne filling my nose, I'm not sure what to say.

"You were late," he asks, it obviously has been playing on his mind all night.

The deep crease of worry between his brows makes me brave. "Did you think I was going to miss this...?" *Miss you.*

His eyes soften. "Then where were you?"

"I had a hard time getting dressed."

His eyes drop slowly over my body like he's drinking me in. "You could wear a paper bag and still look hot. If I wasn't here on this fucking boat right now..."

"It's a yacht," I interrupt with a smirk.

"If I wasn't here at this stupid celebration, I'd be..." He stalls.

"You'd be what?" I breathe, desperate to hear the answer.

I need him to finish that sentence like it's my next breath.

He leans so his mouth is an inch from mine. My breath hitches. Is he going to kiss me?

Please...do it.

"I'd rip that fucking dress off your body and kiss that lipstick right off your mouth."

My mouth parts at his declaration. I don't think I could wait until we're off this damn yacht. The party has picked up now, and we are heading farther into the ocean every minute. It's been a long build up to now. We've talked, flirted, and now he's staring longingly at me.

With a few glasses of champagne in my blood, I feel brave. I bend forward, feeling his warm breath on my lips. I move to seal our lips together when someone clears their throat.

I straighten up, looking over Jeremy at Grant.

"There you are." Grant walks toward us.

Closely behind him is Poppy and Dalton. They look around until they spot me.

"I was looking for you two." I point at them. Specifically leaving Grant out of it to make it clear I'm not interested in him.

"I thought you fell overboard." Poppy hiccups, but there's a small lift in the corner of her mouth. I'm not sure she realizes she's doing it, but with the way she's swaying on her feet, it's easy to see she's had a lot to drink.

"Looking for the bathroom." Dalton points at Poppy's head from above her. "Someone's not feeling the best."

She moves to the edge of the yacht, holding on to the side next to Jeremy. He turns to check on her and my heart swells. I'm about to offer Poppy help to go to the bathroom when Grant whispers, "Jeremy isn't what he seems."

I blink rapidly. *What?*

He's warning me.

Or is he jealous?

I'm about to ask what he means when Jeremy interrupts, "Excuse me, I would like to show Nova to the sun deck."

I look over and Dalton is walking Poppy away.

"Nova care to join?" Jeremy pushes when I don't answer.

"Sure." I nod toward Jeremy. I don't want to be around Grant anymore.

He takes my hand and pulls me in the opposite direction.

Grant narrows his eyes. "But you were headed to the upper deck."

This guy is observant and makes me a tad uncomfortable after his threat.

When there's enough distance between Grant and us, Jeremy asks, "What did he say to you?"

"He was warning me away from you."

We walk along, but before we get down to the sun deck, he stops and turns. His body is tense. "This back is mine to touch, not his. Hell, not anyone else's." His seductive deep tone melts me.

I stare back at him, enamoured. "I thought the attraction was just one-sided," I mumble.

"You have no clue, do you?"

I shake my head.

"Do you know how much I want you right now?"

I blush at his words. "No. I thought I had some silly little crush on you. You're way out of my league."

"Nova," he says as his hand touches my shoulder, then moves up to my chin. He tilts my head back so his eyes can bore into mine.

It's definitely not a one-sided feeling here. And it's the anticipation that's killing me. I think if he was just to kiss me, I would work him out of my system. I'm sure I'd get over this silly crush but the fact that he keeps tempting me and making me wait for the kiss. It's killing me.

"You don't come from the same world as me," I admit. Honesty comes as easy as breathing near him.

"You get me more than anyone ever has. Are you sure I can't change your mind about working for me?"

His words make my heart swell. I can hear the sincerity in them. But I can't. "I can't work for you."

"Why not?" he asks. "I'll give you double what he's paying."

The money...God. That sounds so good. What that money could do for me. For my family. But I keep that thought to myself. If I was to work for him, I couldn't be with him. It'd be going against every rule in the book and that doesn't sit well with me.

"I don't want to mix business and pleasure."

He lets out a frustrated sigh.

My heart races in my chest. "If you were my boss, I wouldn't be able to do this."

I grab the sides of his head in my hand and bring his lips to mine. His lips are soft with a hint of roughness––or is it urgency as if the almost kisses have sent us into a frenzy of desperation. He grabs my sides and pulls me to him.

He is strong and I welcome his passion. It mimics my own. I follow his lead when his tongue hits my lips and I part them. One sweep of his tongue in my mouth and I shudder. He pulls back, staring at me darkly for a long time. We remain silent and the only noise is our heavy breathing.

"It probably wouldn't be a good idea. If you work for me. I'd barely get anything done," he admits with a smile that causes the lines around his eyes to show.

Chapter 16

Nova

I NEED A MOMENT to suck in some air and cool down my body after our hot kiss. I step to the side of the yacht and look out into the night. "It's so pretty, don't you think? But it's a bit cold..."

And before I've even finished the sentence, he's behind me. He wraps his arms around me. I don't dare fight his warmth. I sink into his hard body. He's tall and so manly. He covers me perfectly, and yep, I can feel that hardness against my back. He's aching for me too. With that knowledge, I'm encouraged to wiggle my ass over him.

"Hey," he whispers darkly into my ear and bites me.

I gasp. "Remy. What are you doing?"

His touch on my skin feels good. When was the last time a man had his hands on me?

A very long time.

I wish I could grab them and place them on my body. Specifically on parts that are aching for him.

"Warning you. Don't do that again. I know you felt how hard I am for you. You don't need to drive me nuts. Otherwise, I'll bend you over right now. And go against what I said earlier and fuck you hard as you hold that railing there."

"What if I want an audience?" I say.

His mouth is still close to my ear. "I'd give it to you if you really wanted it."

I shake my head. "No, I don't want...I don't want to share. I just want you."

He cuddles me tighter. "Good. I don't like to share."

I sink further into him. Keeping my ass away from him and trying hard not to tempt myself to rock my hips against him.

But I will probably get him off and not myself and you know what... If I'm being tortured, so will he.

We stay silent watching the houses, parks, and other ferries. My mind is no longer just freaking out about his presence and his body so close to mine, but also by the prospect of being with a guy after such a long time. I'm about to ask if he wants to grab another drink when he speaks first.

"I told my grams about you the other day," he says.

"You did?" I clarify, turning so now I'm in front of him. My back is to the ocean.

"Yeah. She knew something was up and she made me spill."

I laugh.

"Growing up we visited her and Gramps for Sunday dinners, where we ate chilli and cornbread. She made sure to have a one-on-one conversation with each of us to find out how we were doing at school."

I smile. Enjoying the fond way he talks about his childhood memories. "She would give us candy during our chat. Mom and Dad never knew."

His eyes shimmer with mischief and I imagine his face as a child getting candy behind his parents' back.

"I like her," I reply.

"She'd love you."

"Why?"

I wonder what things we would have in common.

"You're sweet, humble, and funny."

His words make my cheeks tickle with shyness. I'm sure I'm flushed.

"I wouldn't call myself funny but thanks."

"You are, and I've never found that trait attractive but with you..." He reaches out, stroking my neck until his hand settles along my throat and his thumb rests on my lips. He touched me like this before. And it makes my legs weak. "It's captivating. I want more. I can't get enough of you."

His eyes take in all of me. It's like he's trying to read me. His thumb taps on my lip. I'm glad he's confused by us too.

I'm bumped into him from behind. A heavy body colliding with my back sends me forward and into Jeremy's arms. He catches me.

"Watch where you're going," he spits.

I try to turn my head, but the way Jeremy is holding me stops me seeing past his arms. I'm snuggled into him. Wrapped in his warmth and delicious masculine scent. My hands on his chest take in the tight pecs underneath the linen shirt, which I wish was on the floor. I want to explore his body. Like where does the hair end? Does it go directly to his pants or stop?

"I'm sorry man," a guy's voice slurs. It pulls my mind briefly away from dirty thoughts but not for long.

"You should be," he fires back with venom. His voice vibrates under my hands.

Heavy feet tap away.

"Are you all right?" Jeremy asks me.

I nod. "Yeah." I try to step back, but he grips me harder.

I tilt my head and we are inches apart. My mouth parts farther and I lick my lips. He catches it and another grumble or is it a growl leaves his chest.

"Tell me not to do this, Nova." His voice is thick with desire. His hands roam over my back and down to my ass where he pushes the front of me onto his hard cock. Between my thin panties and dress and his hard erection, I moan.

"Fuck"

"Please."

"Nova," he warns.

"Please," I beg, trying to get him to cave. His eyes snap away as if he's still trying to respect me and crap, I shouldn't be doing this. But I can't stop. I try to think about my job, but he did offer me one. He wouldn't take it back after we sleep together, would he?

That's what I want, isn't it?

Yes.

"How long are we on this stupid thing for then," I ask.

"Another ten minutes at least. Given where we are on the river and not docked," he says, his head dropping to the crook of my neck where he nuzzles in.

"I can't wait that long," I breathe, tilting my hips on him.

He looks around, swearing as his mind comes up blank.

"Nova. There's really nowhere here..." he says frustratedly.

"Maybe later."

"Fuck that. I've got an idea." He rasps, his eyes dark and burning with the same desire swirling inside of me.

"Come." His gaze sweeps over my face then down over my body before he grabs my hand and pulls me down the stairs and to a room.

"Where are we?" I ask in a shaky breath.

"In Bentley's office."

I look around at the dark and boring workplace. Where's the books? It looks like a spare room. I'm pulled by the hand by Jeremy. He's leaning on the edge of the desk. A dark smoldering look on his face. I barely have time to think before he grips my hips and pulls my body between his parted thighs.

"Make yourself come," he orders.

My core hits his erection, my breath leaves in a whoosh. "Huh?"

"Rub your wet, hungry pussy on my cock until you come."

I shake my head at his request. "Don't be crazy. I'm not dry humping you here." But my voice is weak, giving away just how much I'm struggling to fight him. I should be worried that I'm in my boss's office, but my desire for Jeremy takes over.

"Nova. Do it."

A thrill powers through me at his tone. "We don't have time," I say in a wobbly voice.

"You have ten minutes."

We stare unblinking at each other. As he really looks at me, I can tell he actually wants this. And so do I. But I've never done this before. This is so out of character for me yet exactly what I want.

Fuck it. I need to live. For five minutes, I'll forget about the consequences of my job and solely focus on Jeremy.

Keeping my hands on his strong shoulders I tilt my hips and feel his large erection jerk against me. His body responds so easily to my touch.

His hands sit above my ass, and he leans over as if he's hugging me. But he slowly leans his ass farther against the desk for more stability and it helps keep him still on the next roll of my hips.

"Yes-s-s," he stutters.

I breathe loudly as I continue to chase the orgasm. Trying to keep the same pace. I can feel myself getting more wet. Being in Bentley's office adds to the thrill.

Jeremy's mouth trails warm air up and down the side of my neck. Never kissing me, just simply tickling me. It drives me wild. I want him to lay those lips on me. I don't know how much longer until I start begging. For now, I swallow a whine and continue. He's grinding his cock against me as I rock down. It hits my clit perfectly, causing my back to arch, and I moan.

He already knows how to read me. Imagine how he could control me if I let him in the bedroom. No clothes. I clench as I imagine his strong body controlling me.

My breaths quicken as my body tightens in response.

"Remy," I mumble.

"You're so beautiful," he rasps, and it takes me over the edge. Unable to scream like I want to, I bite down hard on his shoulder and ride the orgasm out. His fingers grip me tighter.

When I peel myself back, his eyes are feral. And crap, I want him to fuck me right now.

"I'll take you home."

"Is there anything you won't do for me?" I ask in a daze as I come down from an intense orgasm.

"No." He inches closer, dragging his hand along my jaw to the front of my neck, his thumb resting on my chin as he leans forward. Those fingers on my neck sink in harder and my heart beats wildly in response. But he doesn't kiss me.

He pulls away. "Calm down, *star*. Let me get you alone in my bed, so I can rip this sexy dress off your body. I want to see all of you."

"But—" I'm about to argue and say, "I should say good-bye to Bentley."

He shakes his head, and it silences me.

"He's been in the cabin for hours. I doubt he'll be back."

"If I get fired because of you, that job offer of yours better be real."

"Everything I say to you is real."

I swallow the lump in my throat and nod.

With that piece of information, I relax.

"Let's go," he gruffs out then grabs my hand and storms us back upstairs. I look ahead and see we've docked. I bite the corner of my lip with excitement. *Finally*.

I keep up with his steps. We're silent as he texts on his phone like a madman with one hand. We stop next to a private car.

I'm sad it's not a limo––what I would give to get him alone in the back of one of those. Because if we had a privacy screen, I'd be on his lap like a cat in heat.

He opens the door and I slide in. He then closes it and climbs in from the other side. He orders the driver home. We sit in the back quietly. I feel his presence and my gaze drops to the space between us. His knee touches mine, and it's like he's done that on purpose. The anticipation of sitting beside him and not having him is going to kill me. But it will only increase the upcoming passion.

I stare out the window as we drive. Until his voice cuts in.

"It'll be a thirty-minute drive."

My head turns to face him. "Okay." I don't really know what else to say.

His hand taps on his leg. "Come here," he says.

I frown.

"Lie down and relax."

I curl up and lay my head on his muscular thigh. My heart is in my throat when he immediately runs his hand through my hair. My eyes flutter as he repeats the action. It's unusually sweet and pleasurable.

"You do a lot for me. What about you?" I say quietly, my eyes checking to see if the driver heard. He doesn't move, so I'm going to hope he doesn't. The radio is playing so maybe it will drown out our conversation.

"Pleasing you gives me pleasure," Jeremy whispers.

I try to move, but he holds me to him.

"Stay. Let me do this."

Why does he make me so responsive? My body naturally relaxes as if it was made to listen to him.

His hands still stroke my hair. He seems to like it.

I'm tired and my eyes struggle to stay open. He must be watching me because his next words are more orders.

"Close your eyes for ten minutes, but before that, tell me what you feel like eating."

"Nothing. To be honest." My stomach is rolling with nerves about what's to come. I can't think about food.

"You need to eat. We aren't coming up for air tonight. So you need to be well-fed, rested, and hydrated."

"McDonalds," I answer without thinking. It's something I love, and I feel satisfied once I've eaten it.

"Rest your eyes. I'll wake you when it's here." His hand stroking my hair makes it too hard to fight.

So I don't. Instead, I snuggle up to his thigh and enjoy the attention. I've never had it before and it's becoming addictive. He's becoming addicting.

CHAPTER 17

JEREMY

I SLIDE THE HAIRBAND off her wrist. She's asleep, and before waking her, I gather her hair up and tie it. I like her hair down, but I also love to see her pulse beating on her delicate neck. I want to devour her the moment we step into my house.

When she ground her sweet pussy along my length, I was about to snap. She is insatiable and I had to hold myself back from coming right there with her. Her face as she comes is indescribable. Her red lips parted and her eyes bright and heavy with lust. It's as if she glows afterward. I wanted to fuck her on the yacht, but I'm a selfish man and I wanted her alone.

The way that guy, Grant, had his filthy hands on her made me see red. I don't know what's coming over me when it comes to Nova, but I feel protective, and I don't ever want another man's hands on her again.

I pull up my emails and begin working. Work never stops, even on the best days. Before I know it, my driver is telling me we arrived at McDonalds. I stare down at the sleeping beauty on my thighs. She looks delicate and at peace sleeping on me. I put my phone down and rub her back. My back. My Nova.

"Nova."

She stirs mumbling, "Remy please."

I smirk, wondering what she's dreaming about. The way she's begging sounds like a sexy dream. And I love that I'm the star of it.

"Nova," I say a little louder.

Nova blinks her eyes open slowly and turns. I'm looking down, and she starts laughing suddenly. "I can't believe I fell asleep."

"You must've been tired, baby."

"I was..."

"Not anymore?"

There's a sparkle in her eye. "Not anymore."

I know what she means, and fuck, she's everything. With one look that says she wants this as much as I do, I grunt. "Good. Let's order and get you home."

The word *home* slips too easily from my mouth. I don't think she picks up on it. Or if she does, she doesn't say anything.

She sits up and I slip my hand on her thigh, needing to touch her.

"What would you like?" I ask.

"Cheeseburger meal with a coke. Are you eating too?"

"Yeah. Why?"

"I just didn't think you'd eat it." Her voice drops and so do her eyes. She runs her gaze slowly over my shirt before clearing her throat and returning to hold my gaze. "Aren't you used to caviar and oysters?"

A deep rumble leaves my chest. I get her question and if I was her, I'd think the same.

"I'm not a fan of either of them. But shh, don't tell anyone."

She bites down on her bottom lip, fighting back a giggle, and looks at me with these big shimmering eyes. I want to kiss her again like it's my last day on earth.

That first kiss ruined me. I can't imagine what our second one will be like, when we get to do it where we don't get interrupted, or I don't have to stop. Because I don't think I'd ever want to stop kissing her once I start.

She brings out the playful Jeremy. It's so refreshing. I've been working my whole life and I'm tired. I love my job, but she gives me something I didn't know I needed: companionship, friendship, and maybe even a relationship.

With Nova, I can see all those things.

I order our meals. Both the same.

"Are you copying me?" she teases and pokes me in the side of my stomach.

I curl over and my face is closer to hers again. "Yes. I haven't had a cheeseburger in so long. I haven't had Mc-

Donalds in a long time either. So I figured you'd choose well."

Her head rears back. "Hey. Don't put that kind of pressure on me. What if you hate it?"

"I'm sure I won't. I'm sure whatever you choose I'd love."

Her eyes drop down and I can't tell what she's thinking. Her cute nose is pink, and I just soak in her until our order is ready.

The smell in the car is so rich with fat and salt it makes me hungrier.

She sits up. "Looks good." Nova smiles.

I tilt to face her. "It does."

"My love of food is the reason I box."

"Is that the only reason you box? I thought you said it was good for stress."

"It does help with that. It centers me."

"I need to check out your gym."

Her face brightens at my suggestion.

"I'd love that."

She hums and I know she's happy.

It makes my heart swell. One offer to visit her and she's satisfied. God, she's so easy to please.

All my previous flings have been so high maintenance that I couldn't date anymore. Nova is like a breath of fresh air. She's easy and so fucking normal. Usually, I can't ever seem to attract them, so I think I'll have to thank Bentley for his fuck-ups, because it led me to her.

The car pulls into the underground car park.

"Fancy," she says.

"It doesn't change me," I quickly add, suddenly worried my house will scare her off.

Her hand reaches out to touch my shoulder. "Hey. I know that. It's just, you live in everyone's dream suburb, and I'm assuming, dream house."

"You haven't seen it yet."

"But I will," she says with a husky tone that has me licking my lips and twisting them up.

"You will," I say. "Right fucking now."

I lace my fingers in hers and pull her out of the car. My sudden need to have her is taking over.

CHAPTER 18

NOVA

WE GET INSIDE AN elevator. Of course, he has one in his own house. I take deep breaths and his hand settles on my back in a kind gesture. It calms me immediately. The elevator stops and the doors open. His house has the same colors as what I'd seen on the video that one time. It's masculine, clean, and sexy. It screams Remy.

He exits the elevator first and I follow closely behind. We walk past the entry and I'm expecting a tour, so when he stops suddenly, I slam into him. My body's pressed against his. He spins quickly. His hands fly to the back of my head as he towers over me breathing heavily. His strong body feels so good. The way his warm breath tickles my face makes it hard to breathe.

Our eyes collide with so much want. I'm no longer hungry for the McDonalds; I'm only starving for him.

My name leaves his lips as he smashes his mouth to mine. Our lips automatically move in a perfect rhythm. I moan as I feel every part of my body pressed against him. My skin, my apex, my thighs, my hands, and my lips all touch him. I grab his solid shoulders and moan. He growls. I need more of him. I want to taste him.

I run my tongue slowly over the seam of his lips. He opens them as his hands tighten in my hair.

Then one of his hands slips from my face to my neck, his hand pauses to feel the crazy beat of my heart. My tongue enters his mouth and I tilt my head to explore. He mimics it, kissing me tenderly. His taste is addictive and perfect. My tongue tangles with his, and I lean my body into his. I feel his thickness grow against my stomach. I moan again. This time rocking my hips upward, trying to cause friction between my aching pussy and his hard cock. I want him to destroy me. I want to feel full and completely satisfied.

His grip around my neck intensifies and I moan again. I grip his shoulder muscles tighter and he pulls back, breaking our kiss. I pant and open my eyes, staring longingly at him. His eyes are feral.

"Remy," I pant, unable to make a full conversation. I just need him at this moment.

"Fuck." He grunts and his hand slips from my neck.

I almost whimper. I don't want him to stop. I want him to ruin me with multiple orgasms until I beg him to stop. He takes my hand and walks me through the house. His kitchen comes into view and it's incredible. Bright whites and splashes of gray.

He walks me through the house until we hit a bedroom. His bedroom.

I turn to find him staring at me. Waiting for my approval.

How does this handsome man still not know? I've already given him consent.

I push up on my tiptoes and slam my mouth to his. He catches me in his arms and pulls my body into his. His strong, tall, powerful body feels incredible against mine.

The heated, deep kiss is intoxicating. I love the taste of him. A mix of mint and...him?

Our kiss is making the air crackle around us. Especially when his hand settles on the spot over my neck and jaw. It feels so right.

I hum into his mouth as his tongue tangles with mine.

My fingers find his shirt buttons. I unbutton them with shaky fingers. The anticipation is taking over me. I want to take it slow and go fast at the same time.

I bite his bottom lip and he growls *fuck* against my mouth.

The sounds he makes when I do something excite me to try to do more.

I've never been this eager or bold. Definitely not with sex. I've had good sex, but Jeremy is screaming great. The wild streak in him, where the pressure of his hand on me increases, and his control tells me it's going to ruin me for all other men.

How would I be able to compare?

I couldn't. No one could ever compare to him.

My hands touch his ripples and strong muscles. I moan at the touch of his hair and warm skin.

He's perfect.

I'm soaking in every second of this kiss and his body under my hands.

When his shirt hangs open, I pull my lips from him and push his shirt off his shoulders. His tanned body makes me thirsty. I lick my lips.

"*Star.* The way you're looking at me..." He trails off as if he's lost for words.

"I've wanted to touch you for a while now. To see you in real life. This doesn't seem real. You don't seem real," I say, my eyes still roaming over his body until they meet his blazing gaze.

"You have no idea how much I've wondered how sweet these lips would be," he says, running his thumb over my bottom lip with pressure. "They are better than I thought. And now it makes me think how sweet that pussy of yours would taste."

I swallow the lump in my throat. His naughty words. The image of him on his knees tasting me...

"Remy," I breathe. I need him.

I reach for the top of his shorts. Enjoying the feel of his heated skin as I pop the button and unzip him.

"Why do I get the feeling you not trying to remove my clothes is a problem?" I ask, sliding my hands between his shorts and briefs and pushing the shorts down.

"I want to enjoy this moment," he says, staring down at me. His shorts hit the floor, and he stays still.

I pause and undress him as I absorb his answer. "Why? Do you think it'll be our last?"

Our eyes hold. His hand touches my cheek softly as he speaks. "Fuck. No. This is the beginning of us. I've never thought of myself as being in a relationship. But with you, I see a whole future."

"Oh," I say shocked. His words snap me back to his briefs. I push them down, freeing his thick, large cock. Fully erect he's intimidating but it doesn't stop my sex from pulsing. I want him more now.

My gaze drinks him in, starting at his cock and moving up to his quizzical face.

"I'll take care of you," he rasps.

"You will," I reply eagerly.

"Now I'm naked for you. I think it's only fair..." he whispers, leaning into my neck and nipping at my skin.

"Ah."

"This dress is like wrapping paper. I can't wait to tear into it."

Oh no.

But I'm sure one touch or one slide of his thick cock into me and I'll come. I sink to my knees in front of him.

A hiss leaves his mouth.

I stare up at him from under my heavy lashes. Watching as he registers what I'm about to do.

"You want to suck my cock?" His heated gaze watches me.

"Yes," I whisper.

"Good because I've been dreaming of watching your red lips wrap tightly around my dick as I fuck your sweet mouth."

He smirks at my shocked state. His hands run through my hair in the softest caresses. But then, he wraps it around his wrist and pulls my hair tight. It's a delicious sting on my scalp.

"Suck. My. Cock. Nova."

I shuffle on my knees closer to his strong thick thighs covered in dark hair.

My hands hold his thighs before one hand tries to wrap around his cock, but he's so thick that I can't hold him fully.

"You're so fucking eager," he mutters.

I nod. Keeping my eyes trained on what I'm doing. I want to blow his mind. I've done this once or twice before, and I remember reading an article recently that said to use lots of saliva and your hands.

I bring my mouth to his cock and my breath makes it jerk against my lips.

"Don't tease. Suck me hard," he rasps.

His words are uneven, and I love the power I hold already.

"You look so pretty with my cock inside your mouth."

I flick my gaze up and watch him stare down with the hungriest eyes I've ever seen. I smile. His hands are still pulling my hair, and I keep my gaze on him as I take him into my mouth and suck him hard.

"Ah. Fuck!" he shouts.

My hand on his thigh wraps around it, feeling the muscle contract. I flick my tongue over his tip and then take him as far back as I can. My eyes prickle with tears.

"That's it." He grunts.

Make it messy...the article says.

I ignore my head telling me to swallow the saliva and I push away any pain.

Pain makes me feel powerful. I fight the urge to gag and let him rock his hips at the same time I tighten my hold on the base of his cock and take him deep as I suck him deep.

"Nova. You're so fucking good at this," he mumbles through a shaky breath.

His words encourage me.

I let my teeth gently run along his cock before sucking him harder.

"Fuck," he curses and begins to fuck my mouth.

He likes that. He likes that a lot. I repeat it. Until his breathing is so loud and he grows thicker in my mouth and hand. I inhale deeply and continue, loving every second of this.

His hand tightens in my hair, and he pauses. My eyes open to watch his darken.

"I'm going to come. And you're going to swallow all of it."

I smile around him. My teeth graze him again.

"Wicked woman..." he moans as he comes.

His eyes close. But I keep mine on his face, watching it crease.

I swallow him down. And when he stops jerking in my mouth, his eyes open slowly. Staring with such intensity. As if surprised by me.

I've astonished myself.

But maybe it was because I enjoyed it. I've never enjoyed it like I did just now. And I know it's all because of the way he turns me on.

"That was...incredible. Fuck, you're incredible," he breathes, still trying to catch his breath.

His hand loosens in my hair and smooths it down. Then he leans down, grabbing my arms and helps me stand.

"Who are you?"

"Nova Lee," I reply, cheekily.

"Yes, you are. And right now Nova, *my star*, I want to fuck you so hard."

I feel his words between my legs. I ache for him. "Do it," I challenge, my heart beating in my ears at the thought of him doing exactly that.

"Are you wet for me?" he rasps out as his fingers trail over the straps on my dress.

"Yes-s," I stammer.

He groans at the same time a breathy moan slips from my mouth.

He captures my lips and I immediately open my mouth. Our tongues twirl hungrily as if we'd never kissed before. My hands dive into his hair, and he turns me around and walks me backward.

The backs of my legs hit the bed.

He tears his lips away from mine, keeping his face close. We stare wordlessly at each other as he slips his finger under the dress strap, and it drops off my shoulder. He does the same to the other side until it hits the floor.

I'm not one for expensive lingerie, so I have my Target red cotton bra and matching thong.

"Red..." he whispers.

I roll my lips together.

"My new favorite color."

"Is it?' I ask.

"It is now."

Oh.

My lips part as I look up at him. I'm having a hard time accepting that this is actually happening. That he truly exists.

I keep my eyes on his face as he unhooks my bra clasp. My bra falls to the floor, and he sucks in an audible breath.

My nipples are tight, and he grazes his thumb over one.

"Ah."

"So responsive to me."

I mumble, but it's not really a reply. I'm unable to speak coherently.

He lowers me to the bed. "Lie all the way down."

"I don't—" I start to say. "I won't last."

"Multiple orgasms."

Never had that before.

As if he can read my mind.

"Will I be the first guy to do that to you?"

I dip my chin. "Yes."

The wicked grin on his face tells me he loves that piece of information.

And he won't give up until he's had them.

Am I ready for this?

Yes? No?

His mouth closes over my nipple and sucks hard.

"Remy."

"Mmm," he mumbles, popping my nipple out of his mouth with a graze of his teeth. Before licking it again.

I rock my hips into him, but his heavy body sits on top of me, making it difficult for me to move.

His mouth bites my nipple and I arch my back as he trails kisses along the other side. And I know that nipple will get the same treatment. The scrape of his teeth. The hard suck. I moan. I need more.

"I can smell how needy your pussy is."

The dirty talk is so unexpected.

I also didn't realize how much it would turn me on.

"Please," I beg. I'm desperate to come. His rough touch and dirty talk send me over the edge.

"You can come." He peppers my chest and stomach with kisses.

"I need more," I reply.

My skin prickles from his soft lips and warm mouth. He removes my panties as his mouth lays kisses lower until he pauses at the top of my mound.

"Smooth," he whispers against my skin.

"Is that how you like..." I don't want to say *your women*. It feels wrong.

"I like you the way you are." He dips his head lower and lays a kiss just above my clit. "Smooth landing strip, full hair. I don't care."

"Really?" I exhale.

"Do you like yourself smooth?"

I've never thought about how I like the feel of myself.

"I guess. It's easier."

He lays a kiss on the opening of my pussy, and I spread my legs wider.

A silent beg.

"So eager," he mutters before he slides his tongue over my clit unexpectedly.

I close my eyes and tip my head back. "Ah," I pant.

When his mouth lifts away from my pussy, I groan and reopen my eyes.

"You liked that?"

"Yes. But I want more."

"Good. I don't want to stop. I won't come up for air until I feel you shatter on my tongue."

My chest rises and falls with my breaths, the anticipation killing me.

I want him to destroy me with his mouth. His dirty-talking mouth needs to be suffocated by me.

Yeah, I want that now.

He settles back between my legs. His fingers stretch my pussy open, and his tongue slowly licks it. He starts at my opening and licks all the way up to my clit. My hands dive into his hair, holding him against me.

I rock my hips so I'm grinding my pussy into his face. The scuff on his face adding the perfect friction.

He fucks me with his tongue and I'm so close.

His fingers touch my swollen clit and rub it in hard slow circles. My back tingles and my toes curl. I come so hard my eyes roll back into my head.

I'm panting to try and catch my breath. When I open my eyes, he's smiling at me with a glistening mouth. He crawls over me, and his cock hits my opening.

He's ready.

CHAPTER 19

JEREMY

"You're fucking delicious."

She whimpers with a sexy post-orgasm glow. "Please. More."

My cock jerks at her begging tone. I'm settled between her thighs.

The tip of my cock touching the warm spot between them. Warm and wet. Utter perfection.

I stare down, watching as sexy pants leave her mouth. My lips take hers in a strong kiss. Her tongue enters my mouth and I groan. The feel of her strong tongue demanding more drives me wild.

I pull back an inch, staring into her eyes that are roaming my face.

My hips tilt and my cock slides over her wet opening. For a second, I forget myself. "Fuck."

I drop my head and sit back.

"What's wrong?"

"Nothing's wrong. I just almost forgot the damn condom. You're fucking up my head."

She smiles at that.

"Is it funny to you?"

"No," she replies, biting her lip in a naughty way.

I shake my head with a lopsided grin.

I climb out from between her thighs and off the bed. There's a condom in my wallet, so I grab it from there.

I tear it open and roll it on before getting back on the bed and settling between her thighs.

"Is that better?" She lifts her brow with a smirk on her face.

"That was close."

"Yeah, I don't intend to get pregnant anytime soon. I need my job. Next time we need to get it ready."

"Next time...?" I settle my hands beside her head with a quirk in my brow.

"Is this a one-time thing?" she asks with widened eyes and fear.

"Fuck no. I want to repeat this as many times as possible." My voice drops darkly as I continue, "I'm addicted to your taste. Addicted to this perfect body. Fuck I'm addicted to you."

An exhale leaves her mouth at the same time her arms touch mine. She clings to me as I inch forward. I'm teasing the outside of her pussy. I glide through her arousal before

I finally enter the tip of my cock inside her, causing her hands to slide up and onto my shoulders.

Fucking hell. She's so tight.

"Ah. Please. More. Don't stop," she whimpers.

I ease my cock farther inside and stop. Even though I'm so close to just ramming her hard and watching her scream. I'm battling myself because I want to enjoy her, but I want her so badly at the same time.

I'm slightly losing control with her.

"Just give me a minute," I murmur. "I'm thick, so I'm giving you time to adjust to my size."

I drop my lips to her neck, kissing the delicate skin, and then continue up to the shell of her ear. At the same time, my hand moves to her breasts. I roll her nipple between my thumb and forefinger.

"Ah. Remy."

Goosebumps scatter her skin, and her nails dig into my shoulder.

My hand moves to the other nipple, repeating the same movement. As my lips meet hers, I swallow another gasp. With her lips parted, I slide my tongue against hers.

Her hands slide up my neck and hold on to my head and pushes it down to kiss me harder.

We kiss until I feel the muscles in her pussy loosen and her hands release their tight hold on me.

"You ready?"

"Now?" she begs softly.

I growl, loving those words.

With a shift of my hips, I thrust deep inside her then still. Nova's head tips back slightly. "Oh. God. Remy."

I press my lips onto hers and swallow another one of her moans. Then I breathe. "It's okay. I got you."

"Yes," she moans again when I roll my hips. Her eyes roll back into her head as her lips part sexily. Her lips are swollen and pink from the kiss we just shared.

She makes me so fucking hard when she goes feral like that.

"More?"

Her lashes flutter open and a sexy smirk settles on her lips.

"Are you ready?"

She nods. "Yes-s-s." She arches her hips, trying to encourage me, but I don't need that because I'm barely holding on.

My hips pull back before ramming into her and pumping hard. The whole bed slams into the wall behind it.

Cute little noises leave her mouth.

She loves this. She loves me fucking her hard.

We get rougher and I feel her walls suddenly clamp down. "Fuck...Fuck." I rasp, barely holding on, but I have to make her come first.

The way her hands fall from my head and now grip my back, I'd say she's close.

"Yes. Remy," she whimpers again.

"I love that word coming from your mouth."

Her pussy tightens around me. And fuck. I love the way she clenches around my cock.

I keep thrusting and the bed continues to move.

I pull out all the way to the tip and then slam back in. Rolling my hips, stretching her.

"So fucking good," I rasp. "This body is now mine."

"Yes. Anything." She hums in approval.

I look down to where my cock is buried deep inside her sweet pussy. The sight causes a grunt to rumble from my chest.

I pull my eyes back up to her face. She flutters her eyes at me, it's sexy.

Fucking her is perfect.

I don't stop the hard thrusts. She takes it like the good girl she is.

Rolling my hips, I enjoy the feeling of her engulfing me.

It's strange, but something about her feels so right.

There's something about her that makes me fuck her hard. Like she's greedier when I do.

"Come Nova. Come for me."

And she does, hard. Her nails bury deep into my back as her back arches, and she's so fucking loud when she moans.

It's heaven.

When her body settles after her orgasm, she shivers as she comes down.

The pressure at the base of my spine hits me so quickly and I come so hard. Like I've never before.

I'm still sucking in deep breaths when I pull out.

"You're so beautiful." I kiss her again with so much force. The way she makes me feel pouring out from my lips.

"You like it hard?"

She smirks. "I do now."

I fucked her so hard...unusually hard.

"Did I hurt you?"

"No." She shakes her head. "It was amazing. I've never experienced anything like that before."

"And you won't. Now that I've had you, I'll be at your beck and call."

"Oh really," she murmurs.

"Yes." I kiss her briefly. "I'll be right back," I say and quickly get off the bed. After removing and disposing of the condom, I wash my hands and get back in bed. As soon as I lie down, I pull Nova to me. I need to feel connected to her. We fit perfectly together.

It's silent and comfortable, but it doesn't last.

"I should go." She tries to move out my arms.

"No, stay," I beg.

"Are you sure? I'll call a cab."

I tighten my arms around her. "No cab. Stay with me. Please."

Her body sags against me.

"I am pretty tired." She yawns.

"Sleep. I'll be right here holding you."

The next morning, I wake to the feel of soft hair in my face and the smell of roses. As I blink my eyes open, I see brown hair.

She's still sound asleep.

I'm scared I'll blow this. My track record with women isn't good when it comes to balancing work and a relationship. But I want to be better with Nova.

I lay a kiss on her shoulder and dust my thumb along her arm. Her skin is smooth and warm.

Her lashes flutter and she turns in my arms with a lift in the corner of her lips.

"Morning," I mumble.

"Morning."

I kiss her lips. "Are you hungry?"

"A little."

"Let me get us some takeout." I reach out to grab my phone and notice the mountain of notifications. My eyes twitch.

I need to handle this.

"I can cook. Even though I really don't want to leave the bed."

A thrill hums through me. "You're not sore?"

"A little."

"Shit. Was I too rough?" I ask.

She lays her hand to the side of my face. "No, no, no, I just need another minute if we're gonna go for another round. So if I cook, it'll stop the temptation."

"I'm a temptation," I grumble, loving the sound of that.

She rolls her eyes. "Here we go."

I smirk. "Here we go what?"

"Your ego is going to be bigger than the room now."

"Damn straight," I say, tickling her side. She writhes and wiggles. Definitely not helping my morning wood.

I stop tickling her. My body is now hovering over hers. The sparks fly between us.

"The kitchen is all yours. But do you want my help?"

She shakes her head. "No. I've got it."

"Okay, if you're sure. I'll work for a bit. But call me if you need a hand." I peck her lips and hop out of the bed.

She follows and fuck seeing her naked makes me stop for a second and drink her in.

"Incredible," I grunt.

She smirks. "Thanks." Her eyes drop over my naked body. "Not so bad yourself."

A deep chuckle leaves my chest.

I love her playfulness. It's something I haven't found with anyone before.

"Including your monster dick. No wonder I'm sore."

Another roar of laughter leaves me. I take the steps to close the distance between us.

My fingers automatically trailing up her arm, over her collarbone, to cup her face. Her eyes hold mine.

"I'll make you feel better after we eat."

It's a promise.

"I'll use the bathroom, put some clothes on and then I'll cook us breakfast."

I drop my hand and step back. "I'll grab you one of my clean shirts."

Across my room is my closet. I take out a shirt and hand it to her. She spins and heads into the bathroom and I head to my study.

I turn my computer on, and it isn't long before I smell butter and coffee.

Who is this woman?

Cooking me breakfast while I work. This is new. But a heaviness gnaws in my gut. Will this last or is it a fantasy?

I push it aside and focus on enjoying what we have.

I'm working on updating a spreadsheet when light footsteps enter my study.

My breath catches.

Fuck.

She's dressed in my white shirt, which is falling off one shoulder because it's way too big. Her brown hair lays messily in a *just-fucked* look. In one hand, she's holding a white coffee cup and in the other a plate of food.

I'm speechless. She walks toward my desk. I twist my body away from my computer.

She lowers the coffee and plate to the desk.

"I didn't know what you wanted. You have too many options to choose from."

I peer down at the two eggs, turkey bacon, potatoes and whole wheat toast. And then look back at her.

I tilt back in my chair and pat my lap. "Come here, *star*."

She goes to turn so her ass sits on my lap.

My hands on her hips guide her to sit facing me. I want her to straddle me.

Her eyes locked on mine. The chemistry between us is so intense.

"Thank you," I whisper.

She softly smiles before kissing me. A long gentle kiss. My hands glide up her back over my shirt all the way into her hair to deepen the kiss.

My tongue tangles with hers.

Hers twirls with mine just as hungry. I pull back. "You're making me want to change my mind about fucking you."

"Good."

I groan. "You're trouble."

She nods and leans in to capture my lips in another peck. She peels herself away from me to stand. I'm hard beneath my sweatpants. I remind myself she's sore and I need to give her at least a few hours to recover.

She wanders to the shelves of books I have along the wall. Her hand tracing the book spines of the F.X. Toole books. It reminds me of our late night talking.

She continues walking along the shelves, when she stops, pulls out a book and reads the back.

"Take whatever you want," I announce.

She turns her head to face me. "I'm surprised you have fantasy."

"I like having my shelves full of all types of books. I read a lot."

She puts the book back. "My mom and I do too."

"What about your dad?" I say gently, knowing it's a sensitive topic.

A lightness beams on her face. "No way. He won't read at all."

"Not even the newspaper?" I ask.

"Oh, he reads that. Every old man reads the newspaper daily."

"Hey, be careful who you're calling old." I quirk a brow, pushing the newspaper I've been reading beside me.

"You really like to read."

"I do but I also like to keep up with the news and the stock market."

She rolls her eyes. "Boy shit."

"Not just for men. Lots of women are now into stock and shares."

She scrunches up her nose. "Not me."

"That's okay, I still like you." I wink.

"You can teach me poker if you come to boxing."

"Deal. On one condition." My voice drops.

"What?"

I stand, stepping behind her, gathering her hair in my hands and dropping it to one side as I bring my lips to her skin that sits between her neck and shoulder.

She shivers and an eruption of goosebumps scatters her skin.

"It's strip poker," I add darkly.

"Oh."

"Tonight."

"It's not Thursday." Her voice wavers.

I like how she remembers my weekly game night. It's sweet, like her.

"I'd rather play with you. Teaching you––"

"You mean watching me lose," she interrupts.

"Your clothes...Yes."

"Sounds unfair." She pouts playfully.

"I'll make sure it's fair, so I'll lose mine too."

She's silent. Thinking about the proposition.

"I'm down."

"Good. In my shower, now."

I lean down and pick her up, throwing her over my shoulder, and heading directly to my bathroom.

She squeals. "You haven't eaten your breakfast."

"Don't worry about me. I will enjoy you as my first meal before I get back to work."

Her body softens in my arms. She gives up the fight. She likes the idea of my mouth on her just as much as I do.

CHAPTER 20

NOVA

"You what?" Summer shrieks.

I cover my ears.

"I stayed over at a guy's house," I repeat before dropping my hands and grabbing a bottle of water from the refrigerator and a bag of grapes. I'm hungrier than usual since my stay with Jeremy last night.

"Did you go all the way?"

I smile around my bottle as I sip.

"Filthy animal. I knew it," Chelsea adds, walking into the kitchen and grabbing some cookies.

I grab one after a few more grapes. I'm going to train and then visit my parents before Jeremy picks me up at six tonight for dinner...then strip poker.

"I'm jealous of you girls. I would do anything for a single kiss right now." Summer sulks.

"Not desperate, are you?" Chelsea teases. "Even though my relationship is so boring. I have to turn sex down with Bobby now."

"No!" I shrill.

I couldn't think of ever turning down Jeremy. If anything, I want more. I can't get enough of him or the vision of him on his knees licking me while I lay on his bed this morning until I came. Then he took me into his shower, but he had to leave for an emergency call. There was a security threat at his Manhattan Hospital.

She nods. "Yup. It's so forced. I don't know what's wrong with me."

"It's not you. It's him," Summer snaps. She takes a seat with us at the table.

"If you're not happy you should leave," I add.

"I am happy," she replies.

Her tone doesn't convince any of us.

"Anyway, enough about me and my boring sex life. Tell us more about the mystery guy."

"Okay, well, I got a text from a wrong number. His. We talked and he's funny and easy on the eyes."

"Ugh. He's hot, isn't he?" Summer asks.

"Very. Like way out of my league."

"Pfft. He's lucky to have you," Chelsea argues.

I smile. "Thanks, Chels."

"He's crazy rich. His house is incredible," I say.

"I get the feeling you're already wanting to move in," Summer says with a laugh.

"For his kitchen and bookshelves alone, yes. I can imagine cooking in it overlooking the city every day."

"What does he do?" Chelsea asks, fascinated.

"Owns a chain of hospitals," I say.

Summer whistles. "When's he taking you out again?"

"This afternoon."

"Damn girl. He's not messing around," Summer adds.

I laugh.

"Will you stay over again?" Chelsea asks.

I hesitate.

I want to...

"Probably," I admit.

"I can't wait for you to fill us in. Have you told your parents?"

"No, I'll tell them today. I do feel guilty not spending my extra time with them."

I take a bite of a cookie and chew it.

"They would want you happy. And by the look on your face, he makes you happy," Summer says.

I smile stupidly. He does.

"I need to get dressed for the gym and I'll be back. I'll need your help with my date outfit."

"I won't be here, I'll be out." Chelsea winces.

I stand. "It's okay, I can dress myself."

"Hey. I'm here. I'd love to help," Summer says.

Chelsea looks relieved. I lean over and grab her hand.

"Go out and have fun. You do plenty for me." I wink.

"Send me a picture of your first date outfit," Chelsea replies.

"Oh God, it really has been a long time since I went out on a first date," I say with a stomach full of butterflies.

I step through the door of my childhood home, finding my mom and dad in the living room. Dad is fast asleep and Mom is watching a daytime soap. I lower the roses to the counter as I swap last week's out for this week's.

I'm exhausted after boxing. Jeremy seems to lift all aspects of my life. So I take a seat on the sofa and message him.

> **Nova:** Who knew I could train better after being with you.

>> **Jeremy:** Looks like my presence extends beyond a board room. Who knew I was also a secret fitness guru with a monster dick?

> **Nova:** Maybe it's the fear of not keeping up. Survival instincts, you know?

>> **Jeremy:** You keep up just fine. We could repeat?

Nova: I can't, I'm at my parents.

Jeremy: Say hi for me.

Nova: You think I'm going to tell them about you?

Jeremy: Oh. Am I secret fuck buddy?

Nova: No. Of course not.

Jeremy: Then why not tell them?

Nova: Will you tell your family?

Jeremy: Yeah, I will tell my family.

I know I said I don't have time for a relationship, but he makes me happy and forget about the hard days. I'm just seeing where this goes.

Nova: I was going to tell them today.

Jeremy: *Fair enough. But please don't tell them I'm packing. (A monster dick)*

Nova: *Oh God. I'm going. See you soon.*

Jeremy: *Can't wait.*

I tuck my phone away and find my mom watching me.

"Who are you texting?" she asks.

Here goes.

"Um. A guy."

Why is it so hard to tell your parents even as a damn adult.

Her face transforms. "Oh. Tell me more."

Her excitement adds to my nerves.

"Let me make some tea and I'll tell you. I don't want to wake Dad. You can tell him when he wakes up."

"You're fine with him knowing?" Mom asks.

I shrug. "Yeah. You guys know everything."

Mom walks over to me with a warm smile and hugs me.

"My sweet daughter," she whispers into my hair as if I'm still a child.

We pull apart and I smile.

We walk to the kitchen. I make tea and she pulls out the cake she made for the week.

"Looks good, what did you make this week?"

"Lemon cake," she replies, placing a piece on a plate. She pushes it over to the counter where stools sit underneath. I put our cups of tea beside the places. We take our seats and eat.

"So good."

"You always did like my lemon cake."

I sip some tea, preparing myself to deliver the news.

"So I'm going on a date."

"Where to?"

"He's surprising me. He's picking me up at four."

She cradles her cup in her hand.

"I love that element of surprise. Most guys don't do the old-fashioned thing anymore."

Well, we definitely didn't since we had sex before getting married, but I don't dare tell her that. I share almost everything. Some things, like my bedroom activity, are not a topic of discussion with my parents. Friends, yes, my parents, no.

"He is a gentleman. I've just started to get to know him."

"Well, I hope your date goes well and then maybe your dad and I can meet him."

I sip my tea as I stay silent and think about Grant's warning. Is Jeremy too good to be true?

After visiting my parents, I get home and pull my wardrobe apart.

I already have a vision in my head of a sleek, brown dress I own. It's made of silk. It's so soft and feminine.

I think it complements my brown hair and curves nicely, but for confirmation, I need Summer's opinion. So I get dressed, style my hair, pop a little bit of mascara, bronzer and lipstick on.

"Summer?" I call out as I walk out of my room.

"Yeah." She calls back. "Come here, I'm in the living room."

I walk slowly over in my heels, deciding on comfortable over sexy. They're still strappy but they've got a lower heel than my other stilettos.

She whistles as soon as I enter the room.

I laugh. "So I take it this is alright?"

"All right?" she says. "This is hot. He's going to love it. The dress is so flowy that it highlights your hourglass figure perfectly."

"Thanks." I run my hands over my hips and peer down with a smile.

I like this dress. I'm so glad I decided to wear it tonight. I feel really good in it.

I grab my bag out of my room and throw my lipstick and my phone inside. Now I'm all set to go. I checked the time and it's ten to four. Only ten minutes and he'll be here.

Now nerves swarm my belly.

A knock at the door sounds, and my eyes widen. I look at Summer with a giddy smile. She jumps up and down and grabs my hands.

"Are you ready?" she whispers.

I nod frantically. "Yes. You sound more excited than I am."

"I'm thrilled for you. I hope you have the best night. I can't wait to meet him."

I pull her in for a hug. "Thanks so much."

We separate and I take a deep breath and put a jacket on.

She smiles and waves.

I wave and pull open the door, surprised not to see Jeremy.

"Oh, hello," I say to the short, gray-haired man standing at the door with a beautiful smile.

"Hello, Miss Lee?"

"Yes, that's me," I say, closing the door behind me.

"Mr. Lincoln is running a little late. He had to stay back at work. He told me to escort you to the restaurant and he'll meet you there. I hope that's okay."

"Of course."

But really. What else can I say? No and go back inside and not go on the date? He has a really important job to do. I understand that.

I smile. "What was your name?"

"Oh sorry, Miss Lee. I never introduced myself. My error. My name is Terry."

"It's lovely to meet you, Terry."

We take the stairs down to a black car that's waiting.

I can't help the way my stomach feels heavy after being excited to see Jeremy, only for him not to be here waiting for me. "How far is the restaurant?"

"Thirty minutes."

It'll be the longest drive.

All the windows are tinted black. Terry opens the door and I slip in the back.

I pause in the leather seat when I spot a bunch of red roses and a card.

"Are these for me?" I ask, before the door closes.

"Yes, Mam. From Mr. Lincoln."

How did he know I love red roses?

I fasten my seat belt and grab the card, the heaviness replaced by flutters again.

> *Sorry I didn't pick you up. I had to work*
> *late. I'll make it up to you soon, Remy.*

I pull out my phone and text him.

> **Nova:** *I'll see you soon. Thanks for the roses.*

CHAPTER 21

NOVA

THE CAR STOPS OUTSIDE a picturesque winery surrounded by rolling hills and a beautiful vineyard.

Terry leaves the car and opens my door. I unfasten my seat belt and slide out of the car.

A cool breeze hits me. I pull the jacket tighter around my shoulders.

"Miss Lee, would you like another jacket?"

"Oh no, I'm fine. Thank you anyway. Where am I going?" I ask, hoping for direction.

He smiles kindly at me and points toward a set of white glass doors.

"Just through there. Say you're meeting Mr. Lincoln. And they will escort you to him."

"Okay, thank you."

I don't waste any more time. It's too cold out here. I just want to get inside. I quickly make my way across the pavement into the building.

I walk inside, meeting a woman with brown hair tied in a tight bun and glossy lips.

"Hi, I'm meeting Mr. Lincoln."

"Sure. Let me escort you to him." She smiles at me.

I follow her, taking a good look around. It smells fruity but woodsy in here. Beautiful glass windows give a fantastic view of the landscape. It's quiet with only a few other couples in here.

As soon as I turn the corner, my breath catches in my throat. He stands at the bar, his intense gaze fixed on the door, waiting for my arrival. Anticipation hangs thick in the air, causing a shiver to run down my spine. God, he's magnificent. Realization hits me. This breath-taking man is actually waiting to have wine with me. I almost want to pinch myself. The lopsided grin on his face adds a playful edge. It's gonna be a good night.

As I approach, he smoothly pushes off the bar, closing the distance between us. My eyes roam over his suit. Light gray with a white shirt, no tie and his hair styled but more in the messy way that I love. I resist the urge to reach out and touch it; instead, I curl my fingers with restraint.

We don't stop moving until we're directly in front of each other and he towers over me. A sharp intake of breath escapes me when he leans unexpectedly close, his warm breath sending a tremor through me as he whispers, "You look incredible." His hand tightens on my hip and I find myself melting into the intoxicating touch.

"Thank you. You look handsome."

He pulls back with hooded eyes and a devilish smile.

"I thought it was time to trade a dinner date for a winery instead."

His thoughtfulness causes a smile to tug at the corner of my lip. "What's first on the agenda? Make our own wine?"

A deep throaty chuckle escapes him. "No. It's already prepared."

His eyes drop to my mouth and I tip my head back ready for our lips to meet but a clearing of the throat sounds beside us. I momentarily close my eyes, regain composure and turn toward the woman beside us.

His eyes drop to my mouth.

"Lead the way."

He links our fingers together and we walk.

"The air is so fresh here," I say, as our footsteps cause the leaves to rustle.

In the distance, you can hear the birds chirping, insects buzzing, and the vines in the wind. There's no traffic or city noise here.

He leads me into the wine tasting area. The large wooden barrels make a gorgeous backdrop.

"Are you ready to be a wine connoisseur?"

I grin. "Absolutely. I've been practicing my wrist technique."

His eyes widen.

My hand covers my lips mischievously. "Oh sorry, I mean my swirling technique."

"You can show me the wrist one later," he whispers darkly in my ear.

We arrive at a rustic wooden table that overlooks the vineyards. He pulls out a chair and I take a seat.

A friendly woman approaches our table. "Good evening. My name is Shaye, and I'll be guiding you through the tasting tonight. We'll start with a crisp Sauvignon Blanc."

She pours the wine into two glasses, as she gives us the background information about the winery.

Jeremy's phone rings during her talk, and he picks it up straight away. He walks off, and after a few minutes of waiting, I give up and tell her to continue. I'm embarrassed and a little annoyed, Shaye must sense my uneasiness, so she begins speaking again.

I'm enjoying talking to her and learning about all the wine, so when he rejoins I'm relaxed.

The new chardonnay she poured me is really good. Dry but still a hint of sweetness. I take another sip.

I lick my lips of the residue. "That is such a good wine."

As the tasting continues, we make our way through the whites, rose, reds and dessert ones. We share our thoughts and discover a few new favorites.

A charcuterie board arrives and we nibble on that as we sip. Our sommelier walks away, giving us a moment alone.

Simultaneously, we turn toward each other clutching our final wine. We share a soft smile.

"Thanks for bringing me here today," I say.

"My pleasure. Have you been to a winery before?"

"Yeah, but not for wine tasting, just for lunch."

He sits back with a grin.

"I'm glad I could break you in." I don't miss the twinkle in his eye.

"Such a dirty mind." I breathe, not hating it. His desire makes me feel wanted. Which is something I'm not used to.

"Sorry. Whenever you're around, I can't help myself."

I know the feeling, I say to myself. *I know that feeling very well.*

"Cheers to a wrong text," I say.

"Cheers," he replies and we clink our glasses. As we both take a sip, we hold each other's eyes. I wish I could pause this moment, this feeling. Being here feels right.

"What made you keep talking to me?"

It occurs to me that it seems out of character for him. Now that I've gotten to know him, gotten to care for him, he shouldn't have kept our exchange going. But he did.

"I had this need to keep talking to you."

I rub my finger along the stem of the glass.

"I'm not usually distracted."

"I should thank my charming personality for that."

I wiggle my brows playfully at him, earning me a wolfish grin.

"It's definitely what made you stand out to me. That and your beauty."

I feel a warm flush run through me and up to my cheeks.

Gesturing to the vineyards, he asks, "How about we walk through the vines?"

"Yes, please."

I want nothing more than to explore more of this place with him and I alone.

We walk hand in hand through the rows of grapevines. We enter the third row when I notice a couple taking a picture.

I tug on his hand, getting his attention to a couple nestled in a grapevine with the sunset in the background.

"Looks like they're trying to take a picture, but they're struggling," I whisper.

"Mm," he says, looking over at them.

The guy is holding out his phone, but she shakes her head not liking the angle.

"Let me take it for them," I say as we approach them.

"Would you like me to take a photo for you?" I ask.

"Oh, yes, please." The woman's face brightens.

"I can't get the vineyard, sunset and us in the shot."

"No worries. I'll get it," I say, taking the camera and standing back.

I snap a few photos from a few different angles.

"There you go."

I hand over the phone to her. She immediately scrolls through.

"How's that?" I ask.

"Amazing. Thank you so much!" The woman gushes.

"Happy to help," I say smiling.

"Enjoy your evening," the couple says.

We walk off.

"That was really nice of you," Jeremy says.

A smirk tugs at my lip as a thought comes to me. Tilting my head back to look at him. "Can we get a photo?"

He grumbles. "Do we have to?"

I bat my lashes, lean toward him, and say, "Please."

"Only if I take it."

I sigh. "Not just the side of your face."

A small chuckle leaves his chest. "Deal."

I hand over my phone and we edge back into the vines. The sunset is behind us, and we smile. He clicks the photo and I gasp. "You did it."

I grab my phone and face him.

"I did. On the provision you send it to me."

I hit forward and send it to him straight away. His phone chimes with the notification.

The photo is perfect.

"You ready to finish exploring before it's dark out?"

"Yep."

His hand glides over my lower back and then drops to interlace our hands. We stroll along the grass in silence.

"I'm going to have to thank Grams for this date."

I frown. "Why"

"She suggested it."

I squeeze his hand. "I'll have to thank her too."

There's a question I have been wanting to ask Jeremy and I take this as my opportunity to get to.

"You're already aware of my dad's colon cancer. But I don't know who the person in your life is who has cancer."

His eyes drop to the ground with sadness. I let him have as much time as he needs. I understand it must be uncomfortable for him to talk about. So I wait patiently.

"It's my grams. She has breast cancer," he announces.

"When was she diagnosed?"

I keep my eyes ahead. I don't want him to close up on me. The vulnerability is what makes me fall harder for him. I get a better understanding of him and what makes him tick. Not just the sides he wants me to see but the ugly, painful side too.

"Only recently. It's been a couple months, maybe four?"

"What stage is she?"

"Three."

"Oh, same stage as my dad."

"I'm sorry," he says.

"I'm sorry, too."

We stop walking for a moment and face each other. His hands move to the sides of my waist.

"Since your dad was diagnosed, has your relationship with him changed?"

"Yes, I always make time for my dad and mom. Check in almost every day. A visit, a call or text. I need them to know I'm thinking of them, and I work just to give them money."

His tongue rubs along his bottom lip. "You're one of the most extravagant and selfless women I've ever met."

Opening up to him feels natural and like a weight is being lifted from my shoulders. So now that I have started sharing private things, I tell him something that's been playing heavy on my heart.

"I don't know what I am going to do without him to be honest. I don't let myself think about it. I try to avoid reality as much as I can, in the hopes that it will help me not waste the time I have left with him.

"What's his prognosis?"

"Surprisingly good. But he's going through a swollen kidney at the moment. They're managing it well. I'm grateful he has such a great medical team."

"It helps that he's young. Since Grams is older, they avoid any harsh treatment." He exhales, this is obviously heavy on him too.

"You have to keep me in the loop."

"You too. It's actually..." He trails off.

"Yeah," I push, wanting him to finish his sentence.

"It's nice talking about this with someone. I don't speak to anyone about this except for my brothers but even then, we don't often talk openly about it. We definitely don't share how we feel either."

I nod, understanding guys aren't as open with discussing their feelings as women. But I hope he knows I'm here and happy to listen.

"She's our rock, so I know I need to talk about her. She definitely is the *link* in Lincoln. Our family loves and adores her. She's our everything. She is the warmest person you'll ever meet. I actually can't wait for her to meet you. I think she'll end up loving you more than she loves us."

I giggle. "I doubt that."

He smiles, but it fades just as quick. "I think we're all scared. We're fearful to lose her. We're afraid to not have her in our lives anymore. We each spend time with her alone. Every one of us is trying to soak up these last moments because we just don't know how long we will have her."

To think this intelligent and handsome man would ever have something in common with me would have made me laugh only a month ago. Now, as I stare at him longingly, I wonder how I've spent so long without someone like him in my life. His friendship, his tenderness, and his touch.

It's getting dark, the stars are out. A shiver runs through me with the drop in temperature.

"You ready to go?"

My stomach somersaults. "I'm ready to beat you." I'm totally faking confidence here. But it seems to work.

"Do you think you're gonna beat me at poker?" he asks, lifting a brow.

I straighten my spine. "Yep, I've got this."

A dazzling smile takes over his face. "Let's go then. I can't wait to see you try."

I control my mouth to stop a smile from forming. "Is that a challenge, Mr. Lincoln?"

"Miss Lee. It's a given."

He stretches out his hand and I take it.

His fingers tighten around mine and we walk back to the car. Inside we stay quiet. The only noise I hear is the pounding of my heart thumping loudly in my ears.

Terry is waiting beside the car.

"Was he here the whole time?"

"Yes."

"I sure hope you pay him well." I shake my head in disbelief. Not that Terry looks upset. It just seems absurd to me for him to wait the whole time. What does he do?

"I look after everybody that works for me."

I don't doubt it, and after seeing the roses in the car, it reminds me.

"How did you know that red roses are my favorite?"

"They are?"

"Yes," I reply.

He kisses the side of my face, lingering close where his scent hits me.

"I didn't. Lucky guess."

"Lucky indeed," I say to myself.

"Well, that's a nice piece of information. So your favorite flowers are red roses?" he hums.

"Yes. I buy them every week for my mom and I."

He tilts his head. "You buy your mom flowers every week?"

"Yes."

He doesn't say anything else. We climb into the car. He refuses to let go of my hand, which makes it difficult to get inside. I try to buckle myself in, but he takes over, dropping my hand to fasten my seat belt and his.

I suck in a quick breath when his fingers touch my thighs. It's funny how much my body hums whenever he touches me. He places a kiss to my temple and then eases back into the car. We fall into easy silence, so he pulls out his phone and begins typing away madly on it. I turn to watch the city pass until we arrive back at his place.

CHAPTER 22

NOVA

WE EXIT THE CAR and enter his house. He's holding my hand again, like he's unable to let it go and I honestly love it. I love holding his hand and feeling the closeness. It's something I haven't felt in a very long time.

I feel like a teenager all over again.

Jeremy takes me downstairs to his den. I hadn't seen it before. I take it all in. A large TV mounted on the wall, a cream sofa and a big round dark brown table with ten chairs surrounding it. The same relaxed yet moody feel is down here. It's totally a guy's zone.

"Would you like anything to eat or drink?"

I cast my gaze to his to find him watching me with a soft expression.

"No, thank you." I smile.

"Alcohol?"

I chuckle. "Will I need it?"

"No."

I dip my chin and stay staring quietly, as my heart beats out of its chest with anticipation. I know what's coming and all the teasing is making me twitchy.

"Are you comfortable?"

I nod. "Yes."

He breaks our stare by turning and walking to a drawer along the side wall.

I watch with utter fascination. He pulls out the cards and places them on the table.

My chest heaves as he strides toward me, and before I have a chance to speak, his hands grab my waist and pulls me to the chair. My body obeys his silent command naturally. His hands leave my waist to hold the sides of the chair, his whole body crowding my space. He's in control of me and I'm more than willing. He leans closer until his mouth settles on the shell of my ear. "Are you ready?"

"Mm." I nod.

He stands up, breaking our connection, and I have to swallow a groan.

My eyes follow him as he steps over to the table and deals.

It's time to play...

"The game's about to begin," he says when he finishes dealing. His dark smoldering look is mixed with a hint of humor.

He's holding back a laugh. He and I know I'm gonna suck so bad. I'll lose my clothes very fast. But I refuse to let him know that. I want to act like I'm going to beat him. Fake the confidence I don't feel. Isn't that the beauty of poker?

The chairs are surprisingly comfy, which makes sense since they sit in them for hours. They're not supposed to just be aesthetically pleasing.

I try to keep my poker face on. He's matching me with his own stoney look.

He's obviously good at this.

I work hard to keep my face neutral as my nerves finally rear their ugly head.

"Are you ready to play your first round of poker?"

"Yes. I was born ready." I rub my hands together.

His lips twitch.

I pick up my two cards and see a pair. We aren't betting with money today. No, this is all clothing. He reminds me of all the rules and answers any questions I have. My dad used to play with friends, so I do know some of the rules. I haven't told him that with the hope it pays off.

I call and then he puts out three cards.

I show my hand, but he beats me with three of a kind.

My jacket is the first thing I lose. I didn't need to stand to remove it.

I wish I had more items of clothing on right now.

Next, he tosses his gray jacket. I drop my gaze over the way his shirt hugs his muscled chest and arms. The white buttons are straining, and I can't wait to have him remove it.

Yep. I need to win the next hand.

But he wins again.

This time, I stand. He's watching me closely. His eyes hungrily trail the length of my body before coming up to my gaze. I slip the straps of my dress off each shoulder. My body prickles with goosebumps from not only the cool air but his dark, lustful gaze. I want him to touch me already.

When the fabric falls to the floor, he sucks in a sharp breath and mumbles the word, "Beautiful."

I stand there in my beige bra and panties.

He doesn't bother standing, but his hands go to his buttons.

"What are you doing?" I ask. Not understanding. He won.

"I'm matching you. If you lose, so do I."

"I'd say I win. That's not a loss." My words die on my tongue as his fingers push on the buttons on his shirt.

It's alluring watching the man slowly unbutton and reveal his chest. A chest I remember from this morning. It's solid, warm and chiselled with a sexy dusting of hair.

I curl my fingers around the arms of the chair. My fingers are desperate to feel him again. Feel how powerful he is.

He shrugs the shirt off his shoulders, and I think he's going to stop there. But he stands.

My breathing is turning into a pant when I see him unbuckle his black belt. He whips it off and unbuttons his pants.

"Oh, God," I breathe.

"Do you want me to stop?" He challenges with a quirk of a brow.

"No way. Keep going," I breathe.

"I thought so..." he says in a lighter tone.

He begins unbuttoning and unzipping his gray pants. Then he shoves his hands down the sides and slides his pants down. They fall to the floor and now he's standing in only his black boxer briefs. His obvious hard erection causes an ache in my pussy. I want to go and feel the soft skin under my palm or...I lick my lips imagining it in my mouth. It's hard to swallow.

He groans. "Fuck. You need to stop looking at me like you want to eat me."

"I'd say sorry but I'm not. It's exactly what I want to do."

"Fuck."

I look down with a smirk. If I look at him anymore, we will have to stop playing and this has been fun. Even if it's making the ache worse, I know it'll be worth it.

And every time he plays his favorite game with his friends, he'll think of me. Poker won't be the same for him again.

We play some more, and he puts down a full house. Damn it. I lost again.

I stare him down. Wondering do I go for the bra or the panties?

"Bra," he grunts, answering my internal question.

I reach around the back and unclip the bra, letting it fall from my shoulders.

My nipples are tight buds. So much desire is coursing through my veins.

This game we're playing is the perfect foreplay.

I sit back down and wonder what he's going to take off. He pulls his socks off.

"Hey! Unfair." I pout.

"I'll take off my briefs after you lose your panties."

"Why?"

"Once you're naked, I promise I'm gonna fuck you so hard on this table."

My mouth parts. God, I want that. I want that now.

We play, and of course, I lose again. This time on purpose. I'm done. I want him.

I stand shakily but with excitement. Knowing as soon as he's down, he's going to come over here and throw me on this table and have his way with me. And at this moment, I don't care how sore I am from this morning. I want him again.

I need him to ease this ache. I want to come so bad.

I shimmy down my panties.

He stands then pushes his black briefs down. He strides over and picks me up, smashing his lips to mine.

I wrap my legs around his waist and breathe him in as if I hadn't tasted him before.

He grabs my neck, pulling my mouth closer on his. Our tongues tangle in a deep passionate kiss. My hands grab his face, enjoying the way his freshly shaven jaw feels so rough and smooth under my palms. His aftershave so strong. I soak it in.

My hand trails from his face down to his shoulder.

"Remy." I rasp on a breath.

"I've got you, my *star*."

He lays me down on the table. It's hard, but the fabric is soft on my skin.

"Your table will get messy."

"I don't care. I want to remember every time I play how I fucked you here and how good that feels. It'll be like you're with me even on boys' nights."

I shiver.

"You liked that?" he asks.

I nod and hum, unable to speak.

He pecks my lips and moves down to my neck, nipping and kissing his way down to my breasts. He moves to each nipple, giving them a tug with his teeth, and I cry out in pleasure.

"Fuck. you're so perfect. So damn responsive."

"Only with you," I breathe.

He growls and moves quicker toward the heat between my thighs. His mouth kisses my mound and then his hands spread me wide. His pointer and middle finger rub through my wet opening and onto my swollen bud. He rubs it in hard circles.

It helps with the ache. But I want more. My back arches when I feel his tongue on my opening.

"You taste too sweet."

I buck my hips. Desperate for friction.

"And you should see how pretty you look. You were made for me."

I grab his head and hold it on my pussy. He follows my silent order. His warm tongue slides through my pussy up to my clit and then he repeats, harder with each stroke. My hands in his hair are tighter as I feel my body quivering. I'm so close.

"Remy, I'm going to come," I cry out.

It's a warning to him. If he wants me to come twice, I'll happily have one now and then he can get another one with his cock. I'll take it all. I've never been able to come multiple times, but with him, I think he could pull as many as he wanted out of me.

He moves his fingers inside me and curls them up. It feels like I'm peeing. What the heck. My eyes fly open and I'm gasping. My body is shaking all over. He doesn't stop, he continues to lick and curl his fingers, and the next minute liquid squirts onto his face.

I gasp. My eyes roll back as I come so hard, I see stars.

My body softens and I breathe hard. His body moves slowly, and I can sense him above me.

I open my eyes and find him wearing the biggest smirk.

"Fuck, you're beautiful."

"I didn't know I could do that," I murmur.

"Now you do. And it was fucking amazing."

I blink rapidly. How is squirting amazing?

Everything is wet under me.

"I made a mess."

"Yeah."

"Great," I murmur. How the heck will I fix his table? I can't afford a new one.

"Don't be upset. I love it and, if anything, this table might be our new place to explore this some more."

I stare dumbfounded at him. "You want to do that again?"

"Fuck yes. All the fucking time."

My eyes drop to his obvious bulge to find the tip of him leaking. He definitely isn't lying.

My brain is misfiring. "I want you," I say with sudden urgency.

He drags my ass along the table until it's on the edge. Then he grabs a condom and rolls it on, before he lines himself up. "You ready?"

"Yes."

I answer before he thrusts in. The feeling of his big cock filling me is a mix of pain and pleasure. He's so thick and big. I can feel him everywhere.

He doesn't give me time to adjust to his size, he's unhinged, and he fucks me so hard I can barely catch my breath. His fingers dig into my hips as I let him fuck me. My body is firing up again as if it didn't already come.

"You're incredible. I think I'm addicted."

I know the feeling.

His balls slap against me. He's fucking me with everything he has. Truthfully, no one has fucked me this hard before. I love it. I love him feral without hesitation. He doesn't treat me gently. He gives me what he wants, and I take it lovingly. He reads my body and gives me more.

He thickens inside me, and my walls clamp down on him. "Fuck. I'm going to come." He groans.

I feel my back tingle and my legs quake again.

His cock jerks inside me as I throw my head back and cry out his name as I come too.

His body stops jerking and I breathe heavily as I tip my head up and look at him. Both of us thoroughly fucked, dripping in perspiration with crooked smiles on our faces.

"You ready for a shower, baby?"

"I think you'll have to carry me."

"With pleasure."

How he has the energy, I don't know. But when he lifts me effortlessly in his arms, I drape my hands around his neck and cuddle him. His masculine scent is stronger now. It's a shame he's about to wash it away.

CHAPTER 23

NOVA

> **Jeremy**: I miss waking up and seeing your drool on my pillow.

I GIGGLE TO MYSELF as I read my messages during my lunch break.

> **Nova**: I don't drool. Only over you.

> **Jeremey:** You just admitted to drooling.

> **Nova**: Is that something you're into?

Jeremy: *Drool on my pillows? No. But if it means having you in my bed every night, I'll happily let you drool anywhere.*

Nova: *I DON'T DROOL!*

Jeremy: *I KNOW I'M KIDDING. WHAT'S WITH THE SHOUTY CAPS?*

Nova: *You keep saying I drool. When I don't.*

Jeremy: *I'm only joking, Star. I'm sorry. You know I care about you.*

Nova: *Are you going to hurt me Mr. Lincoln?*

Jeremy: *I'd never hurt you. You should trust me.*

Nova: *Do you think that's a smart idea?*

Jeremy: *No. I'll probably be heartbroken, but I have a serious problem.*

Nova: What's that?

Jeremy: I'm addicted to you.

Nova: I'd tell you to see a doctor but you are one...well, at least you were. Unless you're rusty?

Jeremy: Definitely not rusty. My mouth-to-mouth skills are second to none.

Nova: I'd say your hands skills are top tier.

Jeremy: I'm good at getting kinks out. Especially with blockages (Winky emoji)

Nova: I'm never going to live this down, am I?

Jeremy: No, I fucking love it. Come over tonight and I'll show you just how much.

Nova: I'm sorry but I'm having dinner with my parents.

Jeremy: What about before then?

Nova: Who knew you'd be so needy.

Jeremy: Desperate, you mean. For you…yes!

Nova: I go boxing straight after work.

Jeremy: Send me the address.

Nova: Are you serious?

Jeremy: If it means I get time alone with you. I'll take anything I can get.

I stare at his message, and I can't help the smile that settles on my face. Here I was crushing hard on him, but I think he might be feeling the same way. That knowledge is overwhelming as much as it is thrilling. I never expected this to happen to me.

I send him the address and eat my sandwich quickly before returning to my desk. Going back to work is easier now that I can countdown to seeing Jeremy afterward.

I settle at my desk and back into work. I pull up a new client's file and continue on with the numbers when Dalton's voice calls out to me.

"When you were at lunch, Bentley came down to check in on you."

"Does he want me to call him in his office or go see him?"

I really hope I don't have to go up there.

"He said he'll come back after his lunch."

"Okay, well, I don't plan to leave this level until the day is over. I'm sure he'll be able to catch me."

He shrugs. "It doesn't matter if he doesn't. We told him you were settling in fine. Isn't that right, Poppy?"

She sighs heavily and twists ever so slightly. Clearly not interested in joining our conversation.

"Yeah," she mutters.

"Well, thanks, I guess," I say, spinning back around and returning to the spreadsheet.

"What are your plans tonight?" Dalton asks. I swear he doesn't like to stay quiet very long. It's like silence makes him antsy.

"Boxing and then I'm headed to the parents for dinner."

"You box as a workout?" Poppy asks.

I pause typing.

"Ah. Yeah, I go to a gym around the corner from my parents. The owners know me."

"Is it a class?" she asks another question.

What. The. Hell?

I shake my head. "Actually, no, I just use their bag. But they have classes there and I know the teacher, he's really good."

"I might have to try it out. I've always wanted to learn, but I've never known anyone who does it."

All of a sudden, there's a loud clapping sound, and I frown and look toward Dalton. Why is he clapping?

"Look at this, ladies and gentleman. Poppy will hang out with Nova."

"Oh, Dalton please be quiet," Poppy mumbles.

"I am having major FOMO, so even though the thought of boxing and breaking my nose terrifies me, I'd be willing to come and try it out."

"I'd be happy to take you. But remember, it's not fancy. I mean it. It's a cheap, sweaty, smelly gym."

I'm not trying to scare them away from doing it. I'm trying to warn them that this isn't like the gyms they would usually attend. I don't have money for those gyms. They cost way too much.

"Sounds rustic. Just what I expected a boxing place to be like," Poppy adds.

I nod. But really, I just have lost all my words.

I feel like this is a breakthrough. This means Poppy doesn't hate me. Baby steps but I'll take it.

"How's my newest favorite employee?" Bentley's voice booms out of the elevator.

The hairs on my neck stand up. "Good, thanks."

"She's settling in well, like we told you before," Poppy adds with a biting tone.

Yeah, she isn't a Bentley fan either.

"I'm not asking you," he replies.

"I'm settling in well. Dalton and Poppy are great. I'm so grateful for their help and knowledge."

Bentley nods. "Good to hear." He rubs his palms together and wears a cheesy smile. "Dalton, you're quiet today. Cat got your tongue?"

"No, sir. Just busy working."

"Don't work too hard."

Poppy's mouth drops.

I bite back a laugh, knowing Dalton works the least out of all of us.

"Nova, I also have a new financial breakdown I need written up for Mr. Lincoln."

My belly flips at Jeremy's name.

"I thought we finished everything for the ophthalmology instruments."

"We did. But I sent him a prototype of a new product I think he'd be interested in. He said yes but wants numbers."

"That's where I come in."

"Exactly."

"I'll forward you the stuff now," he says before his phone rings. "I better get this. I'll send you the information soon."

I nod.

"You've been a wonderful addition to the team, Miss Lee."

I smile. There's something about hearing those words. Feeling like I belong. Maybe this was the right job for me all along.

"Talk soon. You know where to find me." He winks and strolls off, answering his phone obnoxiously loud.

"Way to go!" Dalton says.

"Mr. Lincoln again? You're the teacher's favorite," Poppy adds.

"Are you jealous, Poppy?" I say without thinking.

The pang of jealousy twisting in my gut feels foreign.

He'd never be interested in her, right?

I trust him.

My sudden insecurity rush makes me want to text him.

> **Nova:** You didn't want a new contract to stay in contact with me, did you?

> **Jeremy:** I don't need to do that, do I?

> **Nova:** No. I just had to check you weren't trying to work with me again.

Jeremy: *Oh, I was one hundred percent doing that.*

Nova: *You're crazy.*

Jeremy: *About you. Yeah, nuts.*

Jealousy is replaced with desire. A more peaceful feeling. Something I needed to finish the day off.

And the next few hours fly by. It's four o'clock and it's time to go boxing.

I drive to the gym, and when I arrive, I scan the parking lot for his car, but it's not here yet. I'm relieved I can get inside and freshen up. I change and tie my hair back. I'm in my black sports bra and black shorts ready to take on the bag.

I wrap each of my newly-healed knuckles, knowing I'm about to bust them open again. It happens every time I box.

I finish wrapping both hands. When I look over my shoulder, I'm disappointed. He's still not here...

The nerves are getting to me, so I decide to box to take the edge off. No more waiting. It's just me and the bag. I jab, punch, hook, uppercut, repeatedly. I do it for what seems like ages.

I've worked up a serious sweat.

"I need to watch out."

Jeremy's deep velvety voice sends a shock through me, causing me to jump. I spin around with a smile.

He looms tall in an all-gray dark suit, white shirt and gray tie. His hair is impeccably styled, showing no signs he's been at work all day.

"Are you planning to wear that?" I ask, eyeing his attire.

He steps closer to me, his presence commanding. "I don't plan to work out."

"Then why did you come?"

He grabs my chin, tilting my head back, and delivers a brief but intense kiss. His heated breath whispers across my lips as he murmurs, "Isn't it obvious?"

"No," I reply, meeting his amused gaze.

"To hang out with you."

"You're cutting it close. I need to leave in ten minutes. I thought you'd be here waiting when I arrived," I confess.

He smirks. "I would've but a meeting ran overtime."

"So you're going to watch me for the next ten minutes?"

"Yeah. Even though I don't like the way guys keep looking at you."

"They are?" I scan the gym but see no prying eyes.

"Yeah, and it's bothering me. You look so sexy right now."

I scrunch up my face. "You're delusional. I'm all sweaty and gross."

He softly shakes his head. "No. You're half naked and flushed. Like, I've just fucked you for hours."

My mouth parts. "Oh."

"Yeah. So all the guys here are looking at you. I can't blame them, but it doesn't mean I don't want to gouge their eyes out. And fuck. This place is dodgy too."

I hesitate. "What's wrong with this place?"

It's not like I don't know, but I don't want to say I can't afford any better. I don't want him offering to pay for a commercial gym. If I can't afford it, I don't need it.

His eyes survey the peeling cream paint, stains on the floor, and other signs of neglect.

"Definitely a few imperfections."

"You mean a massive O H & S issue," he grunts.

I peel off the wraps, wincing as the material clings to the re-opened wounds, forcing me to rip it off.

"Look at your hands," he says, grabbing them to inspect the damage. "They're worse than the night with Eddie."

I shrug. "Yeah, happens every time."

"It must hurt."

"After a couple of hits on the bag, I can't feel them."

He looks up, holding my gaze. I see the wheels turning in his mind, but he remains silent.

"What?" I push, wanting to know his thoughts.

"It seems like you want the pain." His voice is low and pained.

He's right. It takes away from the pain my dad's diagnosis causes. But I don't want to ruin the moment by getting into the heavy details of it right now, so I shrug and then exhale heavily.

He unexpectedly pulls me into his chest, wrapping his arms around me and kissing the top of my head. "If you need to talk, I'm here."

I absorb the slow, steady beat of his heart in my ear, my own heartbeat syncing with his after the workout.

I can never get enough of him. Every touch reaffirms how much I need him. How much I desire him.

"Thank you," I mumble into his chest.

He understands me, offering what I need without me asking. He knows me better than I know myself.

"Let me walk you to your car," he offers.

Crap...not again.

"Don't judge it," I warn.

In the daylight it looks worse. The paint is discolored, and I have worn down tires. I'm in dire need of a new set.

He grumbles, grabbing my hand, "Let's get out of this shithole."

I smack his chest with my spare hand. "Don't say that."

"Why?" We leave through the gym door and walk the sidewalk to the parking lot.

"Someone will hear you," I murmur.

"The guy at reception didn't stop me when I walked in. His eyes were glued to his phone. Now when we left, he did the exact same thing."

"The owners are really nice."

"I didn't say they weren't. It doesn't change the fact this place is crap."

"This crap is all I can afford," I say with light sarcasm. "I know you can have better but don't insult what makes me happy."

He cocks his head and I expect him to argue, but he just shakes his head.

We approach my car. "Here we are."

He stills. His jaw twitching.

I roll my lips, preventing a giggle from his reaction. Yep. He still officially hates my car.

"It looks worse than the other night," he deadpans.

"Yeah, well, it was dark the other night. But she's been good to me. So don't talk bad about it; otherwise, you'll put a curse on it."

"That would be a bad thing?" he mutters.

"Yes. I need this car."

"I—"

"No!" I cut him off. "You're not buying me a car. Don't even think about it."

"I have money and you're my girlfriend now."

Wait, what?

My mind is spinning. We're about to have that conversation.

"Am I?"

"Yes. Of course. That's why I don't want you driving this pile of shit."

"I want a boyfriend not a sugar daddy. I have a job that pays well."

He grits his teeth. He's struggling to figure out how to win this fight. "Then why don't you buy a new one?"

"I can't," I blurt.

He frowns. "Why can't you?"

Shit. shit. shit.

How do I dig myself out of this hole?

I help my parents with their bills. I don't have anything to spare right now. My needs have to wait. The car is fine. The mechanic last saw it over a year ago and said it'll be fine for a while if I don't drive long distances. Which I don't do.

I can't mention any of that. We're way too early in this relationship to have that topic thrown at him.

I don't want him to be with me because he feels sorry for me. I want him to be with me, for me.

"I need to get home. My dad needs to eat by a certain time, and he'll be asleep early. I want to catch him." I say urgently. I'm not lying to get out of this conversation. It's unfortunately true.

"Can I follow behind you in my car?"

I roll my eyes and tap his chest playfully. "No. Don't be absurd, go home. I'll be fine."

His eyes are still locked on my car. He won't leave until he gets something to put him at ease...

"How about I text you when I get there?" I offer.

He stays silent for a long moment.

"Fine," he eventually grumbles.

I grab the sides of his face and bring it close to mine. I seal my lips onto his. He kisses me back. His body softens the longer we kiss.

"I'm still not happy," he whispers between kisses.

"I know," I say back, my whole body sinking into his. "But you'll get over it."

CHAPTER 24

JEREMY

"WHAT ARE YOU DOING for your birthday?" Grams asks. She's sitting beside me in her chair while I'm on the sofa. The TV is on with one of her awful soaps. Who knew that a soap opera could last for twenty-five years? Me. I didn't think anyone would watch it. But I guess I was wrong.

I turn my head to face her, closing the newspaper I was reading. "I haven't made any plans yet. It's not a big milestone."

She waves her finger around. "It doesn't matter if it's a milestone. Everything should be celebrated, I..." She stops herself from talking. "I'd love to meet this woman we spoke about last time."

My mouth lifts at her save.

"I want you to meet her."

I realize I almost said *before you go...* And I hate that it popped into my mind.

Why is it so hard?

Why is life so unfair?

A part of me knows I shouldn't feel guilty, and I should accept what is in the future and have her meet Nova. But none of my previous exes met my grams, so if Nova did, it would be a big fucking deal.

"We just started dating. Throwing her to the wolves might be a bit much."

"We're family, not animals."

"Are we talking about the same family?"

She laughs. "Please. Why don't you have her come here for dinner?"

"A dinner with the family?"

"Yeah."

I try to avoid looking at her radiant face because she knows she's worn me down. "Won't it be too much for you?"

I try one last ditch effort for her to not do this.

"I'm not cooking. It'll be catered."

My gaze watches the actors fake crying on the screen. I can't look at it any longer. I cross my ankles and get ready to read the paper again.

"Fine. Let's have a birthday party dinner."

"I'll tell the family. You tell your girlfriend and her friends to come."

"Hold up. Her friends too?"

"I want her to be comfortable."

"So you admit our family is a bunch of wild animals, Gram?"

"No, but I'm a woman and I know meeting the family is nerve-wracking. It'll help her feel relaxed."

"Okay, well, I'll ask her—"

"Good idea. Call her up and let me know."

I'd argue but between the shit TV show I have to listen to, and missing Nova, I wouldn't mind hearing her voice again.

"Alright, I'll call her."

"I'll make us tea."

"Coffee."

"Yes, well, coffee for you, tea for me."

I get up off the couch and grab her four-wheeled walker, wheeling it in front of her. I hold my hand out and help her up. She stands and grabs the handles.

"I'm up, thanks. Now go call her." She waves me away.

"Alright, I'm going."

I slide open the back door onto the patio and call Nova. She answers after the second ring. "Hey, you."

"Hi, baby, what are you doing?"

"I'm on the couch trying to motivate myself to shower."

I groan imagining her body in a shower. "Wish I was with you."

"You wouldn't fit in my shower."

"I like tight and confined spaces."

She laughs, which sounds a lot like a snort. "Always dirty, Mr. Lincoln."

"With you, I can't help it. It flies out of my mouth."

"I don't know if that's a good or bad thing."

I move closer to Grams' railing on her back patio and lean against it. "I'd say good. Most people get the boring side of me, the business one."

"I am lucky. I know you better than most."

I stare out into Grams' backyard. It's green with a small patch of grass. Beautiful flowers and trees and a veggie patch down the back.

"Better than anyone."

"I am sure I don't know you as well as your friends do."

"To a certain point."

"You go deep with me," she says with a lighter tone. It's almost as if I can hear the smile in her voice.

A deep chuckle leaves my chest. "Very deep. Now this time, you started it."

She laughs. "What are you doing right now?"

"I'm standing outside on the porch in my grams' back-yard."

"Did you go straight from work?"

I sigh. "Yeah, I have a flight tonight so I wanted to stop by."

"That's right, you're leaving me for two days."

"I know. I won't see you until Friday night. Speaking of, it's actually the reason I'm calling."

"So you're not calling because you missed me?" she teas-es.

"Oh, definitely that. Hearing your voice makes it harder. It makes me want to get in my car and see you."

"Do it." She breathes in a soft beg.

I groan, loving how she begs so easily. "I can't."

"Yeah, I know..."

It's quiet for a moment before I remember I haven't asked her yet.

"Friday night, Grams is hosting the family for dinner."

"What for?"

I really don't want to say it. Birthdays aren't my thing. I don't celebrate them. I prefer to buy gifts rather than receive them.

"My birthday," I murmur.

"Your birthday!" She squeals.

"Calm down." I chuckle.

My grams and her will definitely get along. They both love birthdays.

"How old are you turning?"

"Old."

"Haha, smarty pants. Answer please." The begging tone makes it impossible not to spill.

"I'm thirty-eight."

"What does the birthday boy want?"

"A–"

"Mind away from sex."

My lips twitch. "Damn it. It's exactly what I was thinking."

"You'll get that, but I need a gift to bring to the dinner."

"You are my gift. A surprise gift."

"Oh, look at you being all cute."

I turn to lean my back on the railing. "Don't tell my brothers I'm cute."

"Your secrets are safe with me. But I don't count as a gift. Give me an idea."

"I have no ideas. If I want something I buy it. And no one buys me gifts."

"Not even your ex?" she says.

"Not even her."

"Well, that's an even bigger reason to give you a gift."

I look at the wooden porch. "Are you jealous of my ex?"

"No. She isn't around anymore so she's not competition."

I smile and jerk my head back up. I'd never look away from Nova. No one could compare. She's everything to me, even though it's only been a short amount of time.

"So why do you need to worry about a present then?"

"It's the principle of knowing I'm the best."

My lips part to a stupidly wide smile. "You are the best."

"I will be even better with a gift."

"Good luck with that," I say.

"Bring your roommates. Gram insisted."

"You have the coolest gram."

I look into the enormous arch windows, looking around her indoor and outdoor plants to see Grams moving around her large kitchen. "I know."

"I'm excited to meet her."

"I am too." I expected to be filled with regret about inviting her to meet my family, but it doesn't come. Chatting with her now just makes me want more time with her.

"I better go back inside before she calls a search party."

Nova giggles.

"I miss you," I say, standing up from the rail.

"I miss you too. See you Friday."

"I'll see you then."

I hang up and stare at the phone as if it has the answers I am looking for. I'm finding time for her, which is something I didn't think I could or would want to do. Why her? What is it about Nova that makes her so different from the others? I don't know anything other than what I feel in my heart. In my gut. She could be the one.

I open the door and slip back inside.

"Did you tell her you love her?"

"What?" I ask totally surprised by the question.

"Did you tell her you're falling in love with her?"

I snort. "Hell no."

"Don't swear."

"Sorry, Grams."

"You ought to." She huffs her displeasure.

I meet her in the kitchen, with its beige marble counter and floor-to-ceiling wooden cabinetry. Two cups sit on the counter. My grandmother's brown eyes stand out against her pale skin and white hair.

"Why?"

She turns, her gorgeous purple cardigan draping over her white collared dress as she reaches for a plate filled with cookies. Every time I visit, she has a fresh treat waiting. She bakes every week without fail. Even with her chefs, she still makes her own desserts. I reach for a cookie, but she leans over and lays her hand on my cheek, causing me to pause. It makes me feel like a kid again.

"Because you love her."

I shake my head. "I don't." I didn't say I wasn't falling, but I'm not full-on in love with her. Fuck, give me a second to spend more time with her. I'm still scared she'll leave just like my ex. That my work will drive a wedge between us.

"Your face is glowing."

"Grams, are you unwell? I'm sure you're seeing things now."

She drops her hand. "You—"

The doorbell rings.

"Saved by the bell." I wink and grab a peanut butter and chocolate chip cookie and take a big bite.

She shakes her head softly.

As I open the door, I see that it's my parents.

I smile, and quickly greet them both, kissing my mom on the cheek and shaking my dad's hand.

My mother has shoulder length freshly dyed brown hair and brown eyes, while my dad's hair is now gray, although it used to be brown. His beard is neatly trimmed, longer than any of us boys. Both are in their early sixties and retired. Dad and Mom used to own Lincoln Media and Lincoln Gallery respectively. Nowadays, Dad plays golf while Mom teaches painting to those who can't afford college. They used to travel together until Grams' diagnosis. Now they prefer to stay put, with Dad spending every day with his mom.

My mom and Grams want to see all of us boys married with children. So, I take this as my cue to leave. I'll let Gram tell my parents Nova is coming Friday for dinner; otherwise, I'm about to get another woman's opinion on how glowy I look. Like what is that? No, I'm not fucking glowing.

Happy? Yes. Glowy? Fuck no.

I kiss Gram and tell her I'll see her Friday. Before I close the door behind me, I hear my mother and grams' exchange.

"Guess what Jeremy did? He found a girl he's willing to bring home."

"He's inviting a woman—" I hear my mother gasp as I shut the door.

CHAPTER 25

NOVA

IT'S FIVE TO SIX and we're sitting inside her car outside the address Jeremy gave me.

"Are you ready?" Chelsea asks.

I rub my hands on my jeans. "No. I'm terrified."

My stomach is twisting and turning the closer I come to meeting his family. Everyone who is important to him is here.

But giving up, or hiding in the car, is not going to help me. I exit the car, put my bag on my shoulder, and grip my hands together.

"Where's the present?" Chelsea asks.

"Oh." I step back and open the passenger door again. The gift is sitting on the floor.

"How did I miss that?" I mutter to myself.

"I've never seen you like this."

I flick my gaze to her. "I've never felt like this."

Chelsea comes to stand beside me. She rubs my arms up and down. "I've got you."

"Thanks. I'm sure I'll be fine as soon as I've said hello."

I nod. "Stop worrying if they are going to like you. There's a man in there I cannot wait to meet. I know he cares for you, and you care for him so if they have a problem with you, then they will have a problem with me."

My heart explodes at her protectiveness. She's like the sister I never had. "You're seriously the best, Chels. Thank you."

We hug.

I exhale a big breath and turn to face the front door.

"Let's get this show on the road."

Speaking of. "What time are you meeting up with Bobby?"

"At seven. If that's okay. I still feel bad for leaving. You know Bobby," she adds, nibbling her lip.

I do and he's a douchebag. I want to tell her for the hundredth time. But I know in time his true colors will come out and she will see what we all see in him. There's someone more deserving of her out there than him.

"No, thanks for coming. I told Summer not to cancel her plans because I'll have him come for dinner next week and meet you both properly."

"Good idea." Her eyes move to the door then her watch and back to me. "Well, let's head inside, it's six on the dot now."

I nod and walk to press the bell, giving Chelsea another last-minute panicked look.

The door opens and I instantly feel better.

Jeremy's standing there looking tall, powerful, and sexy. I melt when he flashes me a smile that reaches his eyes and shows off those lines along his cheeks up to his brow.

I didn't expect him to answer the door but now that he has, I'm so damn grateful. My gaze drops to take him in—black jeans that hug his frame, black linen shirt rolled up to the elbows revealing dark hair that sends my pulse racing. He stands there, effortlessly gorgeous, a silent invitation in the doorway.

"Hi," he says in a smooth, low voice, his eyes holding a magnetic pull that draws me closer.

"Happy birthday," I say, closing the distance between us with a new-found eagerness. My lips touch his, and I wrap my arms around his neck, feeling the warmth of his hands on my lower back as he pulls me closer. Our eyes lock, and in this moment, I finally feel grounded.

"You smell good," he murmurs into my hair.

My hair is down and wavy today. I step back, tuck a piece of my dark hair behind my ear and offer him a small bag. "Here."

He looks at the bag, and then back at me, his expression a mixture of curiosity and a hint of something more. "I said no gifts."

"I had to," I argue with an amused tone.

He will like this gift.

The corner of his lip lifts. "You found a gift. I'm shocked, but I'll open it later."

As he takes the bag from my hands, his fingers brush mine and send a rush of electricity up my arm.

"Good idea," I breathe.

He grins wider. He understands it's meant for no one else to see.

"This is my friend Chelsea."

My eyes flick between the two.

Chelsea stares warmly at him. And just from the face she's wearing, I can tell she has a good feeling about him.

But when her eyes meet mine, I see her eyes are misty.

Panic floods me. I want to ask her what's wrong, but she shakes her head.

She faces Jeremy with a smile. "Hi. I'm Chelsea. Nova's roommate."

He extends his hand with a smile. "It's a pleasure to meet you. Come in and meet everyone."

"Is everyone here already?" I whisper.

"Yeah. But they haven't been here long."

Shit, I better up my game if I'm going to impress him and his family.

We enter the house and pressure builds in my chest as we walk closer to the sound of people talking.

It's not as loud as I thought it would be.

If Chelsea wasn't here, I'd be dripping in sweat. I would never have thought to bring a friend along when meeting a guy's family for the first time.

We walk across the rich hardwood floors to enter the living room, which leads to the luscious green backyard.

The same patio he rang me from the other day.

The doors that lead to the patio are open, allowing me to see how far the garden goes. The whimsical path design complements the herringbone hardwood floors inside.

There are no coverings on the arch windows. The natural light beams into the house. There are big pendant lights, smart appliances, and greenery in every room.

Five people—four men, and one older woman with white hair––are scattered in the open living and dining room. They engage in conversation while holding glasses of alcohol or nibbling on the charcuterie board resting on the coffee table.

The entire room falls silent as we enter.

"Not subtle at all," Jeremy grunts, clearly annoyed.

They quickly try to go back to talking as if we hadn't entered the room.

Chelsea giggles beside me. It makes me laugh too.

"Come on, you two, let's start the round of introductions," Jeremy says.

"Can we get you drinks first?" A sixty-year-old brunette in a pair of black pants and a navy shirt asks.

"Thanks, Mom. I totally forgot to ask them," Jeremy says.

"That's okay," she says.

"Mom, this is my girlfriend Nova and her friend Chelsea," Jeremy says.

I can't help but look at him when he says girlfriend. It's a weird feeling. But the sparks between us are palpable.

"It's lovely to meet you both."

I smile and Chelsea and I both say, "It's a pleasure to meet you too."

He never mentioned her name.

"Eliza." She smiles, knowing he forgot to mention it. "You're both so beautiful. And I'd say I've heard a lot about you Nova, but I haven't." His mom looks at Jeremy. He doesn't seem phased.

"I wanted her to myself." He shrugs.

"Now you have to share her," his mom replies.

"I know," he mutters. Not happy about that either.

"What can I get you two ladies to drink?" Eliza asks.

She bears a resemblance to Jeremy in the way she looks at me.

"We have wine, beer, whiskey, soda, water, tea."

"What my mom is trying to say is that we have everything," Jeremy says, irritated.

"I'd love a glass of wine," Chelsea replies. "A small one. I need to drive."

"Should you be drinking at all?" A tall, dark-haired man stands next to Jeremy.

Has to be a brother or his cousin based on the fact he looks similar to Jeremy but younger.

"I'm twenty-seven. Not twenty-one," Chelsea says, in a sickly-sweet tone.

Now if you didn't know Chelsea, you'd think she was being polite. But that tone in her voice means she's annoyed.

"Harvey, don't be rude to the guests," Jeremy sneers.

"Yes, as your mother I'm embarrassed," Eliza adds in a deeper tone. I think I'm witnessing her mom's voice.

"Hey, calm down, everyone. I'm playing. I'm sorry..." Harvey pauses with his hand toward Chelsea, gesturing for her to say her name.

"Chelsea," she says with a tight smile. Yeah, she doesn't like him. She shakes his hand but is quick to remove it.

"I'm sorry, Chelsea I was teasing. I probably should've waited until I got to know you," Harvey says.

"Probably a good idea," she replies smartly.

"I'd love a white wine too," I cut in, talking to Jeremy's mother and wanting to shut this conversation down.

"This fucking idiot here is my youngest brother," Jeremy says.

"I heard that!" a voice calls out from the living room.

Jeremy winces. "Grams has the best hearing, and she hates swearing," he explains. "Sorry Grams." He shouts.

"I'll be back." Eliza wanders off.

"I'll give her a hand." Chelsea follows.

"She's upset, right?" Harvey asks.

"Are you seriously asking? Isn't that obvious?" Jeremy snaps, smacking the back of his head.

"I don't know women." Harvey shoves his hands in his pocket.

"Clearly," Jeremy adds.

"Looks like we need to be introduced too." Two other guys slide up next to Jeremy. One squeezes Jeremy's shoulder, the other nods beside him.

Jeremy looks at me. "These are my other brothers, Evan and Oliver. This is Nova, my girlfriend."

Eliza and Chelsea arrive back with drinks.

"Thanks," I say, taking the glass. I immediately take a sip, enjoying the fruity Riesling.

"Evan and Oliver, this is Nova's friend Chelsea."

Oliver steps forward, his hand ready to shake hers. "I'm one of Jeremy's younger— "

"And dumber," Harvey teases.

"Great, there's more of you," Chelsea mumbles to me. Then drains half her glass.

I smile into my wine glass before drinking some more.

"What do you do for work, Nova?" Oliver asks.

I move my gaze to his to answer. "I'm an accountant."

"Impressive."

"What about you?" I ask.

"I own Lincoln Gallery."

"Nice."

Evan is quietly standing there. He doesn't say anything. He's not angry or scary looking. He's obviously the quiet one. Happy to assess the situation and only speak when spoken too.

"Evan, what do you do?" I ask, wanting to get to know him.

"I'm the CEO of Lincoln Media."

"I've heard of that. The paper has been around for many years," Chelsea says.

"Look at all of you. Good jobs and good looking," I say.

"Only me, right?" Jeremy cuts in.

"Settle down. We don't want your girl." Oliver chuckles.

"Just clearing it up."

"No need. I've only got eyes for you," I say.

Jeremy winks.

"Cue the sick bag," Harvey says.

The corners of Evan's lips slightly curve up.

"Oh, you two are so cute," Eliza says.

We all stand in our circle, some holding alcoholic beverages and some soda.

I'm enjoying myself so far. Everyone in his family has been welcoming and lovely. My gut instincts don't raise any alarms about rudeness, or any unsettling vibes from anyone.

"Remy, introduce me to your girlfriend."

I blink rapidly.

Remy...

The nickname I use for him.

The one I googled.

He never said a word.

I've noticed so far no one else has called him Remy, including his mother and brothers.

"Let's go introduce you to the final link in Lincoln, baby." He winks.

Why does that one line make my stomach twist? The nerves are eating me alive.

I put my glass of wine down and take his outstretched hand. I refuse to show my anxiety. I swallow hard and follow the voice from the living room. She's sitting on the beige fabric sofa when we stand in front of her.

Her hair is white, short and styled as if she just left the salon. She's dressed in a collared pale blue dress, white cardigan, stockings and shoes.

So elegant and beautiful.

"Grams, this is Nova. Nova, this is my Grams, Iris."

His hand touches my back in a comforting manner.

I smile warmly at the woman who is so dear to him.

"Hi Iris, it's a pleasure to meet you. I've heard wonderful things about you."

His grams' eyes widen, and she tilts her head to look at Jeremy.

"Is that so?" she says.

"Nice things, Grams," He cuts in.

"Of course," I add.

She brings her eyes back to me and smiles.

"Well, come on and let's get to know each other." She takes my hand and waves Jeremy away.

I want to laugh. Jeremy's face is full of uncertainty. It's like he doesn't know what to do.

"That sounds lovely," I reply.

"I guess I'll—"

"Go find your brothers. We won't be long," Iris says as an order.

I bite the inside of my cheek to prevent a laugh. She is the boss of the family. I can see it.

"It's so lovely to meet you, Nova."

I smile. At least her genuineness is helping me calm down.

"It's wonderful to meet you. I've heard a lot about y—" I reply honestly.

"About my cancer you mean." She says with a knowing expression.

"He did open up to me about that when I told him about my dad."

Her brows pull together. "Your dad?" She squeezes my hand.

I look down at our joined hands.

My eye pricks and I look up to her.

"He has colon cancer."

Her head dips. "I'm so sorry. When was he diagnosed?"

"Three months."

"Does he have a good prognosis?"

"He's stage three."

"He's young. He won't be going anywhere. He still has to watch you grow up, get married and have children. That'll be enough of a reason to stick around."

Those words are what I hope for.

There are milestones in my life I want him around for. So much, like getting a job. That was just a start to many positive things to come.

"Is that what is the most important for you too?"

Her head dips. "Yes, my grandchildren. My boys mean the world to me. I want them all to find love and happiness and I hope I get to be around to see them all get that."

She speaks so much about love that I wonder...

"I hope this isn't too personal..."

"Never. Ask away." She squeezes my hand again as a way of encouraging me.

"What happened to your husband?"

A soft sigh leaves her lips. "He died of a heart attack ten years ago. But he was the love of my life. We had been together since we were 17."

My heart swells at how her face lights up at the mention of him.

I can see on her face that she likes to talk about him.

"Do you miss him?"

"All the time. It's the part of the afterlife I'm excited for. I want to go to him." Her eyes shimmer.

I hope to feel that way someday.

Could it be with Jeremy?

I hope so.

"I see the way Remy looks at you." I stare at her confused, not knowing which look she's talking about. "He's falling for you."

"He is?" I ask in shock. He hasn't said anything or done anything that makes me think he's in love with me. At least not yet.

"Hard. I've never met any of Remy's girlfriends."

"None of them made the cut." I laugh.

"He wouldn't bring you to meet me if he didn't see a future. You must be special."

Based on how he's treated me so far, I can envision a future with Jeremy as well.

"He's a rock I didn't know I needed. He's also the lightness that I wanted. Learning about my dad's diagnosis changed my life. My days feel better with him around."

"He'll be there for you. He needed you in his life too. In all his success, he hasn't had this aura. With you he's glowing."

My chest feels tight. "I feel the same way about him."

"I'm excited for your future. Now go to him because I can't stand him staring at us for a second longer." She giggles.

I peer over my shoulder to find him staring at me.

I smile at him, giving the reassurance he clearly needs.

He's definitely stressing over there. His wide stance, hard lines, and hands buried deep in his pockets give him away. His face settles a little as he turns to his brothers and parents.

I haven't met his dad yet, so I'd like to get up and do that. Also, I need to find Chelsea.

She's due to leave soon.

I turn back to Iris and smile. "Thanks for the chat. I'll go back to him now."

I stand and she nods with a knowing look.

I wander back over to the kitchen where Jeremy is. He wraps his arm around my shoulder, pulling me into him. I sink into his body, welcoming the warmth he's giving me.

He leans into my ear. "What did you two talk about?"

"Wouldn't you like to know?" I tease.

His hand curls around my waist bringing my body closer to his. "I can't change your mind on telling me?"

"Nope, that won't work."

He chuckles and he moves my arm.

"Worth a try."

I know he's tense and vulnerable, so I decide to give him something.

"She was just getting to know me. Everything about my job, my family, and my dad."

I don't want to give away everything we shared. All that matters is we get along and that she knows I care deeply for Jeremy.

"Where's Chelsea?" I tilt my head back and ask him.

"She went out the front a while ago."

My heart rate picks up. This isn't like Chelsea, unless her dick of a boyfriend bailed on her again. Dammit, if he has, I think I'll lose it. I can't sit back and watch my friend be treated this way.

"I'll be back. I need to check on her."

"Of course. Do you need me to come?"

I shake my head. "No, it'll be better if you don't. I'll fill you in later."

He caresses my lips in a kiss. "Go find her."

I slowly slip out of his embrace and move to the front door. I pull it open and step out, pulling the door behind me closed. A breeze picks up and I wrap my hands around my middle as I take the stairs down the front porch. Her car is still parked out front.

I move and I'm about to call out her name when I hear voices.

I walk closer. I can see the back of Jeremy's brother, Evan. A pair of hands loop around his back. He's rubbing her back, up and down.

The woman peels back, and I almost topple over. Chelsea.

Why would he be comforting her?

I want to ask.

But I think she needs another man to show her the good out there. I don't know a thing about Evan, but knowing his family, I can say he is a better man than her current shitty boyfriend.

Instead of interrupting them, I turn around and return inside.

I head straight back to Jeremy's side.

"Did you find her?" he asks.

"Yeah."

"Is she okay?"

"She will be," I say with hope.

"Ready to meet my dad?"

"Yeah, let's go," I say with a smile.

Sebastian is quiet and sweet. Not the least bit scary. Actually, come to think of it, no one in his family has made me uncomfortable.

Except for his brother Harvey. He's a bit of a dick. But only one out of all the ones I met today are pretty good odds.

"Dinner is served," Grams calls.

I twist to look at the front door, wondering if Chelsea is coming back in, but I don't know.

Should I get her?

But just as I think about going, Evan steps through the door and closes it behind him. His face is blank so I can't get a read on him.

I don't know much about his brother other than he's quieter.

My phone sounds. I pull it out and see a text.

> **Chelsea:** *I went home. So sorry. I'm not feeling well.*

> **Nova:** *Oh no. Do you need me to come home?*

> **Chelsea:** *No! Stay. Enjoy Jeremy's birthday. He's lovely. I'm so happy for you. :)*

> **Nova:** *Thanks. If you need me to leave, just text me.*

"Is everything all right?" Jeremy asks.

I twist my head to look at him. "Yeah. Chelsea left."

"Do you need to leave?" he asks. I blink up at him.

He understands how close I am to my friends; they're like my family.

How did he know that was the right thing to say?

CHAPTER 26

NOVA

I love his offer, but with Chelsea's blessing I say, "No. Let's go eat, birthday boy."

He gives me a wicked smile, and we wander to the long wooden table where silverware, plates, glasses, and food are all laid out. It's a feast.

"This looks delicious. Thank you," I say to his family, as I pull out a beige fabric chair and sit.

"It's our pleasure. We're so grateful to meet you," Eliza says.

I smile and begin eating, starting with bread and butter.

"How did you meet my brother?" Harvey asks.

"Yeah, we haven't heard this story," Oliver adds between bites of food.

I'm still chewing my food and I tilt my head in Jeremy's direction. His face is amused. I laugh before facing everyone at the table; they all seem ready to hear the story. It makes me feel so special to have six people all wanting to hear our story. And I love how it started.

"It was actually a wrong text."

"A wrong text?" Gram asks.

My gaze moves to hers. She cuts into her chicken.

"He was given my number by mistake—"

"Whose number was it meant to be?" Sebastian asks.

"My boss Bentley," I explain.

"How does your boss give a wrong number?" Iris asks.

"If you met Bentley, you'd understand, Gram," Jeremy says.

"Sounds incompetent," Evan scoffs.

"Oh, he is," Jeremy quickly replies.

I look at Jeremy. Putting my hand on his forearm, I say, "If it hadn't happened, we wouldn't be here."

His gaze holds mine as he speaks. "I would have bumped into you at the office."

"There's no guarantee we would've had time to chat," I add.

"Hmm maybe," Jeremy murmurs.

"Well, I'm glad it happened. Let's raise our glasses and cheer for them." Eliza holds up her glass.

"Mom, we've already eaten," Harvey says.

"Just do what your mother says." Sebastian urges.

Everyone holds out their drink including me. My eyes drift to the man next to me. A wide smile settles on my face as I say cheers. I watch him over my glass as I take a sip. He copies me and when we lower our glass, he leans in and kisses me.

"Gross," Harvey teases.

Our lips part, and I giggle. My gaze moves to Oliver.

"You're just jealous," Jeremy taunts.

"Of having to put work aside for a woman. No thanks. I'll pass," Harvey argues.

"I thought that once," Jeremy insists.

His work remains a priority, but his drive is one of the aspects that attracted me to him in the first place. However, at times, I wish his phone would remain silent, or he didn't have to be distracted by emails, emergencies, phone calls, or meetings.

"No one is changing my mind." Harvey snorts.

"I agree," Evan says, and I almost fall off my chair. His quiet brother finally gave me a piece of information. At least I know he's single, so touching Chelsea is not a big deal. Even though she's in a relationship. Unhealthy or not, she can't be with another guy until she ends things with Bobby.

"Do you wanna bet?" Jeremy challenges. This is exactly what I thought having a sibling would be like. Healthy rivalry. I can't help but love watching it all unfold.

"Jeremy is right. You guys just haven't found the right woman. And to make your Grams happy you all need to settle down, get married, and give me grandbabies."

The table groans at Eliza's statement.

"No," Evan replies.

"Never," Harvey adds.

"Grams please," Oliver pleads.

I continue eating, watching these grown men softly argue with the queen of the family.

"I'm right. One day you will find a woman and I'll let you eat your words," Jeremy says.

His words leave me momentarily stunned.

"Don't settle," I add, thinking about Chelsea. My eyes shift to Evan; he must sense it, because he looks up, but I can't get a read on him. He just looks down at his food and continues eating.

I'd love to know what he and Chelsea spoke about.

I'm full and the table has finished eating. The staff clears our plates as dessert arrives. Cake, ice-cream, tiramisu.

"I'm going to roll out of here. Or maybe I'll go extra hard at boxing tomorrow," I say rubbing my stomach.

"You box, Nova?" Iris asks in a high-pitched tone.

"Yes, I've found it to be a really good outlet."

"She's really good," Jeremy adds.

I look at him with a smile, remembering the two times he's seen me train. I find it endearing that he wants to support me.

"Thanks," I whisper to him.

He winks.

"I think it's time we go," Jeremy announces as soon as dessert is cleared.

I thought it might be too soon, but his brothers all stand and announce they're leaving too.

"Good idea," Iris says, obviously ready for us all to leave now.

"Thank you all for hosting me. It was a pleasure to meet you all and thanks for dinner it was delicious," I say addressing everyone.

"You're very welcome," Eliza says.

"Anytime. Please come back," Iris adds, remaining seated.

I nod and stand. Jeremy laces his fingers with mine. I say goodbye to his brothers and leave.

Jeremy's car is here today. No driver.

It's a two-door black sports car. I don't have a clue what make or model it is, other than it looks expensive. He pulls open the door and I sit on the cream leather.

The coldness is refreshing on my boiling skin.

Meeting his whole family has exhausted me. I'm ready to go and fall asleep. Preferably in his arms at his house.

He gets into the driver's seat and starts the car. Neither of us speaks for the ten-minute journey to Jeremy's.

All we did the whole time at his grams was talk. Now I want to relax.

He parks his car in the underground garage and when he opens the door with one hand, he holds the present in the other. I know as soon as we get inside, I'll want him to open it. One is a joke present; the other is a thoughtful one I had made.

We head to his bedroom on instinct. Neither of us needs to say that's where we are headed. We just both knew it's the place to go.

Inside his room, he lowers the present to a set of white drawers.

"Open your present," I command when I realize he is going to store it away for later.

He grabs the present and brings it to his bed to unwrap it. I can't contain the stupid smile sitting on my face.

"A towel and cards," he asks, puzzled.

"The towel is more for me. You need to open the cards."

The poker cards are matte black with black foiling, but his family name is in gold and personalised.

"I don't want the towel. I told you I want you on my table. Scratch that. I want you everywhere. I want my house to be full of you. By the way, I plan on doing that every time we're together."

A thrill of longing courses through me. I'd willingly let him repeat that every single time.

Including right now, and by the way his eyes darken, I know he's thinking the same.

He lowers the present and steps closer. The words *look at the cards* are on the tip of my tongue, but when he grazes his thumb over my jaw, I shudder with desire.

He can see them after. I had a perfect night meeting his family, but now, there's nothing else I need but him.

"You were incredible tonight," he whispers.

"They're wonderful, Remy," I say honestly, knowing I had a great time.

He grips my jaw and tips my head back; a gasp leaves my mouth, and he swallows it.

Our mouths crash in a frenzy. My hands grab his head. His hands grip my arms. Our bodies are smashed together. My heart beats widely with the need to have him.

My hands slip over his head, down his neck, to the front of his shirt. I remove his buttons without breaking our kiss. The touch of his lips on mine is too hypnotic to stop. When I've made quick work of his buttons, I slide my hands over his pecs and up onto his shoulders where I slip the shirt off him. He lets go of me to shake it off. Our lips are still sealed. Neither one of us wants to break this. I breathe in his breath as if I need it to live.

I skim my fingers over his stomach and to the top of his pants. I flick the button off and blindly unzip him.

I push his briefs and pants down at the same time and then reach my hand out, palming his hard dick between us and causing my body to ache.

I need him.

But I want to taste him more.

I rub his length up and down, loving the little grunts leaving his mouth. I swallow each one. Pre-cum leaks from the tip and I slide my thumb over it and smear it.

I break our kiss. His mouth hangs open, breathing heavily. His mouth glistens from our kiss and his eyes are heavy. I sink to my knees.

"Nova," he rasps.

"Remy," I breathe.

His hands sink into my hair. He wants this too. A little smirk curves on my mouth at what I'm about to do. Before he has his way of working me to squirt, I'm going to make him come so hard he sees stars.

I grab his length at the base with one hand and my other one grabs hold of his thigh, loving how it twitches at the contact.

I lower my mouth onto his tip and welcome his salty taste, humming my pleasure.

"You're so good at this. No instructions. You're just so hungry for my cock."

I nod. And bring my mouth over him, welcoming the feeling in my mouth. He touches the back of my throat and jerks.

His hands touch my head to encourage me. I take more as my eyes water and then I pull back and continue the up-and-down motion slowly. I take him all the way again, and his hands curl tighter in my hair.

"You take me so well."

I open my eyes and look up at him, as I slide him to the back of my throat and then swallow more of him.

"Fuck Nova," he grunts, tipping his head back and closing his eyes before he peers back down.

"I won't be able to hold on if you keep doing that. You're way too good at this, baby."

And by doing that, I know he wants my eyes on him as I take him down as far as I can. So I do it again. I want to feel and taste him as he unravels.

I slide up and down a few more times and I feel him thicken. He grips my head, holding me as he stills. I welcome the hot bursts in my throat and swallow. My eyes don't leave his face. His eyes close and his chest moves rapidly, and he grunts so deeply it makes me wet.

His hands soften in my hair and his eyes open and drop down. I remove my mouth slowly from him and swallow.

"You're amazing. Come here." His eyes hold a promise of what's to come.

It's my turn and I couldn't be more excited.

He holds his hand out for me to take, and I stand up and he kisses me, taking me by surprise. I welcome his hot mouth on mine. But then he lifts me into his arms, and I cross my legs behind his back and disconnect my mouth.

My arms curl around his neck as he walks me to his bed.

"Do you—"

"Don't finish that sentence."

"Let's not make a mess on the bed...I want to sleep."

"I've got you covered. You worry about coming like the angel you are, and if you aim right, I'll be wearing most of it."

My mouth opens wider as a mix of shock and excitement runs through me. I begin to remove my clothes, and afterwards he lays me down on the bed.

"Let me," he commands.

I drop my hands away from my top and let him undress me, welcoming his hands on me.

Once I'm naked, he spreads my legs and settles his mouth on me. He licks me slowly and forcefully, causing me to whimper.

He swirls his tongue around my swollen clit before continuing to lick from my entrance to my throbbing clit repeatedly. Until I'm arching my back and moaning out his name. I want more. I need more.

Fingers hit my opening and I flutter my eyes. When I look down, I find his eyes are already there to meet my gaze. I can't see from his mouth down because his lips won't leave my pussy. He inserts two fingers and pumps. I moan but when he drags his fingers in that *come here* motion, I feel that funny feeling again. My mouth is unable to form words. I battle with my need to close my eyes with the reminder of how his face looks so eager to have me on him.

I should be embarrassed but how can I when he's so desperate for me?

I tingle and I can't hold back.

I come on his face.

His face is euphoric, and I swear I cry harder and come harder than ever before.

I come down from the incredibly high and he crawls over me licking his lips. His thick cock hits my entrance.

"You ready, baby? Because that was exquisite, and I just need to fuck you hard now."

I nod. "Yes."

With a smirk, he rolls on a condom, takes me in one hard thrust and I see spots in front of my eyes.

CHAPTER 27

NOVA

I WAKE UP IN his bed expecting him to be there. But the cold empty spot beside me tells me know he's not.

He's probably in the kitchen or his office. Either way, I roll over still tired and achy from last night and easily fall back asleep.

The next time I wake, I see it's been two hours. I tilt my head. He's still not here, so I get up and go in search of him.

I use the bathroom and then wander through the house.

There's no noise but I walk to the kitchen and find it empty. His study is untouched.

I find a home gym but that's also empty. It's a Saturday. What does Jeremy do on a Saturday morning?

I head back to his room and grab my phone.

He answers immediately, "Hey, baby."

His low sexy voice makes me miss him.

"Where are you?" I ask.

"I've come to the office to do some urgent work that popped up. I shouldn't be much longer."

"I'll have a shower and eat."

"Help yourself. The television is there with anything you could need."

"Okay. Well, I'll see you soon."

"Yeah. Then I can take you out. We could do something."

After the amazing time I had with his family, a thought pops into my mind.

"What if we go to my parents' place tonight?"

"That sounds perfect."

A smile spreads on my face. "Well, I might head home first, shower and eat then go to my parents. I'll text you their address."

"I'll come as soon as I've finished here."

I hang up and text him the address.

As soon as I get home, I can tell no one is awake. It's so quiet. No TV noise or food cooking.

I trek up to my room quietly and grab fresh clothes. The feeling of Jeremy around me will wash away the instant I stand under the hot water, but tonight, I'll be in his arms again. And I can't wait.

After I step out of the shower, I call my mom.

"Hi," she answers.

"Mom, hi."

"Are you coming for dinner or are you busy?" Her high-pitched tone lets me know she's hinting at Jeremy.

"Oh, I'm still coming, but I want to ask for a favor."

"Oh, yes. What is it?"

Here we go…I'm asking to blend three of the most important people in my life together.

"Can Jeremy come for dinner too?"

I grip the phone tighter. I'm apprehensive. I'd never bring anyone home with what we as a family are going through, but Jeremy is different.

"Of course," she replies eagerly.

"I'll be there earlier. Jeremy is at work. I told him six. I don't want to mess up Dad's schedule."

"I'm sure we could've worked something out."

"No. He knows Dad's in treatment."

"Okay, love. I'll see you soon then."

I hang up and head downstairs for a late breakfast.

Summer is beside the toaster in her dachshund pajamas.

"Morning," I say.

She twists. The corner of her mouth lifts. "Well, hello."

"What?" I ask. Her expression clearly shows she wants to know something.

"How was meeting the Lincolns?" she asks. Her bagel pops out of the toaster, so she turns back and retrieves it and adds a layer of cream cheese.

I go to make a bagel myself, my mouth watering as I look at hers.

"It was amazing. His family is so welcoming."

"The brothers?"

"They were nice. One is a little quiet and the other a little rude, but I'm unsure if that was deliberate or if he doesn't know how to talk to a woman."

She carries her plate and steps back to give me room to make mine. "What do you mean?" she asks before taking a bite of her bagel.

I put mine in the toaster and explain.

"Chelsea and I were talking and he kind of made a dick of himself about Chelsea drinking."

Her face screws up. "Awkward."

Speaking of Chelsea. I'm worried about her. Did she break up with Bobby? Is that why she hugged Evan and then left?

"Yeah. Hey, where is Chelsea?"

"She went to work, why?"

I exhale heavily.

I look at the front door and debate if I should tell Summer what I saw between her and Evan.

"Tell me."

I spread cream cheese and whisper, "Please don't say anything though."

"Oh shit, what happened?"

"Nothing bad. Can we sit?"

We both sit.

"So she disappeared around the time the douchebag was meant to pick her up."

"He didn't pick her up! I'm going to kill him," Summer adds.

"I'd be angry if I didn't see what I saw."

She pauses her bagel that was on her way to her mouth. "What did you see?"

"I walked out the front and Jeremy's brother, Evan—he's the quiet one—was hugging Chelsea. At first I couldn't see her face. All I could see was his hand rubbing her back."

"Chelsea? No!"

"Uh huh." My lip twitches.

"Woah."

I nod repeatedly. "Yep. I think it would be a good thing to have another guy pull her attention away from Bobby."

"She doesn't listen to us."

"I know but another guy could be the answer."

"It's always the quiet ones." She laughs, hitting her hand on the table.

I laugh too. "Listen, I don't know much about him other than he is the CEO of Lincoln Media."

Summer whistles. "Nice."

"An upgrade from the flake she has now," I add before taking another bite of my bagel, as we sit there in silence.

"I can't believe he stood her up again," I mutter, still pissed about it.

"She really needs to stop giving him chances."

"I think in her own time she'll end things. Well, I hope…"

"Anyway, what are your plans for dinner? I need to get some food from the shops. Will I get to meet the famous Jeremy?"

"Ha Ha, you're funny. Not tonight. Maybe I can see if he can come over tomorrow night?" I offer.

"That would be great. I'd love to meet this family. Maybe there's a brother for me, too." She wiggles her brows at me with a wry smile.

I laugh. "Let me get to know them before all my friends take a brother."

"When you say it like that it sounds weird." She scrunches up her nose.

"Yeah, exactly."

"He's meeting my parents tonight."

"I'm so happy you're finally letting yourself live."

I'm happy for me too.

Three hours later, I'm at my parents' house. It's five o'clock and I'm helping my mom prepare a five-course meal in the kitchen.

Dad is in the living room in his chair watching a football game.

I peel the potatoes as Mom chops up carrots beside me.

"How's work?" Mom asks.

"I'm really enjoying it. The team I work with is fun. I'll be sad to move departments when the lady returns from maternity leave."

"Have you asked your boss about a position within the same team?"

"No, I hadn't thought about that."

I finish peeling the potatoes and pop them in a pan.

"This is a lot of potatoes," I say, knowing that they spent more on food today than usual, clearly trying to impress Jeremy. It makes my chest swell. I'm glad they're excited.

Even if I know my dad will be protective of me. I haven't warned Jeremy to expect a lot of questions. I assume it's a given, considering I'm an only child. Dad is naturally going to give him a run down on everything.

"Leftovers won't be wasted."

"Did you need more money?" I ask Mom, ready to get money from my purse.

"No, love. Keep it for yourself."

"I have enough for myself," I lie.

I'd love to save and not live paycheck to paycheck.

At this rate, I'll never buy a home. But maybe when my dad is in remission, he'll be able to return to work. I can save then.

"What do you need help with now?"

Mom looks in all her pots and pans.

"I'm all prepped, so I think I got it."

I look around, noticing the table isn't ready.

"I'll set the table."

"Then sit down," Mom instructs.

I set the table and check the time. He should be here in ten minutes. This is the first guy I've ever brought home.

I take a seat on the gray fabric sofa. "Is he here?"

I look over to my dad, surprised to find him awake.

"Not yet. How are you feeling? Has the fluid around your kidneys settled down?"

"Yeah, the doctor is happier this week," he says, patting his cheeks.

"But how are you feeling?" I ask again.

"I'm better. I just wish I wasn't so tired. I can't wait to feel like myself again."

"Soon. Once you get through chemo, the side effects should reduce."

That's what the nurses told us anyway.

"Who's winning?"

"The Eels are thrashing them."

"Is that good?" I ask, not having a clue about football.

He laughs. "Yeah, it is."

I smile. When he's happy, so am I. I sit back and watch the game.

After a while Mom calls out. "Did he message you, love?"

I pull out my phone to see no messages or missed calls. "No, why?"

"It's just after six. I don't know whether to serve everything or keep it warm in the oven."

"Let me message him and find out."

I unlock my screen and quickly type out a message to Jeremy.

> **Nova:** Hi! Where are you?

> **Jeremy:** I'm sorry I am caught up at work. I'll be there soon.

> **Nova:** How long is soon? My dad needs his medication and then he goes to bed.

> **Jeremy:** I'm so sorry. Half an hour maybe?

I inhale a deep breath and close my eyes tightly. His absence tonight is disappointing. It shows me he may not value my family as much as I did his, which is unacceptable considering the importance my family holds for me, and he's well aware of that.

My heart pounds so hard in my chest as I type the words.

Nova: *Don't worry about it then.*

I stare at it for a second before I put my phone on silent and tuck it away.

"He said he's still working. Let's eat."

"Of course," Mom says, raising her brows. "But are you okay?"

"I'm fine."

I don't want her to worry about me. I'm ready to enjoy a nice meal with my family.

Five minutes later, Mom starts serving our plates.

I get up from the sofa and help put the plates on the table. The chicken, potatoes, and vegetables look delicious. I'm really hungry now.

"Dinner is ready," I call out.

My father gets out of his chair and leaves the TV on. He walks over to his dining chair and takes a seat.

Mom puts bread in the middle of the table and then takes her seat. We all take some and begin eating when the door rings.

My eyes widen. *Is it him?*

Mom pushes her chair out.

I hold out my hand. "I got it."

Mom brings her chair back in when Dad nods. I stand and go to the door.

I take a deep breath and open the door. A sudden coldness hits my core. He's standing there in a black suit with a downturned mouth, holding two massive bunches of red roses. The black compliments his smoldering eyes and dark hair.

"Hi, Star."

"What are those?" I murmur.

"One is for you, and one is for your mom. I'm really sorry I'm so late."

That gets my brain working.

"You should come in and apologize to them too."

I step back, one hand on the door handle and the other hanging slack by my side. He steps into the house, coming to stand in the entrance and the familiar buzz from being around him hits me.

I turn my face to the table, my parents' eyes are on us standing in the entryway. I lift my hand toward them and in a flat voice I say, "Come."

I walk him through the house which isn't as big as his and we arrive at the table.

"I'm so sorry I'm late, Mr. and Mrs. Lee." He hands my mom her bouquet. And she stares at him confused.

"Are these for me?" she asks.

"Yes, Mrs. Lee," Jeremy says.

Jeremy moves to my dad, who stands when Jeremy arrives with his hand extended to shake my dad's.

"Mr. Lee, I'm sorry I'm so late," Jeremy says, offering to shake his hand.

My dad lifts his chin. "Making a good impression doesn't mean much these days, does it?"

They stand eye to eye. My dad's hard expression makes Jeremy clear his throat and turn to me.

"Again, I'm so sorry. These are for you." The sincerity in his voice and his dull eyes make me step forward and take the bouquet of roses.

My dad will love that he's given us flowers, apologized, shook his hand, works hard, and wears a suit. They are all a tick of approval in his eyes.

"So you got stuck at work?" my dad asks.

"Yeah. I have a few problems with a hospital in Boston. It needed my urgent attention."

"Take a seat and we can talk while we eat."

"Do you want something to drink?" Mom asks Jeremy.

"Water?" he says.

"Sparkling or still?" she asks.

When did my mom buy sparkling water?

When I decided to invite a man over...

CHAPTER 28

JEREMY

"STILL, THANKS," I REPLY.

My eyes drift to Nova and I can't help but want to slip my hand over hers and interlace them together. I hate that I've upset her.

I have this desperate need to touch her to alleviate the tension in the air. But I need to respect her and her parents. I've already left a bad first impression. I'm feeling unsettled and I can only imagine this is how she felt with my family.

After they met Nova, my family proceeded to bombard me with texts and calls to remind me not to fuck this up, to tell me how beautiful and intelligent she is and how happy they are for me. I had to laugh a few times. Do they think I'm unaware of how special she is? I barely looked at a woman before, but with her, she consumes me. Every day. All day.

"Are you able to return back to your job after treatment?" I ask her dad.

Her mom brings a glass of water and I look up and mouth, *thanks.*

She takes her seat, and we eat.

The chicken is incredible.

"I'm on unpaid leave, but I'm due back soon."

I frown. "But you're in the middle of treatment."

"I can't have Nova supporting us any longer. She's our child. I don't want this life for her. I want her to have her own life." There's a bite to his words and I don't know if it's at me or the fact he hates Nova supporting them.

"I understand," I reply. My brain is working overtime. My eyes drift to Nova whose flushed cheeks let me know she didn't want me to know that certain piece of information. But I'm going to pay her rent and her parents' mortgage. She's going to fight me on it because that's Nova. She's strong and independent. But she needs to know she can still help them without sacrificing her future or anything she wants to do.

I want to help her. It will be a good way to make up for being late too.

After we leave, I'll sort it out.

I'll worry about how she reacts when the mortgage is already paid, and her rent is done. I'd buy that property, but I don't want her living there forever.

No, she's my forever girl, and I want her to live with me.

"If you're unable to go back to that job, quit, and I'll find you a job. There are so many people I know and so many jobs within the hospitals. I can help you out."

"Would it include all the benefits?"

"Of course. Better pay and conditions I promise you, Mr Lee."

Her dad nods. "I'll think about it. I can barely stay awake for 5 hours let alone 8-to-10-hour shifts."

"You need to concentrate on treatment. Gain your strength back." I grab my wallet and pull out a business card, sliding it across to him. He picks it up and stares at it before looking at me.

I smile. "Call me when you're ready. I'll look after you."

He looks over to his wife and I see a misty look in Nova's mom's eyes. Then I move my gaze to Nova, who's staring at me with a glassy stare. I think that means whatever I said was right.

We eat in silence around the compact wooden table before Nova speaks.

"Do you watch football?" Nova asks me.

"A little, why?" I reply.

"My dad watches it."

"Who do you follow?" I ask as I eat a portion of the buttery potato.

"The Eels. You?"

I want Nova's dad to like me. I don't want to fail over football. "No specific team but maybe you could convince me to root for the Eels."

He dips his head at me. "Good choice."

I smile and my hand slips to Nova's knee under the table. I give it a gentle squeeze. Nova turns to me, and I wink at her.

We finish dinner and Nova stands when her mom does to start clearing the plates. I go to stand to take my plate to the dishwasher, but Nova holds out a hand to stop me.

"Stay. I'll bring you a slice of the blueberry pie."

"I was going to say I am full, but if there's homemade pie, I'll find room."

"You won't regret it. Mom makes the best pie."

"Is your mom the reason you know how to cook?"

"Yeah. My mom will tell you all the stories about teaching me to cook."

"It's been our thing since she was a little girl," her mom gushes.

"I just get to eat it all," her dad says with a chuckle.

"I can't blame you, sir. I'd happily be the taste tester. Except I'd probably gain a ton of weight."

"Nova is a great cook," her mom continues.

"I learned from the best," Nova responds.

Her mom hugs her, and I love the warmth they all share.

I watch as Nova's mom pulls the pie from the oven. The pastry is the perfect golden color. I lick my lips with anticipation.

The room is infused with the rich buttery aroma of pastry.

Nova's mom cuts up pieces and serves us all a big slice of pie. I pick up the whipped cream and pour a decent helping and then eat.

It's so good. I can't help but moan. I don't take a breath until I've finished my entire slice. "I'm so full but Mrs. Lee that was a feast. Thank you. You didn't have to go to so much trouble," I say, leaning back in my chair.

"I know but I'm glad you enjoyed it," she replies with a warm smile.

Her dad yawns beside me.

"Dad, take Jeremy to the couch while I clean up with Mom. Watch a little bit of the Eels before we go," Nova orders.

My lips twitch at her telling us what to do.

"All right," her dad says without a fight. He's obviously used to it. I'm not, but I actually don't mind her commands. It's sexy.

"Are you sure you don't need a hand?" I ask, feeling bad leaving the girls to clean up all the mess on their own.

"No, please sit with my dad. Mom and I have mastered this." Nova's expression is almost pleading. Like she wants me to spend time with her dad.

I refrain from probing further and instead walk through her cozy family home, which exudes a humble charm. Family pictures hang on the walls, telling stories of the years gone by. Taking a seat on the well-worn sofa, I listen as he explains the rules in detail. His excitement is palpable, especially as the Eels seem to be winning, and I can't help but join in the excitement with a shout of my own.

Nova and her mom join us to watch some of the game before it's time for us to leave.

We say goodnight so her dad can go to bed and as soon as we are outside beside my car, I can't help but kiss her.

I've wanted to do it all night.

She moans and kisses me back with so much passion. Her hands on my shoulders move to my neck. She's so handsy and not afraid of touching me everywhere. I love it. I love that she shows me how much she wants me.

I move my hands down her back to the top of her round ass. I push her against me. Where she finds me rock hard. She whimpers and grinds against me.

It causes me to snap. "Let's go home," I say, my voice hoarse.

"What about my car?"

"Terry will sort it out." I pull open the car door and she climbs in. I get in the car and drive off, trying not to speed my way home.

On the drive back, I ask her the burning question. "Why didn't you tell me you were helping them out?"

She exhales and stares out the window. "I knew you were going to bring this up."

"It's huge," I say softly.

"It's not. My parents are struggling, and I can afford to help them."

"And how long were you intending on helping them?"

She shrugs. "For as long as needed."

I grow quiet.

My admiration and respect for her deepens as our connection strengthens overtime.

I park in the garage and then open her door. Without exchanging words, she gets out of my car gracefully. I take her by the hand and lead us inside.

We don't speak. I just walk through my house all the way until I have us in my bedroom. I need her. The pressure to have her has been burning all night and right now I'm about to pop.

As soon as we enter my room, my mouth is on hers. A deep feral growl rips through me.

I walk her backward until we're close to my bed. My tongue skims her lips to encourage her to open them. When she does, our tongues collide––hers is demanding inside my mouth.

And I hate the knowledge that I can't have this or her all the time.

I've never thought or asked this of a woman before, but with Nova, I want it. No fuck. I need it.

"Come live with me," I rasp between hot kisses.

Her hands unbutton my shirt as she gazes at me longingly.

"When?"

"Now."

"I can't..." she whispers.

"Why not?"

She blinks and she's pushing my shirt down my arms until it falls to the floor.

"It's too soon," she breathes.

"To who? My family adores you as much as me. Your family seems to like me. Would they be opposed?"

She snorts. "No. You have their approval."

"I do?" I ask surprised. I knew her mom liked me, but her dad was hard to read. I try to remember what they said tonight that would gain that much confidence from her.

"Trust me. You answered all my dad's questions, and you watched football with him on the sofa. You have him. Mom was in the kitchen gushing over how perfect you are and how you look..." She trails off.

When I realize she won't continue, I push to hear the rest. "Look what?"

"How you look at me differently."

My mouth curves slowly and seductively. Not hiding the fact that I know I do. "Oh, I do. You shine so bright when you're in a room. You make it impossible not to stare. I'm addicted to you. *My beautiful star*."

I sound like such a wimp, but I can't help the way she makes me feel.

Her hands trail over my hot chest to the sides of my face. She rises on her tiptoes and kisses me. "You have no idea how powerful you are. Always working hard. You're admirable."

I think my heart stops.

"You think me working hard is admirable?" I ask in disbelief.

"Of course," she says.

Nova doesn't get jealous or worry. And I'm glad because I don't want anyone else; I only want her.

Whenever I'm on my phone or when I'm not with her, I'm working. I didn't become successful by doing the minimum. I work hard and I hope with my future, I can play harder.

Being able to pay her parents' mortgage or her rent for a year is nothing but small change to me. To them, it's a life raft.

If I wasn't already falling for Nova, this is proof.

"I need you, Nova."

"I need you too."

"Get on the bed," I command, grabbing a condom and rolling it on.

She blinks at me but doesn't waste another second before she climbs on my bed, lying back on her elbows and waiting for me.

"Fuck. The way you look at me kills me. You make it so hard to concentrate. I should punish you."

She gives me a wicked-as-sin smile. "Do your best."

Chapter 29

Nova

I STRIDE OVER TO the bed. My gaze drops over his toned chest before meeting his eyes. He crawls up over me, and I swear I can't breathe.

"I hope you're ready because I'm about to bury myself deep inside you."

"Please," I moan.

He reaches between us and grabs my top, lifting it up until I whip it off and toss it across the room.

His fingers trace from my neck, over my beating pulse, down to my chest and over my ribs. I shiver. My whole body erupts in goosebumps.

He's going to make a mess of me. It's written on his face. I'm already welcoming the way he'll destroy me.

His mouth moves to my shoulder where he nips all the way up until my neck meets my ear.

"You taste so sweet."

He nips me one last time before he moves his mouth to my breast.

He bites my nipple and I cry out, "Ah."

I'm arching into his mouth because I want more. He doesn't give it to me though, He looks up with a crooked smile.

"You will get what you've given."

I exhale a shaky breath and nod.

He moves his mouth to my other nipple, biting it hard.

I whimper at the hard bite. My center is achy and wet.

He laps up the bite with a lick of his tongue.

The contrast is too much. "Please," I beg.

"You want more?"

"Yes."

"Do you want my cock in your tight pussy?" he asks with a dark smile. His eyes drop to the sweet spot between my thighs.

"Yesss," I stammer.

"You need to wait and earn my cock." His hand slips between my legs and he cups my pussy hard.

I squirm, desperate for friction.

His hand slides up to the button on my pants. He makes quick work to undo them and then pulls my pants and panties down together.

Yesss.

He roughly removes them and settles between my thighs, and without warning, he licks my pussy.

"Ah."

My hands fly to his hair. On the next lick, he thrusts his tongue inside me, fucking me hard with his tongue as his hands hold my legs wide open for him.

He doesn't come up for air; instead, he continues to tongue-fuck me. He's so good at this. I whimper when he removes his tongue.

"You taste so fucking good."

Without warning, he moves his mouth to my swollen bud and bites it.

My head tips back from the mix of pain and then pleasure. "Ah," I whimper.

He lifts his head to watch me intently. His hands move to my entrance, and he inserts two fingers. He pumps them in and out, then adds a third finger.

"You feel so good. So tight."

My body is on fire. I don't know how much more I can take. Especially as I hear the sound of my wetness.

As if he knows I'm on the edge, he pulls his fingers out and I whimper at the loss.

I watch him bring his three fingers to his mouth where he licks them clean. It's so hot. To watch him enjoy the taste of me. He's so hot.

"You taste incredible."

He shuffles on the bed, so his knees are between my thighs. He drops to his elbow to kiss me in a violent kiss.

When he pulls back, he lines his hard cock up with my wet core. Without warning, he slams into me all the way to the hilt.

"Oh...my God," I gasp.

He doesn't slow down, instead he picks up the pace.

I wrap my legs around his waist as he thrusts in hard. He's not holding back. He fucks me relentlessly. My erratic pulse is unable to slow down. With every hard thrust, my tits bounce. He tries to go deeper even though it isn't possible. He fucks me harder. And harder. His balls hit my ass and I quiver with the need to come.

"Fuck, your pussy was made for me. You take me so well, baby."

I can't take much more.

"I'm going to come," I breathe.

"I'm coming too, so fucking hard," he grunts.

His hips still slam repeatedly into me until I come. He follows. He pauses when he's deep inside me and I feel his dick jerking.

He smiles down at me. I blink and look lazily up at him as if he has answers to what that was.

How is it possible that sex gets better with Jeremy every time?

CHAPTER 30

NOVA

I GET HOME FROM work, not bothering to go boxing tonight. I need to prepare the house and then dinner. Jeremy is coming over.

He's meeting Summer. Chelsea will be here too, but he's already met her.

This is the first time he's been inside my place for dinner.

I clean the floors while the girls are out. Chelsea went to pick up wine for dinner and Summer is in the shower.

I finish putting the vacuum away when Chelsea steps through the door.

I wash my hands and begin prepping the crumbed fish. "Did you want a hand?" she asks.

I lay out all the ingredients, pouring flour, egg, and breadcrumbs into bowls.

"No. I'm good. I need to keep busy, so I don't watch the time."

She flicks the kettle on to make tea. She sits down on the stool waiting.

"You've really fallen for him, haven't you?"

I don't bother hiding it.

"Yeah. I have."

She stays silent and I worry about her with Bobby. Her phone chimes. I assume it's the devil himself.

"Is everything okay with Bobby?" I ask softly.

"Yeah, why?" She frowns, looking up from her phone.

The kettle has boiled, so she gets up, tucks her phone away, and makes tea. "Did you want tea?"

"No, I'm good. At Jeremy's birthday dinner, I went looking for you and I came outside to find you hugging Evan."

She returns to her seat on the stool. I've finished breading the pieces of fish and now I move on to deep frying them.

"That was nothing. Bobby cancelled our plans, so I was upset. I didn't want to tell you and ruin your night. Evan came out to take a business call and saw me."

"Are you still with Bobby?"

"Of course. There's nothing going on with me and Evan. I hugged him and that was it. I love Bobby."

I look over at her and the hearts in her eyes kill me. I wish she didn't love him. She deserves better. But it's not my life.

"Okay, okay, I'm just asking. But that was nice of Evan though. He seems quiet, so I was surprised to find him comforting you."

She laughs. "He didn't exactly have a choice. He asked if I was okay, and I pretty much cried and threw myself onto his chest."

I giggle, picturing her doing that.

"Did you tell Jeremy?" she asks with horror-filled eyes.

I shake my head. "No. I wanted to talk to you first."

"Please don't say anything," she begs.

I groan. "I don't want to keep secrets from him."

"This technically isn't a secret. No point in telling him when I'll never see his brother again."

I agree. "Fine, but if you do, I'm telling him."

"Okay."

I continue to cook the fish as I turn the burner on for the pre-cut vegetables.

"Something smells good," Summer calls as she enters the kitchen.

"I hope you're hungry, there's plenty to eat."

"I'm always hungry. And I can always take leftovers for lunch tomorrow," Summer suggests.

"What time is Jeremy coming?" Chelsea asks.

"6."

"That's now." Chelsea replies laughing.

I frown. "Really?" I frown. "He's late again," I murmur to myself, glancing toward the door.

"Yeah," Summer replies.

I push it aside and focus on getting myself ready.

The girls must see my panic-stricken face.

"Let me take over cooking, you go and freshen up," Chelsea offers.

"You look pale," Summer adds.

"Jeez, thanks, I won't be long. I just want to freshen up."

"Take your time, we can entertain him until you're done," Summer says.

My mouth falls open.

"I don't mean to entertain him like that. Jesus, woman," Summer says.

I laugh. "I'll be back soon. Keep an eye on the food, please, Chelsea."

"Don't you trust me?" Summer calls out as I head to the bathroom.

"You don't like cooking," I shout as I reach my room.

I pull out a pair of jeans and a knitted sweater. I shower and dress. Then put a little makeup on. It's been half an hour, so Jeremy should be here. I return to the kitchen. Chelsea and Summer have put the food onto plates. I look around and don't spot him.

"He isn't here?" I ask the girls.

"No. Give him a call," Chelsea says.

Summer pours wine into the glasses that are on the set table.

Everything is ready for dinner. We're just missing Jeremy.

I call him. It goes straight to the voicemail.

My phone buzzes with a text message.

> **Jeremy:** I'm stuck in a meeting. I'll call you when I'm done.

> **Nova:** Will you be coming for dinner?

> **Jeremy:** Sorry, something came up at work. Can we reschedule?

My heart drops. I understand he has to work, but meeting my closest friends was important to me. I can't help but be angry. I was disappointed in him coming late to my parents but now cancelling with my roommates has snapped something in me.

Our lifestyles are just too different. I should go back to only focusing on work and my dad.

> **Nova:** No.

My phone rings in my hand. Jeremy's name flashes on the screen. I inhale a deep breath and answer, "Yes."

"I'm really sorry. I'm down a few workers."

I glance down at my bare feet. Usually, I'd just accept it, but I can't this time. He broke something in me.

"Meeting my parents was important to me but you were late that night. And tonight, you cancel."

"I'm really sorry I messed up again."

"You're not prioritizing our relationship. I need someone to be there when it matters."

"I am. I'm coming over now," he says in panic.

I sigh, not wanting to argue right now. "Don't. I think it's best for both of us to take a step back."

I pinch my lips tight to stop them from trembling, but it doesn't stop the tears that fill my eyes. I want him to myself. His last relationship ended due to his workaholic tendencies. I had a hard time grasping how bad it must have gotten. I thought I wasn't as high maintenance. I thought I didn't need all his time, but I guess I was wrong.

I hang up, and before I can take back the words, I turn my phone off and swat my tears away and walk back to rejoin the girls.

"Let's eat," I announce. Even though I'm not at all hungry now. My heart is in my throat from asking him for space.

"What about Jeremy?" Summer asks.

"He's stuck at work."

"Oh damn. So I won't get to meet him?" Summer asks.

"Unfortunately, not. I asked for some space."

"You what?" Summer gasps.

"He's always working. Last night he was late meeting my parents and now not showing up toni—" My voice cracks.

"Here." Chelsea hands me a glass of wine.

"Thanks." I sniff, taking the glass.

Summer puts her hand over my shoulder, guiding me to the sofa. A mix of emotions pulses through me, each one a sharp stab of pain. I'm torn between the memories Jeremy and I shared, and the painful need to let go. The weight of it all suffocates me, as I struggle to make sense of the shattered pieces of my heart.

CHAPTER 31

NOVA

A FEW DAYS LATER, I'm typing out a report that should've taken me half an hour to complete, yet I've been at it for two hours and I'm still going. The numbers aren't flowing, and it makes me second-guess everything I'm writing. I've rewritten and triple-checked everything and I'm still not happy. I'm blaming this uneasiness on my lack of sleep last night. I kept waking up to check my phone to see if Jeremy called. Every single time I found nothing.

I get up and make a coffee in the break room and return to my desk.

"Mr. Spencer," I say when I walk back to my desk to find him perched on it with his arms crossed over his chest.

"Nova, the report was due an hour ago. I see you haven't finished."

His eyes drop over to the computer. He read it while I wasn't here.

"I'm sorry. I'm making sure it's perfect," I admit.

"I don't need it to be perfect. I need it done."

His angry tone has panic filling me. I can't lose this job.

"I'll have it for you in the next hour."

"Not a second longer. I hate having grumpy clients."

I nod.

He exits the room and I exhale heavily, taking a sip of my coffee and sitting down.

"Is everything okay, Nova?" Dalton asks.

"I'm struggling to finish this report. Any chance you can help?"

He grimaces. "I can't. I have a meeting to get to."

"That's okay. I need to learn."

"I can help," Poppy's voice calls out.

My eyes widen at the fact she's willing to help me. Now this is progress.

"Yes. I'd love some help," I reply desperately.

Her heels click and I know she's making her way over. I get up and grab her a chair. She stands close and I take her in. Her hair is pulled into a sleek pony and her black suit fits her so well. She is every bit sophisticated. To have her help me means more to me than she will ever know. She takes a seat in the chair and moves closer to the computer screen. I'm about to explain what I need help with when Dalton speaks.

"Look at you two being besties." Dalton winks.

"Go away," Poppy says, not bothering to turn to look at him.

"I'll see you two when I get back." He walks off.

"Bye," I call and then explain to Poppy what I've done and where I'm stuck. She reads through everything, then sits back in the chair and shifts to face me. "This is really good. Very thorough. Way more than you need?"

"Should I delete some?" I ask.

"No, I think to shut Bentley up, send it as is," Poppy says as she stands.

"Thanks for helping," I say.

She nods and walks back to her desk. "You're good, Nova. Get out of your head."

I pinch my lips together. She has no idea how much I've been in my head today and it isn't about work. No, my head is filled with thoughts of Jeremy.

A few hours later, I'm sitting outside on a chair in the crisp New York air. No one is up here. Workers tend to go to the break room or walk to a local bakery and eat lunch. I've come here to be alone and make a phone call.

"Hello Mom," I say as soon as she answers.

"Hi, love. Are you on your lunch break?"

"Yeah, I called as soon as I could."

She sent a message to call her when I got the chance. I needed to finish and email the documents to Bentley in order to keep my job.

"No rush. I just had a question."

My brows pull together. "Yeahhh." I draw out.

"Did you pay our mortgage?"

"No, I transferred you the money you need for the week. Did you get it?" I ask, with a sudden rush of panic. I'm about to hang up and check my banking app.

"Yes, we got the money, but when we tried to pay, we had issues. I called the bank who informed us that the mortgage had been paid in full."

"No..." I grip the phone tighter. What's going on?

"Yeah. I'm wondering if you had anything to do with it?"

It wasn't me, but I suddenly knew who did.

"Maybe, let me call you back. I need to check something."

I hang up and see a message from Summer.

> **Summer:** Did you pay a year's worth of rent today?

> **Nova:** No, but I think I know who did.

> **Summer:** I need a sugar daddy.

I grimace. I hate that she thinks of Jeremy like that because it hasn't been like that. But I need to find out if he did pay off my parents' mortgage and our rent.

I dial his number. His deep voice answers. "Hey, baby."

His nickname for me makes my muscles weak but only momentarily. "Hi."

"I'm still really sorry. The Boston Emergency has been a nightmare."

I take this as another chance to be honest.

"You should've called."

"I fucked up, didn't I?"

"Yeah."

"I'm sorry. It will never happen again, I promise."

The genuineness in his voice makes it hurt less, but I can't give in. I need to wrap up this phone call.

"Did you pay my parents' mortgage?"

He doesn't miss a beat. "Yes."

I squeeze my eyes shut. "And my rent for a year?"

"Yeah, that too."

I'm stunned silent for a beat before I open my eyes and sit up. "Why?"

"Why not," he argues.

"Jeremy."

"Nova," he mimics.

I sigh. "Why?"

"Because I can. It's nothing to me. But it's everything to you."

"I was doing it."

"You were, baby, but you weren't living your life. I want you to spend your money on you. You work hard."

"I do."

"Now you can spend the money on whatever you want. Investments, savings, a house, a new car."

"It's too much," I breathe, squeezing my eyes shut.

"For you, it's never enough. I want to give you the world."

I stare out at the courtyard flowers. "I don't need the world."

"I need you."

I hang my head as my eyes prick with fresh tears.

"I have to go," I say and hang up.

Later that night, it's five thirty and I'm curled up on the sofa in sweats under a throw blanket watching *Million Dollar Baby*.

Summer isn't home from college yet and Chelsea is at work.

I'm alone feeling sad and sorry for myself.

A knock on my door sounds and I throw off my cozy cream blanket and walk to the door.

I suck in a sharp audible breath. It's Jeremy. He's here. I take in his appearance as if I haven't seen him recently. My gaze starts at his brown styled hair and travels down over his navy suit that accentuates his broad shoulders and black dress shoes that complete the look.

The sight of him sends my stomach into a frenzied somersault, excitement bubbling within me at seeing him again.

In his hands, he holds a big bouquet of red roses. I run my hand over my sweater, making sure it's clean and that it didn't have any chocolate stains on it.

"Hi," he says.

I frown and look over his shoulder. "What are you doing here?"

"I was thinking we could have dinner tonight. I could make it up to you," he offers.

"So you can bail on me again?"

He winces. "I deserve that."

I accept the red roses and turn, leaving the door ajar so he can close it behind him. "Was there a shortage?" I tease, throwing away the week-old red roses and arranging the fresh ones in the vase. I had meant to get new ones for both my mom and me, but I hadn't been in the mood to do it.

"As a matter of fact, there was. I wanted a big bouquet and most had sold out," he explains, and I find myself biting my lip in response.

"Are you laughing at me?" he asks, walking over to close the distance between us.

"Never," I reply, turning to place the vase on the counter, attempting to put some distance between us.

"I should've put you first. I'm not asking you to forgive me."

"Then what's the point?" I question, my tone guarded.

"I want another chance. I want to show you that I can be the partner you deserve. I'm serious about making things right."

When I asked for space, it wasn't a decision I made lightly. Yet. here he stands, with those pleading puppy dog eyes, and it tugs at something inside me. I want actions not words. And he's here.

He deserves a chance.

"Fine, but let me get ready."

"You look beautiful."

I roll my eyes. "Sit on the sofa. The remote's there. I won't be long."

I'm showered, dressed and back downstairs in half an hour.

I'm about to open the door when he stands in front of me. He takes my hand in his. I drop my head and look at how well we fit together.

I feel the weight on my shoulders drop as I tip my head up. He leans forward, brushing his nose with mine. God, I've missed him. I've missed him so damn much. My hand immediately grabs the lapel of his suit to bring him closer to me. His aftershave is so strong and his presence stronger. He tips his head, so his mouth crushes on mine. He's freshly shaved, and I can't help the whimper that leaves my mouth the moment his tongue glides inside my mouth.

"Let's go, baby. I'll kiss you so much later, your lips will be bruised with my apologies tonight."

His hand settles on my lower back and guides me to the car. The simple touch ignites my body.

He opens the passenger door. I put my seat belt on, and he opens his driver door and takes his seat.

"You're driving today."

"I am. Is that a problem?"

"No, the opposite. It means your hands are busy but mine aren't."

His head whips to me in a flash. Surprise stretches across it before his dark gaze sends a shiver down my spine.

"Yes," I say with pure excitement running through my veins.

My hand glides over to his thigh resting on it as he starts the car.

"Where are we going?"

"A surprise." A guttural growl leaves his chest when my hand moves up his thigh.

I bite on my lip, loving how I have power over him right now. It's not often I have it, so whenever I can get it, I take full advantage.

The sun is setting, and he drives us through the city. The radio plays softly in the background. And this simple drive fills me with so much love.

His phone beeps. My back muscles tense. Work. I expect him to grab it. So I bring my hand back to my lap. I have my favorite red lipstick *BRAVE* and my rose scented perfume on.

He punches the hang up button furiously.

"Is everything okay?"

"No, the progress I made with the Boston hospital is falling apart. But I told them not to disturb me."

"What do you mean?"

"There's a building delay because they can't get building materials. Pushing the project out six months."

"Is there anything I can do to help?" I offer. Maybe I can type while he drives.

"No, I'll ignore it, and when we stop, I'll switch it off."

"Do you want me to drive so you can answer it?" I offer, seeing his pinched expression.

"No. I've got it. They're not important."

I love that he's trying hard to make this right. I at least want to meet him halfway. I don't expect him to never work with me around. I understand. Work is important to me too. It was more important than anything, except my family. I never wanted love or a partner. I was all about work. I needed the money. But now that I'm with Jeremy, he's more important. And that's how I want him to make me feel.

We're at a set of traffic lights waiting for them to turn green. We've been driving for fifteen minutes, and I have no idea how much longer we have until we reach our destination.

His phone buzzes again, and he opens the message. "Fuck off!" He slams his fist on the steering wheel. It makes me jump in my seat.

As the lights change colors, he doesn't see the car that's running a red light. He hits the accelerator and I scream as headlights come at me.

And everything goes black.

CHAPTER 32

JEREMY

An alarm sounds in my ear. Fuck my head hurts.

I wince as I turn my head and open my eyes. The bright lights make it so hard to see.

But the sirens don't.

What's going on? Why are there sirens? I remember being in the car with Nova.

Fuck. Nova.

I focus on the body beside me. She's not responding. Her body's limp in her seat. I try to move, but my head is screaming in pain.

I can't recall what happened, other than work distracted me. Now I'm waking up with my girlfriend unconscious beside me.

I try to speak, but my throat hurts.

Fuck!

I jerk in my seat, frustrated that I don't hear my voice and am unable to move. I'm trapped.

A surge of panic courses through me. I'm trapped and so is Nova. I have to help her. This is all my fault.

"Sir, please, stay still; we are getting a stretcher. We need urgent scans to make sure there are no severe internal injuries."

I want to tell her to focus on Nova and forget about me. That I deserve to die. She doesn't.

But when I open my mouth, nothing but a rasp of air leaves my throat.

"I'm going to put a neck brace on now."

I don't bother responding because I can't.

I'm at the paramedic's mercy.

She puts the foam around my neck and explains how she's going to get me out. How I don't need to move. I tune her out. My eyes are trying to find Nova.

I'm out of the car, but my body is on fire. The pain from my waist takes my breath away.

"I'm going to give you some pain relief. Do you have any allergies?"

I try to shake my head. It must work because she replies, "Good. This should make you feel a little better."

The pain reduces, but my head feels groggy.

I can't feel or see Nova, but I have to know if she is alright.

"Nova." I finally manage to say.

"We are taking care of her. We have to take you to the hospital now."

"No," I choke out.

"You can't stay here. The quicker you're assessed, the quicker you'll be able to see her in the hospital."

She pushes more pain relief into my veins. It helps the pain in my hips but not my heart. My eyes close, too tired to stay awake. "Nova…" I call out before I fall unconscious.

A few hours later, I wake to new beeping sounds. I groan. I've never wished for silence and darkness, but today I do.

My eyes slowly adjust to the light as I slowly look around the hospital room. It's not one of my hospitals, which is good. I don't want any special treatment. I don't deserve it. I hurt Nova.

I touch my neck, realizing the brace is gone. But the pain in my body is still a big reminder of the crash. But I deserve the pain. It's only a fraction of the pain I've caused Nova.

I look around for any of my belongings. I need to find Nova.

I can't see a single thing of mine. I'm in a hospital gown with a stupid IV drip and monitors attached to me.

I peer around the room. I try to find a phone or plan my escape. I touch the IV in my arm. I'm ready to remove it when the door to my room opens. I drop my hand away.

I turn my head to the sound. Mom and Dad enter.

"Oh Jeremy, you're awake," she exclaims, tears filling her red-rimmed eyes. She's obviously been crying.

"I don't deserve to be," I grumble.

She rushes forward, setting her coffee cup on the table, and hugs me.

Her body shakes as she cries.

"Please don't cry, Mom. I'm fine."

"You scared us, Son," my dad says as he stands on the other side of the bed. He reaches out to touch my cheek as if he can't believe I'm awake.

"I'm sorry," I murmur.

Mom sniffles. "Are you sore? Do you need me to call the nurses?" she asks, pulling back to take a good look at me.

"No. I'm fine. But where's Nova?" The tension in my voice mirrors the sudden knot in my stomach.

My mom looks over at my dad and my heart drops.

"What?" I choke, the weight of uncertainty settling over me. The backs of my eyes begin to sting and I fight to hold back tears. My parents have never seen me cry. I'm not a crier but fuck, for Nova, I'm a pussy and would cry over her.

"She's in an induced coma," my dad says.

"What. Why?" My eyes dart between the two of them.

Mom inhales a deep breath before gripping my hand and explaining. "She has a broken pelvis and internal bleeding, Son. They are trying to stabilize her."

A numbness settles within me, rendering me speechless. I gaze blankly at the end of my hospital bed and mumble, "It's all my fault."

Mom attempts to comfort me by stroking my arm, but I pull away. I don't deserve warm touches. My girlfriend is in a coma because I was reading an email from the board of directors of the Boston hospital.

I'm a selfish prick. That should be me in the induced coma not Nova. She's innocent. I'm not. I'm a criminal. They should lock me up and throw away the key. I deserve any punishment thrown at me.

"The driver who ran the red light died at the scene."

I don't know how to feel about that. Should I be happy? They could have made a mistake like me. One single mistake cost him his life; I just hope it doesn't cost Nova hers.

"Is she at this hospital?"

"Yes, but she's in the ICU."

"And where am I?"

"On the medical ward. You're lucky you missed surgery. You have a few cracked ribs and a lot of bruising, but you'll recover."

I grow quiet. Unsure what to say. I don't feel lucky.

"When can I see Nova?"

"I don't know. We'd have to ask the doctors and nurses," Mom replies.

I find the call button and press it. I'm not waiting a second longer. I want to go see Nova. Need to see her. Tell her I'm sorry. Tell her. Fuck. Tell her I love her. I've never said those words to her. I've felt them for so long, but it wasn't the right time. Now I worry I'm too late.

A nurse walks in. My parents back away from my bed to give her room.

"Mr. Lincoln, you're awake."

"Seems so," I say.

She walks directly up to the machines and assesses them. I watch her intensely. She presses buttons and then she is putting a cuff on my upper arm.

"I'm going to check your vital signs."

She takes my temperature and other signs before informing us that they are all within the normal range.

"Do you need some more pain relief?"

"No."

I'm tender but not enough to require painkillers. I want the pain as a reminder of what I did. What I've done to Nova. If she's in pain, I need to be too.

"Are you hungry?"

As soon as she asks the question, my stomach grumbles.

"Yeah."

"A man of few words, aren't you? Well, I'll call the kitchen to bring you some food."

She looks like she is leaving.

"Wait," I call out.

She spins around. "Yes, Mr. Lincoln?"

"When can I go visit my girlfriend, Nova? She's in the ICU."

"You need to be seen by the doctor before you can leave the room. So it won't be until tomorrow at the earliest."

"Tomorrow? I can't wait that long."

"I'm sorry, but you don't have a choice. You also need to rest."

I want to argue, but I know it's pointless. I blow out a frustrated breath. I need to see her with my own eyes.

I don't say any of that out loud. Instead, I just stare at the nurse who looks at me with pity.

Guilt fills my stomach. Does she blame me? Does she know I was typing an email and wasn't paying attention to the road?

I don't deserve Nova. This is why I could never be with a woman. All I do is let them down by working too much.

This time it cost me more than just a breakup. This time it could cost a life.

The nurse leaves the room without another word. My parents are sitting in chairs silent. I'm grateful for the silence because I'm not in the mood to chat.

I'm too busy rolling around in self-pity. Mom and Dad are on their phones typing away. Reminding me...

"Where's my phone?"

"You're not planning to work, are you?" My dad says, his disapproval evident.

I haven't even considered working or checking my emails. Right now, thinking about it fills me with self-loathing and a nauseous sensation.

"No. I'm just asking."

"It's probably in the bag of personal items the police put together," my dad replies matter-of-factly.

"Which is where?" I ask.

"In the cupboard." Mom answers.

"Can you get it?"

"Ask her nicely, Son," my dad says sternly.

"Please, Mom."

I know I'm back to being grumpy, but I'm mad at my-self.

"Sure." She stands, giving me a smile.

She heads to the cupboard and pulls out a plastic bag. The room door opens, and I turn my head, hoping it's a doctor who will allow me to see Nova. But I see my family. Oliver, Harvey, Evan, and lastly, Grams.

They say hi to Mom and Dad before coming to me at the bed.

"Don't you look happy," Oliver teases.

"Shut up, dickbag."

"Good to see your mouth still works," he replies.

"Excuse me! Did you forget I was in the room? In the hospital or not, no swearing," Grams says.

I wince and the tension causes pain in my ribs.

"Sorry, Grams." I grunt through the pain.

"Do you need me to call the nurse?" Evan asks. His face contorted.

I shake my head. "No, I'll be alright."

"No prizes for not taking your pills," Harvey argues.

"I'm not trying to claim a prize, I'm trying not to rely on them."

"You're not going to become addicted. You're in a controlled environment here," Evan adds.

"I want to be alert in case a doctor comes in and allows me to see Nova."

No one speaks after I say her name, which means they all know she's not well.

Why aren't they angry at me?

I don't deserve their love and support.

A thought comes to me. I can't be there in person, but I can do something that will let her know I'm thinking of her and I'm there with her in spirit.

"Evan?"

"Yeah." He calls out standing beside Mom who's putting away my stuff.

Mom's clearly taking it all home to wash. I don't care what she does with it. She puts the phone on my tray table.

"Come here."

He comes closer. We have an audience.

So when he's close, I whisper, "I need you to go to the florist shop and get red roses for Nova. The biggest bouquet they can make and deliver it to her room, please."

"When?"

"Now."

"Anything else?"

I want to say all the things running through my mind, but they have to come from me when she wakes because she is going to wake up from this nightmare. I can't have her leave me now; I only just found her.

"Sure." He answers by squeezing my shoulder. "I'm glad you're okay."

I dip my chin. And watch him leave my room.

"I need a moment alone with Remy. Can you all go grab me a tea from downstairs and give me some time with him?" Grams requests.

No one argues with Grams. So they all begin to rise from their chairs or walk straight to the door, telling us they will be back. As soon as they leave, she takes a seat on my hospital bed and reaches out to squeeze my cheek.

"How's my handsome grandson doing?"

"Okay."

"No, tell me, really. No lying to me." She leans in a little.

"Better than I deserve," I answer honestly.

"You're paying a price for your mistakes. You're human. It's okay to make mistakes, it's what you do after that's important."

I let her words sit with me for a few moments before I pour my heart out to her. The person other than Nova I feel I can be vulnerable with.

"Grams, I can't lose her."

She holds my hand and looks me dead in the eye.

I know I'm about to get my ass handed to me by just that one look. "If you're adamant that she's the one then you need to show her. So far, you're doing a good job at pushing her away."

"I don't mea—"

She puts up her hand and looks to the side. My mouth closes.

"I'm not done speaking. You need the hard truth. You work too much. You're thirty-eight. Unmarried and without children. Do you want things to stay this way, or are you ready to get your girl?"

If you had asked me this before I met Nova, I would have said no. But now, I want everything with Nova.

"Yes."

"Then quit working so much. Focus on what matters to you. There's no point in having money if you're lonely. It won't fill the void. This was a wakeup call. Use it wisely. I'd hate to see you let that sweet girl go because you're a damn workaholic."

"I don't know how to quit working so much."

She pats my hand. "I'm not a fool Remy and neither are you. Figure it out. You were always good at challenges and this one is your biggest yet."

"I love her."

"I know you do. So prove it to her. She's got a long recovery ahead of her. And I'd hate to make you feel worse than you do, but you did this to her. You better be there as she heals. She needs you."

The door swings open again, and I expect my family has come back, but it's the kitchen bringing in my food. Grams lets go of my hand and takes the seat beside my bed. Having her here makes me feel settled. I eat the sandwich, juice and crackers. It doesn't fill me up, but it at least gives me something.

My eyes feel heavy, and I'm suddenly tired. Grams stands.

"Don't keep yourself awake. I'm going to go down and tell them all to leave. You need to rest."

"Thanks, Grams."

"Also, can you go back to the nice Remy. I don't like this grumpy version."

I chuckle. "Is that so?"

"Yeah, your parents said you're back to the days before Nova."

"I'll try but no guarantees."

She rests her hand on my cheek. "That's all we can ask for."

She turns with her walker and leaves my room. I don't even remember hearing the door click before I'm fast asleep, yet the same horrors fill my dreams. Nova in the passenger seat covered in blood and unresponsive. I wish it was a dream, but it's not, it's my reality.

CHAPTER 33

JEREMY

I watch the sunrise from my hospital bed. Even though my mom got my phone out, I haven't been able to bring myself to switch it on.

I still haven't decided how I'll handle work. I know the emails and to-do lists will be piling up, yet that still can't get me to touch it. My brothers are keeping my personal assistant up-to-date, so she can answer people when they call. Leaving me to *rest* as they say. None of them know that the sound of Nova's screams still haunts me. It was so high-pitched, laced with fear. It's the last thing I remember.

I try to push the bad away and focus on the good memories we've shared. Like the time when my phone didn't scare me, and I looked forward to the cheeky remarks Nova messaged me. Or the time in the lift where I held her close for the first time. And speaking of...our first kiss. The touch of those red painted lips on mine was addictive at the very first touch. I miss the way she tastes and smells.

I want to see her already. I'll lose it if the doctor doesn't come by today and let me see her. I need to see her.

First thing I need to do is shower and change. I can't see her in a hospital gown.

I press the bell for the nurse, and she assists me in the shower. She adjusts the length of the drip so I don't have to take the whole device into the shower. She says if I eat and drink enough water today without feeling sick or needing pain relief meds then the doctor said I could have it removed.

Afterward, I decide to sit in bed and nap. Doing even the most basic tasks, like showering, is exhausting.

An hour later, it's eight and I see breakfast has been delivered. I sit up on the side of my bed and eat. The door opens behind me and heavy steps stride in.

A doctor.

Thank fuck.

Getting to Nova feels like a step closer now.

"Good morning, Mr. Lincoln. I'm Doctor Andrews."

"Morning, Doctor Andrews."

"How are you feeling?" he asks, grabbing the chart from the nurse's outstretched hand.

"A little tender but otherwise good." I don't bother lying because that won't get me any closer to seeing Nova.

"You're not taking much pain relief," he murmurs, flicking the papers on my chart.

"It's not that bad."

"And you're moving. I see you've had a shower."

"Moving just makes me a little tender, nothing I can't handle."

"I'll keep the drip in your arm today and if you're fine, it can come out tomorrow and you could look at going home."

"Really?"

"Yeah, but let's see how you do today. Do you have any other questions."

"Just one. Can I visit my girlfriend Nova in the ICU?"

"If you have a family member that can take you in a wheelchair and you promise me you won't spend all day there, then yes."

"Thanks Doctor."

"An hour or two max."

What? That's not long enough. But right now, I don't have a choice and I'll take anything.

"Any other questions?" he asks.

I shake my head. "No."

He closes my chart, hands it back to the nurse, and looks at me. "I'll see you tomorrow, Mr. Lincoln."

As soon as they leave the room, I grab my phone and switch it on. I ignore the number of messages and focus on finding my brother's name.

I call him and tell him to go to my house, grab me some clothes and get his ass here asap. I explain that the doctor cleared me to see Nova.

He promises he'll be here soon, so in the meantime, I hang up and take another nap, knowing I'll need the strength for later.

A knock and the door swings open.

"It's me," Oliver calls out.

I swing my legs off the bed in anticipation.

"You look like your ugly self again."

The edge of my lip tilts up. "Thanks."

He comes to me and holds out the bag of clothes. He's in cream chinos and a white button-up shirt. This is his version of casual.

"I had your maid pack stuff because I wasn't going through your drawers. It didn't feel right."

"They're clothes, not sex toys."

"That's what I was scared to find. I don't need to stumble upon shit that I'm not supposed to, because then I'd never look at you the same."

I shake my head and the first real laugh in days rumbles from my chest.

"You're an idiot. Give me the bag so I can get changed."

I rip open the bag and pull out sweatpants and a t-shirt. I dig around until I find the sweater and clean briefs. I start to undress.

"Woah, man. Give me a warning before flashing me your Crown Jewels...fuckkk."

I continue putting on my pants. "You have a set yourself. Or are you jealous I have a bigger dick than you?"

"I didn't look long enough to take that much notice, idiot."

"Your loss. I'm not showing you again."

"Never said I wanted another look." He's looking outside my window.

"I'm all covered and ready to go."

Oliver turns away from the window. "Let me tell your nurse and grab you a wheelchair."

"I don't need a fucking wheelchair."

"It's a long walk and there's no way you're walking that far."

I stay silent deliberating starting a fight.

"Don't fight me on this. I'll push your ass the fastest I can."

"Fine!" I sit down on the bed.

"Don't sulk. You'll be back to yourself before you know it."

With that, he leaves the room. I grab my phone and turn it off before putting it away.

Oliver is back and one look at the chair causes me to grind my teeth.

"Don't say a word. Get your ass in the chair and let's go."

I huff but step over to the chair and sit.

He doesn't wait, he pushes me straight out of the room.

"Did you tell my nurse?"

"Yes. Now, let's go."

I want to ask him if he has any updates, but I don't know if I want to know right now. I decide it's better I wait and see.

I grip the sides of the wheelchair and look at every sign we pass, searching for the words ICU.

I'm sure Oliver knows where he's going, but I can't help but point and tell him the direction when I finally see a sign.

My heart pounds knowing I'm so close to her now. As soon as I see the nurse's desk, I'm edging from the chair.

"Stay in the chair." Oliver grunts from behind me. I twist my head to see perspiration beads on his forehead. I forgot he had to push a 180-pound man around in a hurry.

I sit back down.

"Hi. We're here to see Miss Nova Lee."

"Unfortunately she has family in there already, so I can only allow one of you."

"I'll stay out here. Go in, I'll be here whenever you're done."

"Are you sure?"

"Yeah, I have work to do. I'll sit on those chairs and do it."

Work. Something I'm avoiding and should feel guilt-ridden about, but I don't.

Oliver's hand squeezes my shoulder. I cover my hand with his and squeeze it as a thanks. He turns and strides over to take a seat.

I turn and the nurse pushes me into the room. My heart is already in my throat, creating a painful lump, as the door swings open to reveal Nova.

Tears fill my eyes at the haunting scene. There are wires...everywhere.

My eyes well up with tears, and I struggle to breathe properly. I blink rapidly as my vision blurs. Tears roll down my cheeks, each droplet carrying the weight of my guilt, which only intensifies the longer I stare at her unmoving, lifeless body in the bed.

"Jeremy?" a familiar voice calls.

I turn toward it. Her mom.

I prepare myself for the lashing I deserve. I put their daughter in danger. She could die because of me.

But her mom comes over and hugs me. I'm shocked at first, but when I understand what's happening, I bring my arms around her and hug her back. She cries in my ear at how glad she is that I'm okay.

I don't deserve her kindness.

A hand touches my shoulder, it's gentle yet firm. "Son, she's okay, but we need to talk." Her father's voice hits my already vulnerable state.

Her sick father. A man who doesn't deserve this pain. A sob leaves my mouth. I can't stop the waves of tears that unleash now. Lydia's arms squeeze me tighter and I keep howling my lungs out like I've needed this as much as I needed her to wake up.

Once I've cried my heart out, I peel back from Lydia's arms and turn to Charles.

He dips his chin and walks out the door and I follow.

We move away from the others. This is a private conversation.

Once Charles sits down, I position myself so I'm facing him head on.

"How are you?" he asks.

"Better than I should be."

He shakes his head. "The accident wasn't your fault. I'm not here to blame you for this. This is an adult conversation between us."

"Mm," I reply, so he knows I'm listening.

"You know I'm sick. And I won't be around forever. So, I need to make sure she's with someone who is going to be there through thick and thin."

"I will, sir."

He shuffles forward in his chair, hands on his knees. "I'm at a point in my life where I need to make sure you're going to be there for my daughter in the bad times and good. So if this isn't what you want, I need you to let her go."

This is the moment where the father lays down the law and wants to make sure I'm not going to hurt his daughter's heart.

Fuck. I don't plan to. Her being gone from my life for a few days almost killed me.

"I promise you she's it for me. I need her in my life. I'll give up work, money, anything." I throw my hands up in the air. "All of it just to have her."

His lips part. "You don't need to do that. You just need to show her that you've got her back. That you'll be there when I'm gone."

My throat constricts. I hate hearing him talk about him dying. He isn't, not now.

"I don't plan to leave her side ever." *Again.*

"Good." He grabs my shoulder and squeezes it. "You're good for her. I like you. Now we will give you some time alone with her."

No. My fear says.

"Thanks." My heart answers.

"She's been waiting for you."

At those words, one fat tear rolls down my cheek.

CHAPTER 34

JEREMY

I WHEEL CLOSER TO her bed, my gaze fixed on Nova.

Her frail body looks so helpless right now. The door gently closes behind me, leaving only Nova and me in the room.

"Baby," I murmur, lifting her hand and cradling it in mine, carefully avoiding the IV attached on the back of her hand. I recall the moments when, holding her hand, she would interlace her fingers with mine. Now, she remains unresponsive.

Not having her touch is agonizing and the weight of regret settles heavily on me.

"I'm so sorry."

I look around at all the machines beeping and making all different noises. Medicine dripping into her vein. That's what's keeping her in an induced coma.

How long will she stay like this?

"I hope you can hear me speak." I sigh.

My thumb follows the bumps in her knuckles. I feel so helpless. What can I do to fix this?

"I wish you'd wake up and talk to me. I need to tell you something I should've said ages ago."

Why do we wait until something happens before we realize we should have said something, but we didn't?

"Your parents have been so kind. I thought I'd walk in here and your dad or mom would throw me out for endangering their child. You have the best parents. You missed me crying like a baby in your mom's arms. Would you believe me if I told you I don't cry...like ever. Yet walking in and seeing the damage I've caused you sent me into a puddle. I'm so sorry I was distracted with work and not paying attention. I was selfish and careless. Now I can't bring myself to look at my phone and I definitely cannot work. I don't know when I'll be ready to open that door, but at the moment it doesn't feel right."

I realize I'm talking about nothing and yet everything that is inside me. No one prepared me for what it's like to speak to someone you love on a ventilator. It's horrific and my stomach is twisting in pain.

There's a book on the table. I'm guessing it's her mom's, but I pick it up anyway, opening it to chapter one, and read to her. I hope she can hear the words as she sleeps.

I know she loves reading and I love her. Right now, I need to bring her joy and stop the guilt that's wreaking havoc in my gut as I watch the crash on repeat in my mind.

Reading her the book will make me focus on something else. A new world. A new scene.

I begin to feel my voice tire so after a few chapters, I close the book and put it where I found it.

I stay quiet after that and continue to stroke her hands with my thumb. The door opens, and I don't want to let her go.

I'm not ready to be alone in my hospital room. How will I know when she wakes up?

"Jeremy, it's nice to see you. They told me to come in here and see how you are." I tilt my head, seeing Chelsea behind me.

"I don't want to leave."

"I know but you will eventually have to. You can come back tomorrow."

Tomorrow sounds so far away. I just want to be around her the whole time. Suddenly, an idea sparks inside me.

"I can come back," I murmur.

I place my lips to the top of her hand.

"I'll see you later, baby."

I push my chair back and Chelsea helps me out the door. Nova's parents see me and rush over.

"I'm heading back to my room now. You spend more time with her and please let me know if there's any changes. I know I don't deserve it, but I'd appreciate being kept in the loop."

"We accept your apology, Jeremy. You need to forgive yourself too."

Not yet. Not until Nova wakes and I beg for her forgiveness.

My brother stands and asks me if I'm ready to go.

I nod. Remaining silent, letting him wheel me away. The pain in my chest is worse than any of the injuries I sustained in the accident.

Later that night, I couldn't sleep. I need to be with Nova. I ask the nurse on shift if I can visit her. I'm charming her on purpose to get what I want.

She says yes but not for too long.

This time, I walk. When I reach her room, I see she's alone. No one else is here but me. I sit in a chair by her bed and hold her hand. My body is finally tired as if it feels like it could rest now that she's here. And if she wakes, I'll be right here. So I lay my head on her bed beside our joined hands. I'm not leaving her tonight. They'll have to force me to leave.

"Mr. Lincoln," a voice calls from afar.

I grumble. But I don't move.

"Mr. Lincoln." A touch on my shoulder startles me.

I jerk in my chair, finding a nurse beside me.

"You need to go back to your room now."

I wipe my face and look at the clock. Eight o'clock at night. An hour past visiting hours.

"I don't want to leave her."

The nurse offers me a compassionate smile. "I know. But you have to leave."

In other circumstances, I know I could get my way. But I'm not in charge here. She is and she knows it.

"How about I'll call your nurse if there's any changes?"

I nod. "Thanks." I stand and stare at Nova one last time before I turn and leave her room. Every time I leave her, my heart breaks further. Is it fear? That she might not wake? I don't know, but I take my shattered heart and head back to my room. Rather than going straight to bed, I sit by the window and look out at the stars. She reminds me of them. So bright, so beautiful and unique.

A light knock and the door opening have me opening my eyes. I'm reminded instantly that I'm in my own room at the hospital. I don't remember falling asleep.

"Are you ready to go home today?" Mom asks walking in.

"Yeah, I'd like my bed back."

"But?"

"No buts."

"Son, your face is unconvincing," she argues.

"I just don't want to miss her waking up."

"Why don't you stay with her until you need to leave. We can take your stuff to your house."

I sit up straighter. "That would be great."

The door opens again and Doctor Andrews walks in.

"Looks like you're ready to go home."

"I'm ready to go visit my girlfriend."

"Well, let me check you over, and if there's nothing else, you can go home and rest."

The doctor checks me over and discharges me. I make my way back to Nova's room. Her friends and parents are here.

I don't go in the room until everyone else has had a turn. I'm not in a rush. I plan to be here the whole day and night. I'll be right here until they kick me out, which happens at seven o'clock that night.

I turn up the following day promptly at eight a.m., as soon as visiting hours commence, bringing a large bouquet of red roses. I want her to wake up and see her room filled with them. Today I brought my laptop. I plan to tackle work. I'll be working through it. But I also had an idea during my lack of sleep last night. It won't happen overnight, but I'm appointing a new CEO to take over. It's the best decision. Even if Nova chooses to end our relationship, I want to take a big step back from work. I need to do something else. Like travel. And if later on I decide to work, I can start up a new business. Study something new at college or even volunteer my time.

Today as I wait by Nova's side, clutching her hand, waiting for a miracle, a doctor enters the room.

Her parents welcome him, and I learn that he's been the doctor treating her. My stomach tightens with anticipation. What is he going to say?

"I want to start to slowly reduce the medication and begin to wake her up. Nova's injuries aren't going anywhere, but the swelling and bleeding are no longer a concern."

"How long will she take to wake up?" I ask.

"12-72 hours."

"When will you begin to reduce the medication?"

"Today."

I'm relieved but also worried. What if she doesn't wake up?

What happens next?

When she does wake up, what happens if she wants to throw me out of her room and break up with me?

No. I won't let her. I'll explain what I'm doing and how much I care about her.

The doctor leaves and the medication is reduced. Now we play the waiting game. No one wants to leave her room today. We are all desperate for her to wake up.

Twelve hours pass and nothing.

Not one movement.

And then the nurses kick us out.

Meaning I'll have to wait another 12 hours at least before I can come back in. I'd hate for her to wake up alone. I don't want her scared.

I reluctantly leave her room.

Returning the next morning, I take the same seat I did yesterday. She looks the same, except they removed the breathing tube from her mouth. There's oxygen in her nose. I don't know why I expect her to look different, but I do. I want the flush of color back in her cheeks.

I didn't bring my laptop today, with hopes she'll wake up. Work isn't important. She is. Her eyes opening and seeing me there waiting for her.

I sit silently and when her parents come in, my nerves scoot up higher.

Hours pass but I can't get up and get food or do anything else. I just sit and wait.

A grunt and a groan come from the bed and I jump out of my chair. Her parents come closer to her bed too. We all watch as she moves, touching the nasal cannula on her face. Her eyes are still closed but her face is screwed up. I want to see her eyes. Those hazel eyes with gold flecks. God, I've fucking missed them.

Her mom is crying and soothing the hair on Nova's face. I feel like I'm holding my breath waiting for her to take hers.

My hand holds hers watching and waiting for her eyes to open when her fingers twitch. I drop my gaze to her hand when she squeezes mine. My eyes prick with fresh tears. God. I've wanted this for so long it doesn't feel real yet. I'm watching intently so I know I'm not imagining it.

"Mom?" She gasps.

"I'm here, love," she replies, touching her face and bringing her face closer to Nova's, blocking my view of her face.

"Rem-y," she rasps.

"He's here too." Lydia sobs.

A lump of emotion forms in my throat, so I clear my throat before speaking. "Nova. I'm here."

Her lashes flutter, and as her eyes open, it feels as if my chest is tearing apart. Those hazel eyes find mine, and a tear escapes from my eye.

My heart feels so much for her. I wish I was alone with her right now to tell her... Tell her, I love her.

Chapter 35

Nova

The instant I open my eyes, I lock my gaze with Jeremy's glassy eyes. However, I don't miss the tear that falls, tracing a path down his cheek. My hand twitches in his grip. Part of me wants to swat the droplet away, while another part yearns to kiss away the pain etched on his tormented face.

Mom is on one side, and my dad on the other, with Jeremy positioned beside my mom, holding my hand. I know it's his hand by the familiarity of the touch. A minute later, a nurse enters and asks them all to leave the room. I want to protest, but the quicker she checks my vital signs, the quicker they can return. I'm desperate to spend time with Jeremy, assure him that I'm okay, and emphasize that I don't blame him.

I move in the bed to relieve some pain, but it makes it worse. My hip area is on fire. And when I ask the nurse, she explains how I have a fractured pelvis.

She leaves and brings me back pain relief that she pushes through the IV. After the nurse takes my vitals, she tells me she'll let everyone back in.

I expect my parents to come in, but when Jeremy steps into my room alone, the corner of my lip lifts.

"Hey." My voice cracks.

He takes my hand and sits in the chair closest to the bed. "Nova." He starts to say in a voice that breaks.

He looks at our joined hands. "I'm so sorry. I did this to you. I was so scared I was going to lose you," he rambles.

I reach out to touch his face, enjoying the way the scuff of his beard feels against the palm of my hand. I hold it against his cheek as I speak. "I'm fine, Remy. I don't blame you. The guy ran a red light."

He shakes his head but still enjoys the touch of my hand on his skin. "I wasn't paying attention. Too busy working. I was always working."

"Was?"

He swallows hard and explains. "I'm cutting back. This was the biggest wake-up call. The most important thing in my life isn't work."

I stay silent for a beat, observing the way he breathes heavily. His face pinched with concern, evidence he's been struggling to see me in the hospital. I hate knowing he's riddled with guilt. I've forgiven him, and now I need him to forgive himself. However, it's clear his dedication to his work was consuming him more than I realized until recently. The signs were there, showing up late or cancelling, when he never did before. "There's nothing wrong with working, but I think you need to find a balance."

As I stare into his conflicted eyes, a sense of calm washes over me, a combination of the pain relief taking effect and his presence in the room. I wish he could wrap his arms around me and hold me. But there's still lots of wires attached to me.

"I didn't tell you something I should have, and I was scared I wasn't going to be able to," he confesses.

"Yeah?" I respond, my curiosity piqued.

He stands abruptly and leans forward. His intense gaze holds mine as he utters the next words. "Nova, I love you. I have loved you for so long. I can't believe I've never told you. But from today onward, you'll hear it every day."

Before I met him, I was not living, but now, I feel like I've been given a second chance and I'm not wasting it.

I smile adoringly at him. "I love you too, Remy. So much."

His lips take mine in a gentle, careful kiss. He's trying to avoid the tube in my nose. He's pouring his heart into this kiss and it brings tears to my eyes. I blink through the blurry vision, tasting salt on my tongue. Pulling back, he lays his forehead against mine and he cries too.

"I haven't cried since...fuck, I can't even remember and yet now in the last few days I've cried three times. What are you doing to me?"

I part my lips as a wide smile takes over my face. "I don't know. But I hope it's a good thing."

"With you, everything is a good thing."

He moves his lips to my forehead. Laying a gentle warm kiss there before pulling back, allowing me to admire him in his olive-green sweater and blue jeans.

"So, if you're not going to work, what is the next chapter in your life?" I ask, knowing he wouldn't pull out of his commitments without a plan.

"Right now, you. You have a long recovery and I want to be there every step of the way."

As lovely as that sounds, I know I want to go back to my new career. I worked so hard in college to get there. "I will be getting better so I can return to work. Bentley will have me back."

"If he doesn't, he's crazy, and I have plenty of jobs I can give you."

"Is that so?"

"Like a head job," he teases.

I smile. "Are you being dirty, Mr. Lincoln?"

"Never." He winks.

"I don't know how long I'll be out of commission for."

His hand comes up to cup the side of my face, tilting my head back so I meet his eyes. "We won't be doing anything until you're ready. You need to heal."

"I assume I'll be here for a few more days and then to rehab."

"Would you be opposed to coming to my house? I'll have the best physio visit you daily at my house."

"Seems excessive," I argue.

"Not to me. I want to take care of you." He adjusts the blankets on my waist, tucking them in gently, careful not to hurt me.

"Is this because you feel guilty?"

"Part of it."

That makes me queasy. "Please don't. I don't want you caring for me because you feel sorry for me and are wracked with guilt. I want you to care for me because you love me."

"I do love you. I'm crazy about you. I want to bring you breakfast and coffee every day."

"You'll make me breakfast?" I ask, biting back a wide smile.

"Yep. And what's funny about that, Miss Lee."

I roll my lips before answering. "Nothing, I just look forward to having someone cook me breakfast. I've never had that treatment before."

"Well, get used to it. As soon as I can take you home, you will see a different me."

I push out my bottom lip in a pout. "I don't want a different you. I'm not fragile."

He raises a brow at me.

I roll my eyes. "Well, maybe a little. But only for a short time."

"I won't be a different person, just more caring." He skims his fingertips down the side of my face in a soft caress.

"Don't go all soft on me." I huff, trying to hide how much his touch affects me.

His thumb rubs hard over my lips. "Trust me, as soon as I can, I'll show you how hard I am."

That makes me smirk.

"But I can't live with you."

He frowns but his eyes are flicking between mine. "Why not?"

"I should be home. My dad? I haven't been helping out. I didn't do a lot but still my mom must be exhausted..."

The next words that leave his mouth have me awe stricken.

"I sent your mom her flowers and they now have a chef, cleaner, and a driver."

A tear slips from my eye and trickles down the side of my temple.

"Thank you," I breathe, not bothering to argue because they deserve the help. I can get better and help out when I can.

"Not going to fight me on it?"

"No," I say with a soft smile.

He gives me a matching one as my room door opens.

Damn it. I was enjoying our time alone. I need more.

"You look so much better already," Mom calls out, entering my room with my dad following closely behind her.

"I'll grab you a coffee and I'll be back." He says kissing my lips before leaving. I moan and grab his hand before he walks away. "Thanks for the roses."

"I wanted you to see them when you woke up in case you woke up without me here."

My heart swells at how sweet he is. My gaze shifts to the massive bouquets. Red roses. My favorite, of course. I don't know how I'll get them home, so I'll probably leave them for the medical staff here as a way of thanks for caring for me.

He slips out the door and my parents come right up to me. I hug them so hard.

I ask them to fill me in on everything I've missed.

Summer and Chelsea arrive next. They both burst into tears at seeing me awake.

My parents leave us to chat while they sit outside the room.

"God. You aged me by about ten years," Summer sniffs.

"Sorry. This wasn't planned," I joke.

"One would hope not. Now let's get you home. It's been too quiet without you," Chelsea replies.

"Quiet? Or are you two sick of cooking or getting takeout?"

They give each other a look before Summer looks at me, the twist of her lips giving her away.

"You girls will have to carry on without me." I laugh.

Chelsea frowns. "Why? You're awake now so surely you'll be discharged in a few days."

"I am, but Jeremy is taking me back to his place," I admit excitedly.

Shock settles on their faces before Chelsea speaks. "He's been a mess without you."

I believe her after seeing his face today.

"He told me he loved me today."

"I'm surprised he waited to say it. The guy has been a smitten kitten for ages," Summer adds.

"A smitten kitten." I laugh, but it hurts too much, and I grimace. "Don't make me laugh. It hurts."

"Do you want me to call the nurse?" Chelsea asks.

I shake my head. "No, I had some pain meds not that long ago. I don't want too much because it'll make me drowsy. I want to stay awake."

"So should I pack up your stuff?" Chelsea asks with a smirk.

"Not everything. I'll be coming home."

Summer laughs. "There's no way that fine man is letting you out of his sight. You mark my words, you won't leave his house."

I wouldn't mind living there permanently, as long as he treats me like a girlfriend and not a sick patient. I couldn't handle that.

"Sounds like you're trying to kick me out," I tease.

Chelsea grabs my hand. "I'm not. I need to know where your head's at."

"You planning on filling the room with someone?" I ask.

Summer snorts. "No way. And Chelsea isn't allowed to move Bobby in."

I look over at Chelsea, who wears a sad expression.

"You okay, Chelsea?"

She sits in the chair beside my bed. "Yeah, fine."

"Well, I'm planning to move home eventually. I'll keep you updated with any changes. But Jeremy has started changing part of his house to accommodate my arrival."

"I bet. I've never seen a more gutted guy than when he visited you."

I run my hands through my hair and wince. "I can't imagine why he didn't run. My hair is so greasy. I can't wait to shower. I feel disgusting."

"Minus your hair, which is a bit oily, I'm not going to lie. You look surprisingly well," Summer replies.

"Jeez thanks," I mutter, shifting in the uncomfortable hospital bed.

"It's true. I'm sure if I was in your position, I would feel gross too, but I promise you don't look that bad," Chelsea adds.

"I'll have to ask when I can shower and wash my hair. I can't be going on like this for much longer."

"It won't be today. Maybe tomorrow?" Summer says.

"Hmmm maybe," I reply.

I hope so...

The doctor is the next to come in. My parents follow him in. He explains I'll have a couple days here and that Jeremy has already spoken with him about the plan for me to stay with him and have a personal physio. I look toward my parents who don't flinch. I should've already guessed he'd debriefed them and asked for their permission.

How could they say no?

He's so charming and guilt-ridden. I think anyone would give him anything he wanted. And my parents would prefer me getting private physio in the comfort of a home instead of a hospital. They just couldn't afford it, but with Jeremy, they know he can afford it.

I'll be here for a week. It's going to be a very long one. I already can't wait to be with Jeremy at his place.

CHAPTER 36

NOVA

THE NEXT FEW DAYS feel like the longest days of my life. Jeremy has been visiting everyday, but I can tell something is on his mind. He tells me that he is anxious over all the construction at his house, making it ready for me. But I sense there's more to the story. I don't have to worry anymore because I'm leaving the hospital today. I've showered, dressed and now I'm waiting for him to come pick me up.

Right on cue, Jeremy strides through the doors, his charming smile in place.

"Morning."

"Good morning," I reply, leaning forward to meet his outstretched neck and kiss him on the lips.

I missed him.

"You ready, baby?"

I nod. "I've been ready for hours."

He chuckles darkly. "So I guess I don't need to worry about you being too comfortable here."

"Definitely not."

"Alright then, let's get you home."

I like the way he says home.

I stand and sit down in the chair. I'm on a strict physio plan with how long I can stand and sit.

My bag is packed. Mom did it last night to help me. I need more clothes from home, but I'll get the girls to bring me some when I'm settled in at Jeremy's.

He picks up the bag and stands behind me. I expect the chair to move, but his hand slips onto my shoulder and he squeezes. I tip my head back and see him staring at me.

"I never thought I'd be here. I thought you'd hate me and tell me you never want to see me again."

The sincerity in his voice makes my heart squeeze for him.

"I couldn't imagine being alive and not having you. You're not a monster. And neither is the guy who made a mistake. He lost his life, and we were lucky to come out alive. I take this as a wakeup call to remind me how much I never thought I had time for a guy or hell needed one. Until you. Now I don't want to go a day without you."

He stays silent, unmoving, until he finally speaks. "You're too good for me."

"Don't say that. We are perfect for each other. We need each other for us to be one."

"I need you. The last week has been horrendous. And I'm ready to put that chapter behind me."

"Let's go home. I want to sit on your ridiculously comfortable sofa and watch a movie with you holding me."

"Is that right?"

"Yeah. Unless you have other plans."

"The only plan I have on my calendar is you."

"I promise you. You will get sick of me. You'll need to work eventually."

"I'll worry about that when you're back at work. For now, I'm at your beck and call."

He pushes the wheelchair to the elevators as we pass the reception. I wave at the nurses at the desk. I'll miss their warm and friendly smiles, but I won't miss this place. I want to go where Jeremy is.

"That could be dangerous."

His mouth drops and his breath tickles the shell of my ear. "Don't tempt me."

"It's not tempting. It's a promise."

"You need to be careful."

"There's plenty we can do where I won't be standing, or it won't hurt my hips. Do you need me to ask the doctor?"

"No." He grunts, and I can imagine how uncomfortable he is. I bite my lip hiding my smile.

We take the elevator down to his private car. His driver steps out.

"You didn't want to drive?"

"I'm not ready to drive you yet."

"Did you buy a new fancy car?"

"By fancy you mean the world's safest car they offer right now? Then yes. I bought a new car."

I don't push him. Understanding driving wouldn't be easy anymore. Hell, right now I'm queasy being a passenger again.

I slip into the back seat without saying a word. My hands settle in my lap after I buckle up. Jeremy joins me on the other side. He reaches for my hand the moment he sits inside. Even if he doesn't know I'm panicky, I'm grateful he feels the need to touch me because as soon as the car moves my heart is in my throat and it doesn't calm until the moment we pull up at Jeremy's.

I wonder when I'll get used to a car again. Or will this be my new normal?

I truly hope not...

Jeremy opens my door and walks me into his personal elevator. Here I was thinking how ridiculous a personal elevator was but now I'm grateful for it. He guides me into the house, and I'm immediately overwhelmed by all the red roses throughout the house. Every room is littered with them.

"Wow. You really are excited to have me here."

"You have no idea."

"I think the amount of red roses in your house tells me you're obsessed."

"Damn straight, baby."

"Good. Because I'm so obsessed with you too. But I think you bought the whole city's supply of red roses."

"I definitely cleaned out a few florists."

He pauses next to his sofa and as soon as I can I stand, I kiss him. This time I hold him so close and don't stop kissing him until I need air.

"Come sit, we have all night for that."

A grumble leaves me at his all-night comment.

I've missed him.

"Right now I need to hold you in my arms alone here."

"I can do that," I say with a smile.

"The physio is set to come after lunch today."

"Thanks," I say. I'm not looking forward to the session, but I know every session will bring me closer to healing.

We take a seat on the sofa.

He sits with his legs apart and he drags my body between his. I recline into his body, welcoming his arm that snakes around my waist pulling me closer.

"What did you want to watch?" he asks as we flick through the channels.

I don't have the heart to tell him I'm too tired. So I say, "Anything."

He kisses the top of my head. The love and warmth he surrounds me with makes it hard to resist sleep. Eventually my eyes flutter and my heavy lids close.

A few hours later, I stretch, and a stupidly happy smile spreads across my face as I remember he's here with me.

"Did you nap too?"

"You made it impossible not to."

"Oh baby, are you sad?"

"No, I've barely slept in a week, so I enjoyed your body wrapped in mine."

I smile. Knowing exactly what he means, because I too have missed him, and I haven't been awake to see him in a hospital bed looking like death.

I'm glad I wasn't able to see the state I was in. Seeing myself in the mirror the first time I showered was enough.

And a part of me worries he won't look at me the way he used to when he sees the bruising, scars and damage from the accident.

I want him to be rough with me, the first time we do it again. I don't want pity eyes; I want the loving eyes of the man who wants to eat me alive, making every whimper and moan sound like ecstasy to him. Yeah, I need that man. This tender one is nice, and I crave this part of him, but when we're together, I don't want nice.

"What are you thinking about?"

I tilt my head back to look into his eyes. The little wrinkle between his brows lets me know that he's aware I've been quietly thinking the last few minutes.

"How happy I am to be back in your arms." It's a half-truth. I just kept the dirty memories out of it. But, of course, he picks up on my body language.

"What?"

"So you're not ready for more?" I say, with a smile.

"What do you mean?"

"I want you, Remy."

"You need to rest."

"I'm fine, please."

"I've missed you, *Star*. But we can wait."

I grab his thigh in a firm squeeze. "No! I need you."

His brow lifts and his eyes darken seductively.

"And you're recovered enough to have your legs spread wide."

His dirty mouth leaves me speechless. But I recover quickly.

"You worry about yourself. Leave my legs to me."

He tsks. "You know I can't do that." His finger draws slowly up and down my arm in a shivering trance. "I care about every single part of you."

The doorbell rings.

I groan, closing my eyes with frustration. "Who's that?"

"A surprise."

He strides to the door like a man on a mission.

"Hi, Mr. and Mrs. Lee, come on in."

"Mom? Dad?" I say, sitting myself forward on the sofa before getting myself into the wheelchair.

I wheel myself closer to them. They come inside and I smile wide because this is the best surprise.

What are they doing here?

"I organized dinner for us. I wanted to celebrate you being home and I thought your parents should see where you live."

My head turns to Jeremy. I'm too bewildered to speak.

If I thought I loved him before, I just fell for him all over again.

CHAPTER 37

JEREMY

HER PARENTS LEAVE THE house after a nice family dinner. I love watching Nova with her parents. The bond they share is similar to my family.

I showed her parents the house. I don't plan on letting her return to the rental. I almost lost her once; I couldn't cope with her not living with me.

Am I totally obsessed with her? Totally.

Do I care what other people think? Not at all.

No one has almost lost the love of their life. Because if they did, they'd understand where I'm coming from.

"Are you ready for a shower?"

I'd ask her if she wanted a bath, but from the amount of times I've seen her yawn or rub her eyes, I'd say she needs to go to bed soon.

"Yeah."

She doesn't fight me on it, or give me any sass, which lets me know she's going to need help.

"Stay here. I'll get the shower started. Let it warm up before you get in."

She nods. "Good idea."

I set up the shower, and when I return, her eyes are closed. My footsteps have her eyelashes fluttering open.

"How are you feeling?"

"Tired," she mumbles.

I love how she doesn't lie. I'd see right through it anyway.

"But are you sore?" I ask, wondering if a shower is a good idea.

"Tender but I'll have a quick shower before I take the pain meds."

"You knew I was going to ask if you wanted the meds, didn't you?"

"I did." The side of her mouth lifts.

She slowly steps into the bathroom and goes to grab her hairbrush, but I grab it first. I run the brush through her hair, and when it's smooth, I tie her hair up. She moans seductively while I am doing it.

When she undresses, I suck in a breath. My beautiful girl is bruised.

"It doesn't hurt," Nova says when she notices me staring at her hips.

The purple, blue, and yellow staining is killing me inside. And then there's the stitches on her lower stomach.

If I didn't already feel guilty, this just made me beat myself up all over again.

"I'm sorry," I whisper, drawing closer to hold her cheeks in my hands.

"Stop. I forgive you. Don't look at my injuries as a bad reminder, use them as a good one."

Her words sink in.

"Remind me how lucky I am to have you in my life."

She nods. "We have a second chance. Let's not waste it."

"I won't. I promise that until you take your last breath that I am yours. I'm committed to you forever while you're on this earth."

"I love you, Remy."

"I love you, Nova. Never forget."

I kiss her, but I'm able to stop.

She grumbles, enjoying every sweep of my tongue over hers.

Her hands grip my neck, trying to pull my head closer to hers. As if we aren't already close. Our bodies are smashed together as one.

Once we're both out of breath, I tip my head and lay my forehead against hers.

She's so beautiful. And I can't wait to continue looking after her in the shower.

"Now let's shower and clean you up. Then we can go to bed. I want to hold you tonight."

CHAPTER 38

NOVA

IT'S BEEN TWO MONTHS since I left the hospital. And it's the first day I've returned to work. I'm no longer in pain or taking any medication. I walk with a slight limp, but the doctors are adamant it will correct itself in time. Time heals all wounds, they keep reminding me.

I just wish it was faster.

Walking through the glass doors into Spencer's Health brings me joy. I walk to the elevator and take it up until I arrive on my level. The walk to my desk turns to a shuffle. The emotions of returning are relief and excitement. I dump my bag on the desk and walk straight up to Dalton. He swivels at hearing my approach. I'm not in my usual work pumps because they hurt my hips when I tried them on this morning. So I went for a pair of black closed toe flats.

He scans me quickly before he stands up out of his chair. I open my arms at his hesitation. He smiles and we hug.

"It's so good to see you. How are you feeling?" he asks, pulling back, but his hands stay holding my shoulders to get a good read on me.

A small laugh leaves me. "I'm fine."

"Are you sure you're okay to be back at work?" He drops his hands from my shoulders.

"Yes. I need the stimulation. Being at home was fun," I say, biting the inside of my cheek to prevent myself from smiling too wide. Memories of the last two months suddenly replay in my mind. Jeremy spread me wide and sank himself deep into me. Many times, I didn't even bother getting dressed for the day. There isn't a surface we haven't been on in his house. But it wasn't our mind-blowing sex, it was the little things like leaving his phone at home or in another room. He's way more present with everyone around him.

"Fun?" he asks frowning.

"Yeah, I spent the two months in holiday mode. Watching too much TV, physio, and reading a lot of books. Which was great but I'm ready to return to work," I explain.

Jeremy also needs to find a new passion. Well, other than me. I know he stepped down from his company, but he has a lot of knowledge to offer. I don't want to see him waste it. He just needs to find the work/life balance, but we can work on that together.

"Well, I must admit, picking up your slack has been annoying," Poppy adds from behind Dalton.

She walks up with a smirk. I open my arms and we hug.

"Welcome back," she says.

"Don't be too soft on me you two," I say when we pull out of our hug. I point between the two of them. "I mean it."

"You won't get soft from me. I know how capable you are. If anything, I'll push you more," Poppy says with a sparkle in her eye.

The words excite me. I'm ready to get back to it.

"Let me check my emails and then do you have time for a debrief. I need to know where we are with things."

"Then we can handball them back to you," Dalton adds.

"Yep." I say, returning to my desk and taking a seat to fire up the computer.

"Shit. I can't remember my login details."

A loud chuckle comes from Dalton. "Trust you to do that."

Poppy stays silent, but I can imagine her rolling her eyes.

I flick through my desk, remembering I scribbled them down somewhere on my first day.

In a drawer, I find a notepad with the login details.

"Got it," I call out to both of them.

"I'm glad. Now get to work," Poppy adds.

Clearing out my emails takes hours, but after that, I take a well-earned break. I make coffee and grab a blueberry muffin and an apple. Inside my lunch bag I see a white piece of paper.

I scrunch up my face as I pull it out. *What is this?*

I unfold the note and read.

Star baby,

After work, instead of going home, I'll pick you up. I have a surprise waiting for you.

Remy

P.S. I love you.

I pull out my phone and quickly type out a message.

Nova: I still have five hours of work. Can't you give me a hint?

Jeremy: A new place for us to christen.

Nova: You didn't buy a new house?

Jeremy: No. But you know I would if you wanted to.

Nova: No, don't be silly. Your house is amazing.

Jeremy: But it's not ours.

Nova: It is. Wherever me and you are together is a place to call ours.

Jeremy: So you like the table where I make you squirt?

I look up feeling a rush of blood flood my cheeks. I'm blushing as if someone is reading this over my shoulder, witnessing how turned on I am by his sexting.

> **Nova:** *I'm at work.*

> **Jeremy:** *So? I'm assuming you're on a break. You don't answer your phone unless it's a break because you're such a good girl.*

His words cause a deep ache within me. This is going to be a long five hours. I'm glad it has been so busy I haven't had time to breathe because; otherwise, I'd struggle the rest of the day.

> **Nova:** *You're killing me.*

> **Jeremy:** *I promise I'll let you come so hard in the new place.*

I trust that Jeremy wouldn't push boundaries I don't feel comfortable with. He isn't a man that likes to have others watch me. He wouldn't be into it. The one time in Bentley's yacht was as far as he would go. Well, unless I asked, which I've never tried, but I'm not keen to right now.

> **Nova:** *I'm going back to work now.*

I tuck my phone away and drink the rest of my coffee and eat my muffin and apple then head back to my desk.

I've had my debrief with Dalton and Poppy, who handed over all my clients, and I began working on the priority clients.

A new email pops up at 3p.m.

I open it when I see it's from Mr. Spencer.

Nova,

Welcome back. I hope you're settling back in.
Can you come to my office for a chat?

Bentley Spencer

Spencer Health

I quickly type a response.

Mr. Spencer,

I'm feeling great. Glad to be back and working. I will head upstairs now.

See you soon.

Regards,

Nova

"Guys, Bentley wants to see me in his office."

"Now?" Dalton calls out.

"Yep," I reply as I stand and leave my desk.

"Good luck," Poppy calls out.

I walk to the elevators and head to the top level. It's funny how stepping into an elevator after a car accident like mine has changed me. I'm no longer fearful or anxious about stepping into it; however, cars make me hold my breath and give me a try not to vomit type of feeling.

I lost one problem and gained a new one. I hope in time I relax about driving again.

I leave the elevator and his personal assistant says he's waiting for me.

Arriving at his door, I knock. He's facing the windows looking out over the city. It's a nice view, but he still irks me. I can't put my finger on why, but it doesn't matter because just as I suspected, I barely have to deal with him. Dalton and Poppy are wonderful, and the work I do is truly exceptional.

Like a dream career. But worry swarms my gut and has me wondering if Bentley is about to deliver bad news. I've been off early into my contract. I'm sure he's pissed off.

At the sound, he swivels in his chair. He sits reclined with an ankle draped over the other, wearing a cheesy smile.

"Nova," he says and sits up, dropping his foot and then standing.

"Mr. Spencer, you wanted to see me?" My voice is a tad shaky, giving away my fear of losing my job.

It's not like I'm worried about paying for my parents' house or giving them money. But I do love working. I want my career. If I lose it today, I have to go and find a new one, which would be difficult right now as I'm still recovering from the car accident. I want to stay here.

I know I'm a great asset. I just hope he doesn't throw me out without giving me a chance to prove myself.

"Yes. Take a seat." He gestures to the seat in front of his desk as he sits on the side of it.

I move toward the chair. His eyes drop over my dress. I see nothing has improved in the last month, except he doesn't rake his eyes over me for as long. Still annoying, but right now I want him to put me out of my misery more than I want to call him out for being a jerk.

I take a seat and my hands automatically grip the chair. I'm waiting for the blow.

"I want to inform you…"

Here we go…

"Your position here at Spencer Health is safe."

I exhale. "What?"

"Fern has decided not to return after her maternity leave is up. Leaving me a gap to fill. I'd like to offer you that position."

My mouth opens and closes before I'm able to speak. "Yes. I'd love that. Thank you so much."

"Right, well then, it's yours."

"Will you give me a contract?"

"Let me call HR and get one organized for you." He stands to turn around. He picks up his phone and talks to HR to draft up a contract for me.

He hangs up. "They will have it ready soon. If you want to head down there, before you head back to your desk."

"Thanks, Mr. Spencer."

His phone rings.

He looks at the screen.

"I must get this." And the way he says it has me thinking it's a personal call.

I stand and practically rush out of his office. More than happy not being the center of his attention now.

I leave on a high. I don't even remember the elevator ride down to HR. When I step out, they, in fact, have it ready for me to sign.

I walk away with a copy, and I can't wait to tell Jeremy. I think about calling him, but I'm an hour away from being finished at work. Then I can see him.

I'll wait to tell him. I have so much work to catch up on anyway.

Walking into my office, I wave my contract. "You two can't get rid of me now."

They both turn their heads and stare at me in confusion. They are waiting for me to explain.

"Fern resigned and so Bentley offered me the job and I officially just signed the contract."

Dalton claps. "Congrats. This is awesome."

"I'll miss Fern, but Nova you deserve this," Poppy adds with a quirk in her lips.

"Thanks, guys. Well, I better get back to work. I only have an hour left and there's still so much to do." I step to my desk with the contract laid out, so I can look at it as I work as a reminder of what I've achieved.

As I finish work for the day and say goodbye to Dalton and Poppy, I call my parents. When I inform them about the new contract, my dad and mom are filled with joy. I promise them we can have dinner tomorrow night to celebrate—Jeremy included, obviously. Mom enthusiastically offers to cook up a feast. Dad says he's feeling better, still tired, but the fluid has settled and the chemotherapy is proving effective.

I know the reality is we aren't out of the woods yet, but as a family, it's better than hearing the alternative.

As I hold the phone to my ear, I see my man waiting for me. He leans his tall solid frame against the car. His ankles crossed and his hands in his suit pockets.

The motherfucker has the nerve to smirk with one of his panty-disintegrating smiles.

"Remy,"

"Hi, baby," he purrs. "You seem extra happy to see me?"

"I am, and I've also got some good news."

"Damn it. Here I was thinking only I could make you light up like that."

"You do, but this isn't everyday news."

His brows pull together.

"Bentley gave me the full-time accounting position."

"Congratulations, baby. You know I hate the guy and want you to work with me, but I gave the company to Harvey."

"No, things happen for a reason. This was supposed to happen and so is your step down."

He grumbles.

"What?" I ask.

"I think I might buy another hospital."

I smile. "Yeah. What made you decide that?"

"This one is close to my heart," he murmurs across my lips as his lips touch mine.

"Oh really?"

"Mmm. It involves more ICU beds and trauma wards."

I part my lips, but he swallows my breath, and of course, kisses me so my brain can no longer think. All it can do is follow his direction. My hands skim over his broad shoulders, up to his neck, and into his hair.

When he finally finishes kissing me, he speaks. "Every time I think of that time, I get so damn emotional, and I just have to have you. Remind myself that you're really here."

"I'm really here."

He kisses me hungrily. I swipe my tongue in his mouth. Enjoying the way he kisses me back.

"What are you doing?" I ask when I take a breath. Seeing everyone around on the sidewalk. I peek out the corner of my eyes, watching people stare or shake their heads as they pass.

"What do you mean?"

"You're getting attention."

"I don't care about anyone else," he says.

"I do."

"Why?"

"I'm jealous of others looking at you. You're wearing a suit that looks like a second skin. You're hot and you know it. Then you flash me a sexy smile after sexting me all day."

"You don't like our texts?"

"I didn't say that."

"I just find it hard...to concentrate."

"Okay, what if I promise to keep it PG during office hours."

He runs his nose across the pulse on my neck.

"Yeah," I reply, shakily.

"Let's get in the car and I can give you the surprise."

I sigh.

He chuckles. "I promise to relieve you when we get there."

"But other—"

"We're alone there," he cuts me off.

"Oh."

"Get in the car, baby, before I show you how much I'm yours and no one else's."

He pulls back and I feel unsteady on my feet from the air without him in it. He holds the car door open for me and I climb in. He slides in beside me.

"How far away is it?"

"Ten minutes. Close to home."

"Home?"

"Yeah, the one we share. The one I gave you a key for."

"Not to borrow? I thought I'd go back to the girls?"

His lips twitch. "There's no fucking chance your living with anyone other than me. If you're my girlfriend, you live with me where I can treat you like one."

"I love living with you. But I wouldn't mind a dog."

"A dog?"

"Yeah, I want a golden lab or a golden retriever."

Yeah, I picture my man cuddling one of those and I swear if we weren't busy right now, I'd beg him to find one to buy now.

Kids and marriage aren't on our agenda just yet—but it might be fun to start out with a fur baby. I want to fill the house with a cat and dog and anything else he'll let me have.

I haven't had a pet since I was a little girl. The last one passed from old age. I'm so ready for a new dog.

"Let me think about it. And research what kind of dogs they are."

I smile and settle into the cool leather seats, thinking about him holding a puppy and welcoming the coolness on my overheated body. His hand grabs mine and he entwines our fingers together.

Ten minutes later, we arrive at a building that looks no different to any other luxurious one here.

We get out of the car, and I follow him to a door.

He hands me the key. "Open the door," he instructs.

I don't bother arguing, I just take the key and open it. Inside, I can hardly believe my eyes. It's a fully-equipped gym. Red rose petals all across the floor. Bunches of red roses along the sides.

I hold back tears. As I walk in farther, I gasp at the boxing setup. My fingers touch my wobbly lips.

What the hell? He did this for me...

"This is yours, baby."

"No one else's?"

"Maybe me if you'll let me use it."

I raise my brows at him. "You bought this for me, and you want to ask for permission."

"Of course. I bought this, so you didn't use that dingy fucking one."

"Oh, so now who's jealous."

"One hundred percent, baby. I don't want anyone checking you out when you're sexy and sweaty."

I screw up my nose at the vision. "It's not a sexy look."

"I beg to differ. The flush on your cheeks and the sweat on your skin reminds me of when I fuck you. The spent look is hard not to want another round right after I just made you come."

We stand face to face. I've looked over the incredible private gym and now I want him. I've been on edge all day.

I drop to my knees.

"Baby."

"Shh, let me thank you," I say as I reach out and grab his belt.

"I didn't buy this for you to please me. Even though you on your knees makes me want to watch you gag trying to say thanks."

There he is. My man. The one pre-accident that wasn't scared to be rough.

"Please," I beg as I unzip his pants.

He's rock hard beneath his briefs. I can't get him out quick enough. His thick hard cock bobs and the precum that's glistening on the end makes me lick my lips. I bring him to my mouth and open.

He fucks my mouth the moment his cock hits the back of my throat and he doesn't stop until I have tears running down my face and he's coming so hard he spills out of my mouth.

Now that's what I missed.

Rough and unhinged Remy.

EPILOGUE

NOVA

"I REALLY WISH YOU were coming with me," I say over the phone to Jeremy.

I'm heading to Bentley's yacht for our end-of-year work celebration.

"Me too," he replies.

I know I encouraged him to go to Chicago for a holiday party to celebrate the grand opening of the newest Lincoln hospital, so I can't be down about it. He and Harvey collaborated on this venture and I'm happy he found his spark for work. I thought he was never going to return to full time after the accident, but with me returning to work he slowly realized work isn't bad. He just had to find balance.

"Do you have your ugly Christmas sweater and mask on?" I ask, remembering when he first received the invitation with the dress code he complained and refused to go.

"Yes, and I look ridiculous," he grumbles. And I can imagine him running his hands through his hair like he does when he's frustrated.

I giggle. "I bet you don't. Send me a picture."

"Don't laugh at me or I might change my mind about going."

A beep alerts me to a new message, so I pull the phone away from my ear and open his picture.

He's adorable. "Aw, you look cute."

"I don't like being called cute, remember?"

As if I could forget our first video call. It feels like it was only a moment ago and not that we've been together, coming up on nine months now.

"But you look so cuddly in your green pom-pom sweater."

"Cuddly?" He groans.

"Where's your mask?" I ask, knowing he has a green one, but I haven't seen it on him.

"It looks stupid with this ugly sweater."

"So? Take a pic. I need to see it."

He huffs, but I know he's doing it. A smile lifts as I hear him rustling.

I get another text notification.

I open the picture and a whine leaves my throat. He's hot.

"Now that's what I want to hear."

He's giving me fuck-me vibes with his camera stare. Even though his mask hides half of his face, it adds to the sexiness.

"Maybe keep the mask," I admit.

"Oh, you want me to wear this mask while I fuck you, *Star*?"

Hearing him say those words is better than the image running through my mind.

I really wish we were together tonight because it wouldn't be a dream; no, it would be a reality.

"Yes," I breathe.

"Done. Well, I gotta catch my flight. Have a good night. I'll call you tomorrow. I love you."

"I love you too."

I hang up and I get a text straight away.

> **Jeremy:** I miss you.

> **Nova:** Don't be so needy. Go to the party and have fun.

> **Jeremy:** Fine.

I put my phone down and head for a shower. I need to get ready.

Later that night, I board the familiar yacht. This time, I'm not worried and I won't be meeting anyone. Jeremy isn't here but my colleagues are.

I see Dalton waving at me, and Poppy is standing beside him.

The wind whips around my ankles that are exposed. My long black high cut sleeveless dress stops at the middle of my calf. I pull my cream shawl tighter. I wish I had brought a thicker one now. I didn't expect it to be so cold tonight.

Poppy has her arms crossed and she's hunched over a little. She's in a 3/4 length sleeve navy dress so I'm not the only one cold. Dalton is in a white shirt and navy shorts.

No jacket to give Poppy who looks to be struggling more than me. I hug Dalton and Poppy.

"I can't believe it's so cold tonight."

I k-know I won't be staying long tonight," Poppy says, her teeth chattering.

"Did you want my cardigan?"

She shakes her head. "No, keep it. I'll be fine."

"What about a drink?" Dalton suggests.

"Sure," I reply.

We wave down a server with the drink tray and all grab a Champagne.

I sip and peer around looking for Bentley.

"He's around here somewhere," Dalton says, obviously watching me.

"I'm sure I'll catch him soon."

"How about now?" Poppy suggests. I'm about to ask why but then he wanders over.

"Evening. How's everyone doing? Glad to see you grabbed a drink."

I nod.

"Can I steal Nova away for a second," he asks, his gaze moving over to Poppy and Dalton. I notice that tonight Bentley is in a black suit and a crisp white shirt. It's more dressed up than the last time I was on his yacht.

"Go ahead," they say.

I turn and follow Bentley. We're walking up the side of the yacht to the front, when I realize we haven't moved.

"What time is the yacht leaving?" I ask. Poor Poppy will be cold for a lot longer now.

"Well, I'm waiting for a guest."

I frown, not understanding why this guest didn't turn up in time. Must be important if we're still waiting.

The air changes and I sense movement at the entry steps of the yacht.

The familiar scent fills my nose. Jeremy. He's wearing an all-black suit with a white shirt and black bow tie.

Immediately my face brightens, and the biggest grin spreads on my face. His face mirrors my joy, breaking into a wide grin as well.

"It seems he's here," Bentley says behind me.

My mind is reeling. Wasn't he supposed to be in Chicago? Why's he here?

Where's the ugly Christmas sweater and mask that I saw a few hours ago.

"What are you doing here?" I murmur, not able to believe what I'm seeing.

Jeremy opens his arms for me. I step into them, welcoming the heat from his body. I'll ask him in a second. Right now, I just want to soak him in and revel in the fact that he's here right now.

"You're freezing."

"Mmm, you're warm."

He shrugs off his jacket and wraps it around my shoulders. I shiver from the warmth. I didn't realize I was that cold until now.

I reach out to grab his hand when I notice his cufflinks. Gold with the initials NL. It dawns on me that the L could stand for Lee but then also stand for Lincoln. Mrs. Lincoln. I shake off the silly fantasy. We haven't been together long enough. Or is this another time where I'm following social expectations, not my own path. The risky, yet exhilarating path.

"Thanks, Mr. Spencer," Jeremy calls, peering over my shoulder at Bentley.

"Enjoy," Bentley adds, and there's something odd about his tone, but I don't get a chance to dwell on it because Jeremy is already linking our hands and walking us off the yacht.

"Where are we going?"

"To my yacht."

As we walk along the timber pier, we arrive at a bigger yacht.

"But what happened to the Christmas party?"

His face tilts down to me and grins. "Don't worry I've got the mask here."

My lips twitch as he helps me step onto his yacht then we take the few steps up to the deck. "Good. But aren't they expecting you?"

I look around at the light wooden floors and warm night lights hanging from the railing.

"No." He continues to walk me until we stop at the front of his yacht. There are red roses all over the floor and bunches of them in vases strategically placed—it's breath-taking.

He spins to face me, clutching my hands as he stares down at my lips. I roll them, knowing I have his favorite color *BRAVE* on.

"Holiday parties are fun but not without you. I told you I would change my life. It was a promise I made to myself."

I take one of my hands out of his and reach out to hold the side of his face. His freshly shaven jaw is smooth against my skin.

"I hope this isn't the guilt from the accident still."

He shakes his head gently and grabs my hand from his face and clutches it between us again.

"I don't. This is my second chance to have you in my life and I'm not wasting it."

My lips part into an easy smile. He's been so attentive and sweet lately; I wouldn't want to go back to the way things were.

"Well, I won't say no."

His face brightens. "Well, that's good to know."

His hand slips from mine and reaches into his suit pocket. My breath catches.

He pulls out a blue box, and at the same time, he bends on one knee. Tears spring to my eyes. I blink rapidly, trying to see him through the blur.

"*Star* baby. You're everything to me. My soulmate. You're the start and end of my days. I look forward to waking up and going to sleep with you...I even enjoy doing the most mundane tasks like food shopping with you. I'm happiest when I'm just simply with you. Will you do me the honor and become my wife?"

I nod and cry until I'm uncontrollably sobbing.

"Is that a yes?"

"Y-yes," I stammer.

He slides the large round-cut diamond ring on my finger, and I stare at its exquisiteness.

"It shines just like a *star*. Just like you," he says as he stands, and I kiss him. A kiss from my heart and soul. I can't form words through my tears. He thinks he's the lucky one, but I don't feel that way, I am.

The End.

BONUS

JEREMY

"ARE YOU READY?" I ask Nova, as she sits with Grams and Chelsea on the sofa. The moment she took her last sip of tea, I stood from my position next to my brothers.

She lowers her cup and peers over her shoulder at me. The gold flecks in her hazel eyes shimmer. "If you are." She bites the corner of her mouth, biting back amusement.

My parents are away on a holiday. We all offered to help look after Grams so they could have a week in Bali. Dad hasn't left Grams' side and he needs a break.

All of us Lincoln brothers had dinner tonight instead of playing poker.

She grabs the cup Grams is lowering. Grams looks up at Nova with warmth and thanks her. Grams' color is better these days. Her skin is still thin and pale, but not as grey as it was.

The attentive way Nova cares for my grams makes my heart so happy. She and Chelsea are the support my Grams needs in a room full of testosterone.

Nova kisses my grams goodbye, I follow, whispering into her ear that I'll visit tomorrow.

We say goodbye to Chelsea, Evan, Harvey and Oliver. Then we leave.

Exiting my car, I walk around to open her door.

"Can we use a different room tonight?" she asks, stepping out. I close the door, and her hand slips into mine.

My brow rises. I step into her space, backing her into the car.

She licks her lips, and it flicks a switch in me. My hand grabs the base of her throat and I kiss her. She moans into the kiss and her hands move to my back, clawing at it.

Breathless, we pull apart. I lean my forehead on hers. "Which room?"

Her hot breath tickles my face. "Guest room."

"Impatient, baby?"

She nods and I love how much she wants me. It makes me feral. I drag her into the elevator, but I don't wait, my hands are on her body, peeling off her white long-sleeve top and throwing it onto the floor. We kiss feverishly between touching. Her hands on my body, undoing the buttons on my shirt. Her sexy cotton beige bra is next. I swiftly remove it. When the doors open, we stop kissing and step onto the floor. We make our way to the bedroom, both of us have removed our pants and underwear along the way. So now we are both naked.

"Get on the bed, baby," I rasp out, unable to hold back my desire.

She sits down on the navy sheets and leans back.

From this angle, I can see her breasts. My gaze stares at how hard her nipples are, letting me know she's aroused.

Her eyes pretty much beg me to touch her.

"You have such pretty breasts," I say, as my hand drops down to grab her full, heavy breast.

Her skin is hot and smooth. My thumb rubs her nipple before tweaking it a little.

She groans and her eyes drift close.

Her nipples are so reactive. I want my mouth on them, but I'm too busy placing kisses up her neck. And the way her skin shivers and goosebumps erupt over her skin lets me know she prefers my lips on her neck right now.

Her head tips back onto her shoulder and when she feels me roll her nipples between my forefinger and thumb, she whimpers. Loving the sound, it urges me on. I pinch her nipple.

"Ohhh," she says in a moan. "Yes. More," she begs, and I follow her order. Because how could I resist?

I give the other nipple the same treatment before I move my hand down over her stomach, where she arches into my hand. I love her body; it's so beautiful, and I love that she doesn't try to hide it from me either.

My hand goes straight for her core, running through her folds.

I grunt when I find it wet. I rub my hand in circles through her wetness and up to her clit. It's swollen. And achy, I bet.

She remains still, and as I softly utter the words against her skin, "you're so wet," I sense her pulse quicken.

I can't help but add a finger, enjoying the way she clamps down on my intrusion.

"Your pussy is so tight. I love it when you tremble. You were made for me."

She quivers harder at my words.

Her head moves up as if she wants to look at me. Hungry, lust-filled eyes stare back at me. She wants more. I can see that; she just can't speak. Her lips move but no words leave her mouth except for a moan. "You're fucking perfect," I say in a grunt then my mouth returns to her neck.

"You smell and taste delicious, but I'm not going to eat you tonight."

She pants heavier. She's melting under my fingers. I stop fingering her to add another finger. Once I slide in, she cries out.

She doesn't move. I watch her suck in breaths of air. She takes my fingers so well. I'm stretching her, knowing we both want more.

She needs more.

Her sexy breaths cause her breasts to rise and fall. I can't take my eyes off them. They're perfect. She's so perfect.

She quivers again as I pump my hand harder and curl my fingers forward, knowing exactly what will make her wild.

Her fingers dig into my shoulders.

"Jeremy," she cries. "I can't hold back. Please."

I love hearing her beg.

I push one more finger in.

She shivers in my arms.

My thumb hits her clit, and she cries the hardest I've heard. My name leaves her lips in a gasp and her whole-body quakes under my hand.

I hold her, though; I'd never let her go.

Her pussy continues to clamp down as she rides out her climax.

I'm careful of her hips. That's why we don't really move, and I make her come like this.

When she recovers from her orgasm, I wait for her to open her eyes. I can't wait to see her post-orgasm glow, and sure enough, a moment later, her head tips back up and she flutters her lashes and gives me that full smile of hers.

She orgasms so beautifully. The pink staining of her cheeks and dusting of pink on her nose give her away.

"I love you," I whisper, crawling over her until I'm hovering above her.

"I love you, too."

ALSO BY

The Chicago Doctor's

Doctor Taylor
Doctor I DO
Doctor Gray

The Gentlemen Series

Accidental Neighbor
Bossy Mr. Ward
The Christmas Agreement
White Empire
Saffron and Secrets
Resisting Chase

AFTERWORD

To keep up to date with my new books releases, including title's, blurb's, release date's and giveaways. Please subscribe to my newsletter.

Want to stay up to date with me? Come join my Facebook reader group: Sharon's Sweethearts

This is a PRIVATE group and only people in the group can see posts and comments!

Acknowledgements

Firstly, to my husband, thank you for always supporting and assisting me with my career. Without your help, I wouldn't be where I am today.

To my kids, you inspire me to have fun every day. I love you.

Next are the women who were willing to read my rough draft and help me turn it into a beautiful story with their feedback. Without you all, I wouldn't be here. My incredible beta's Amy, Kirstie, Sophie, Dee, Salma, and Nicole.

To my editor Julia, thank you for helping me grow, honestly your generosity and knowledge are unmatched. My story wouldn't be as good without you.

To my editor, Rebecca, this is our second book together and I love learning from you.

To Brittini, thank you for making my stories polished and shiny. Your eye for detail is incredible.

My cover designers, Echo and Sherri, thanks for turning my rambling ideas and turning it into a masterpiece. You're both so easy and fun to work with. I'm incredibly grateful.

And thank you, my readers, for taking the time to read my words. Your love and support of my books fill me with immense gratitude.

ABOUT THE AUTHOR

Sharon Woods writes spicy, feel-good contemporary romance novels. Based in Melbourne, Australia, with her husband and two children. She drinks a lot of coffee, loves to workout, explore new places, and has an unhealthy addiction to reality TV.

Follow Sharon:
  Website: www.sharonwoodsauthor.com
  Newsletter

Printed in Great Britain
by Amazon